to be a FAE ROGUE

to be a FAE ROGUE

TRICIA COPELAND

to be a FAE ROGUE

by Tricia Copeland

Edited by Jo Michaels
Proofread by Karen Robinson
Interior Formatting by Jo Michaels
all of Indie Books Gone Wild

Cover by Shower of Schmidt Designs
Published by True Bird Publishing LLC, Superior, CO

Borean
Elita
N
NW
NE
W
E
SW
SE
S

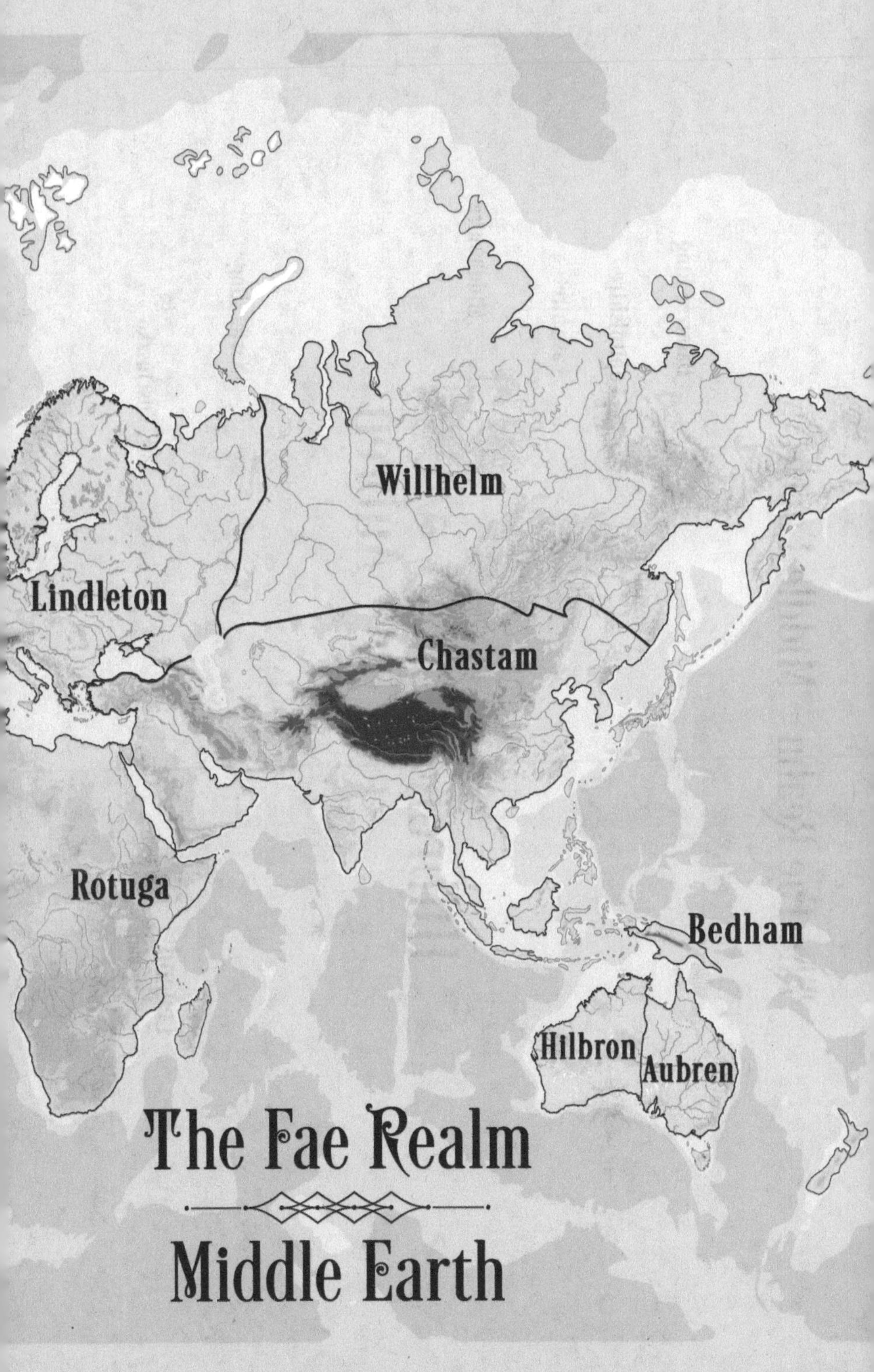

Willhelm
Lindleton
Chastam
Rotuga
Bedham
Hilbron
Aubren
The Fae Realm
Middle Earth

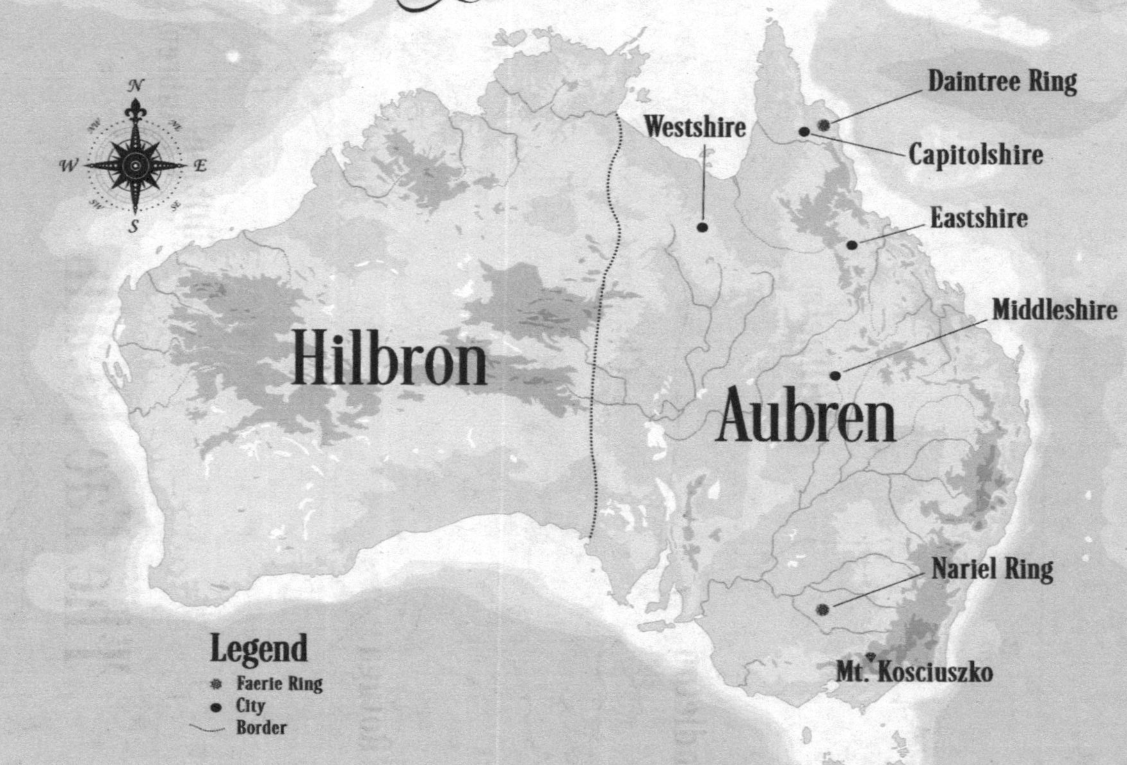
The Fae Realm ~ Middle Earth
Daintree Ring
Capitolshire
Eastshire
Middleshire
Westshire
Nariel Ring
Mt. Kosciuszko
Hilbron
Aubren
Legend
Faerie Ring
City
Border

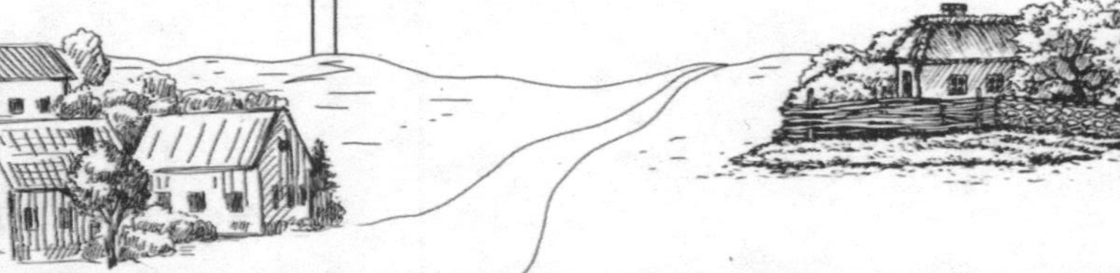

Heaven
Upper Earth
Faerie Ring
The Fae Realm ~ Middle Earth
Passage Between Realms
Lower Earth - Sheol

Chapter

1

Hood low over my forehead, I peer across the meadow as the last light of day basks my castle in orange. I watch the windows as, one by one, lights spring forth as someone within ignites the torches in the passageways. Trying to identify the forms passing the glass panes, I squint, eager for any glimpse of my family. A gale sweeps through the trees, and I hug my cloak to my middle.

"I do not often see anyone in these woods."

I jump at the sound of Grant's voice and fight the instinct to spin to face him. Heart pounding, I assess my options. My Fae at Arms, or former Fae at Arms, will know my voice.

"I love how the castle looks as the last light graces it." I raise my tone an octave, praying he will not recognize me.

"Odd that I have not seen you here before."

"Perhaps I blend into the landscape well then. I come here to be alone and think."

"You should not be in the forest after dark. Even The Queen's Wood shelters danger."

The Queen's Wood? They have named my forest The Queen's Wood? My anxiety at being found mixes with longing.

"It is nice she is honored in this way," I say.

"Did you know the Queen?"

Leaves rustle behind me, and I glance down, catching sight of his boot. "I have only seen her in the village with her cousins."

"You live in the village? I can escort you home." I feel the heat from his body as he approaches.

"No." I tug the sides of my hood over my cheeks. "As I said, I come here often. I will be fine."

"As you wish." The ground crunches, and the air behind me cools.

I tuck my chin to my chest and wait. I catch sight of him exiting the forest and crossing the meadow. As he enters the orchard, his form disappears behind the tree trunks. I jump into the air and weave through the trees. Heart in my throat, I descend to my porch, boots thudding onto the wood planks. That had been too close.

Inhaling, I enter the cabin.

"That sounded like a hard landing," Nicholas, one of my most trusted guards from the palace, says.

I shed my cloak and hang it beside the door. "I saw Grant in the wood, The Queen's Wood. Why have I not been told they named my forest?"

"You spoke with Grant?" Adam, another trusted guard from my palace, jumps up.

"Yes, he found me. He did not see my face, and I tried to alter my pitch. That is not the point." I raise my hands to my hips.

"We did not wish to cause you further strife, and you should not torture yourself by going there. What if you were recognized? What would you do then?"

"I know, I know." Pulling the chair from the table, I slump into the seat opposite my ward. I lift my eyes to meet his. "Were you nice to Adam and Nicholas?"

"Yes, I was nice to my babysitters." Theron, in his fae form, rolls his eyes.

I lean forward. "We do not have babies in Middle Earth. We have younglings."

Adam slides a book across the tabletop to me. "They say this is the last one."

Lifting the thick text from the tabletop, I turn to the page marked with a leather strap. Lines connect names, Lilith to an unknown being, begetting the vampire lines. A second line, opposite the first, links Lilith to an unnamed archangel, creating the witch lines. Sonia's name hovers under the witch lines. *Was she Lilith's daughter?* Surely Sonia, former High Priestess of the witch lines, now transformed into an Archangel who resides in Sheol with Abaddon and Lucifer, could not be that old.

Recalling Sonia's threat, I shudder. *"You've no idea who I am, who my parents are … I will be reconciled, even if I have to move Heaven and Earth to do it. Next time a volcano erupts or an earthquake rumbles through the bedrock, you will be witnessing my reach."*

The fated day above the desert echoes through my psyche. My death, the witches' circumvention of my untimely passing to the afterlife, and the pledge I made scroll through my thoughts. *My reach will be limitless as well.* But here I am, a whole season later, with no clearer a picture of how to stop Sonia than the day I burned the page alerting me of her promise.

Adam and Lilith were set in the garden almost six thousand years ago. Witches' lives span eight hundred to nine hundred years, but Sonia still lived and breathed in human form until the year 2018 AD, or CE, as the humans have adopted now. *What type of being could live six thousand years?* Only one of direct lineage from an immortal being, I could only guess. *Are we to surmise these Sonias are the same?* The fae only know of her activities from about the fifteenth century, when she became bolder with crusades against the vampires.

If the name on the page matches the same being as the Sonia we know, it only follows that she *must* be Lilith's daughter, sired by the Archangel Michael. My brain spins with the magnitude of a life spanning six thousand years. I can barely comprehend the changes my life has seen in the last fifteen months. I was crowned queen, thwarted an attempted coup, and have prevailed over kobold, locusts, goblins, and ogres. I braved more passages to Lower Earth than I care to count. My power has become mine to yield. I have also survived a festival season and being courted by four princes—which may be the most impressive feat of them all. I swallow, not wanting to think about my final act as Queen of Aubren.

My sacrifice could have been for naught if we cannot decipher Sonia's threat. I draw the page to me. Below Sonia's name sits the name of her son, then grandsons—one of these being Theron.

"Terran, that must be you. Your brothers' names are listed here." I press my finger to his former name on the page. "And you contend to not know the name of your grandfather, an aunt, uncle, or any other relative?"

Terran drops a bone on his plate. "I'm afraid no one ever mentioned it. This is your and my brothers' problem, not mine."

"This is the last text to be found. There is nothing more to be known. You are stuck in Middle Earth until your brother believes you are no longer a risk. Help us, and I imagine it will go a long way towards him forgiving you."

"I told you I'm willing to strike a deal. I'll talk after I'm released to Upper Earth."

Hearing a thud outside, my heartrate rises a notch. I push to my toes and look through a slit in the wood panel. Smiling, I swing the door open.

Foster takes my hands, tugging me outside and wrapping me in his arms. His clothes smell of fresh bread and ale, and I imagine he came from dinner with his men. As he releases me, I take in his blue eyes and orange locks, reflecting the light from the hearth. I could look upon him every day for the rest of my life, and I would be the happiest fae ever.

He leads me into the cabin, grunting at Terran, greeting Adam and Nicholas, and inquiring whether they can spare another hour.

"Anything for the Queen and her Chief of Spies." Nicholas winks.

"Nicholas, I am not your queen," I say.

"You will always be my queen. Now, go so I can beat Terran in another round of cards."

Lifting my cloak from the hook, Foster wraps it around my shoulders and raises the hood over my hair. He kisses the largest gem in the center of my forehead, and tiny tingles spread like fire over my skin. Heat rises to my cheeks.

"Can't you guys get a room?" Terran rises.

"We have a room." Foster extends his arm. "We are in a room."

"You peeps don't know anything."

"Yet another sentence that proves you need more time to adopt fae culture. You may never get beyond the confines of this forest, much less outside of Middle Earth, if you cannot adjust." I back to the door.

"Oh, I can pretend, fair Queen." Terran bends at the waist. "I can form sentences without contractions, and I will be happy to lie about how wonderful it is to play cards and stomp my foot to the tune of a fiddle."

Foster clutches my hand, urging me out of the cabin.

"You might want to talk to your Queen about her jaunts to the castle." Adam swings the door shut and turns to Terran. "If you would just be nice for a day, perhaps she would release you, and you may find a fae lass of your own."

"I don't want a fae lass," Terran says.

"Ahhh, every fae needs someone to come home to." Nicholas chimes in.

Foster squeezes my hand. "You have been to the castle?"

"I was not discovered. This hour is about us." I kiss his lips.

"I can be convinced to focus." He wraps his hand around my neck and presses his mouth to mine. Releasing me, he smiles. "Now, let us go."

We leap into the air, staying low under the canopy of branches, small splotches of dim light peeking through. Below us, ferns blanket the ground. The wind from our flight washes over me as we rush past trunks an arm-length wide until we exit the desert plain to the south. Rising high over the sand, the dry air cleanses my lungs. Tightening of my ribs reminds me of those I long to see. This is progress, I realize. For weeks, my chest felt as if a vice were tightening around it, the guilt and shame of leaving my family as I did foremost in my mind and heart.

Sonia should be dead, but she is not. I gave every-thing, left my family and my country, to end her, but her soul lives on. Now, she threatens graver destruction. I pray she only means this for Upper Earth and believes, as most do, I am dead. This tenet gives me the only peace that lets me sleep at night. My absence, faked morbidity, ensures my people and realm are safe, at least from direct threat. For it was I that she wanted. Frustration clouds my mind.

The need to stay hidden limits my ability to help solve Sonia's riddle. *She will be reconciled. With whom?*

I follow Foster's lead, and we alight on the beach.

"You are furlongs away." Foster swings our hands between us. "I wish you would let Alemayehu take Terran to Rotuga. He is ready."

I trace a line in the sand with my toe, fearing what I will face once Terran is gone. His presence gives me purpose. Without him, I have nothing save these few nights a week with Foster. Terran's mentoring and deciphering texts we received from the believers scouring our realm for any mention of Sonia are the only things that kept me sane the past months.

"It is a big responsibility for Alemayehu. He is not a young fae. I am also not sure what I will do once Terran is gone."

"Alemayehu's sons have pledged to watch Terran." Foster's lips form a smile, and he steps forward and brushes a kiss across my lips. "You are to marry me, that is what you are to do."

"You cannot be serious. This is my fault for exposing myself to you." Seeing his wide, round eyes, head shaking in defiance, I grimace. Allowing Foster to know that I live, to visit these nights, is the most selfish thing I have ever done. He pledges his happiness, but we cannot go on like this, him sneaking away to see me. We cannot build a life as such. I must be keeping him from building what could be a normal fae experience with another. Someone he could marry and have children with, grow old and gray with.

"You are free. When we first met, you dreamed of hiding away in a small cottage in the wood where you could live a simple life. Now you may."

"You are right." I straighten my back. "It will be enough."

Pulling me to him, he kisses my lips. "And when I have trained another, I will retire my position, and we shall travel the realm together, living like gypsies."

"What of children? That is no way for a young fae to grow up, untethered to any homeland."

"We shall have younglings, or we shall not. Whatever we decide."

"And what of your family? You would say goodbye, never see them again?" I ask.

"I could return to them periodically for a short bit."

"But they could never know your true life, never share in our happiness."

"Perhaps you could do research for the trinity witches until I am ready to join you. I know you enjoy aiding them. You also have your magic to continue to hone."

My magic, another point of angst in my psyche. I have not used it since my fateful encounter with Sonia, something I have not shared with Foster. Perhaps I cannot even conjure it again. I would not slight the Goddesses for taking the gift. I may welcome the release, for it feels like a curse, a yoke upon my shoulders too heavy to bear.

Leaning over, I rake my hand through the surf and splash Foster. "Why are we talking about this? I do not plan on marrying you. I need to accept my new life, learn to embrace the quiet, simple solitude."

He answers my offense, reaching into the sea and sprinkling water atop my head. "Yes, and I believe you shall attain that goal in a quicker fashion with Terran gone."

"Why are you focused on having Terran leave?"

Pulling me to him, he kisses my lips. "Because then I shall have you all to myself. There will be no need for guards or another to share the cabin with."

His mouth feels soft and warm on mine, and I allow myself to relish his embrace.

As the kiss ends, I smile. "I thought you were withholding spending the night with me alone until we marry."

"I am. The absence of another will make our union more enticing, forcing you to agree to marry me."

"You sound so sure. I feel as if my life shifts as sand in the wind."

"But now it does not. You are not beholden to anything. You are free to be a simple fae."

He keeps saying that I am free, but I have never felt more caged. Perhaps I do not fully trust that Sonia believes me dead. The witches' warning plays through my mind. Theron and I could be in danger if discovered. Theron, in his Terran body, tucked in this realm, worries me less, but my gem-studded brow and brilliant red hair are hard to hide.

I raise my eyes to the portal connecting our realm to Upper Earth, the human realm. The ring of crystals powering the magic glows green, creating a haze of color upon our realm. Thoughts of the lower rings that bridge us to Lower Earth, the realm of the damned souls, swirl through my mind. Sonia still has the power to pass between all these realms.

Archangels have never had power in our realm—or that has been the held belief. They do, however, seem able to influence, control, or somehow assume bodies of other beings, as we witnessed via attacks from kobold, locusts, goblins, ogres, and dragons.

"Your head is with Sonia again." Foster squeezes my hand.

"You do not know that. I could be picturing our life in the forest cottage or with packs on our backs, traveling the realm."

"Why have you not mentioned aiding the witches?" He jiggles my fingers. "I mean, I appreciate it, truly, but my opinion has not stopped you from aiding them before."

Taking his other hand, I hold his gaze. "I have sacrificed much. If I am discovered, it is all for naught."

"You mean to tell me, if there were no danger, you would aid them? That also has not stopped you before."

"If I am discovered, I put all fae in harm's way again. And my sacrifice will be for naught."

"You have your magic, but I see your position."

I bite my lip and drop my gaze.

He leans down. "You do still have the power to wield your magic, correct?"

Jumping into the air, I tug on his fingers. "You see my position? Did you just acquiesce to my line of thought? I say, that *is* rare."

He hovers before me. "And I am sure you have *never* used a distraction to hide an answer before. Your ability to conjure your magic remains, correct?"

I close my eyes and admit that I have not practiced my magic in the three months since I attempted to slay Sonia in her dragon form.

"Please tell me this is a joke. You jest, lest you be overheard by an angelic, or should I say, a demonic, spy."

Leaning in, I whisper, "It is not."

"Now I am more worried than before. You need your magic, Titania. If Sonia or some other enemy found you, or threatened our realm, you would need your powers."

"It brings me pain to think about using my magic again."

"That is why you need more joy in your life. Release Terran, take me as your husband, and let me bring you happiness every minute of every day. Tell me you will consider this." He wraps his warm arms around me, his wings beating in sync with mine.

I take in his hopeful gaze. *How can I not give someone who brings me such joy a portion of the same?* "I will think about releasing Terran to Alemayehu in earnest."

"Alemayehu's soldiers will naturally look after anyone who is new to the ranks," he says.

"I still wish we could stick him with a position like ditch digging."

"In times of peace, did you not use your military for such tasks?" he asks.

"Yes, I did," I say.

"Well, I would think it would be the same in Rotuga. No military man wants to sit around weaving baskets or darning jackets." He swings our arms between us.

I cut my gaze sideways to him. "You would have me weaving and darning jackets? I will devise a test for Terran and have Alemayehu do the same. Customs in Rotuga may differ from ours."

He spins to face me and kisses my lips. "Forgive me. I will task you with building, hauling water, and plowing. I like the test idea. It will put both your minds at ease."

Running my hand through his hair, I smile. "Thank you for watching over me and my family."

Shifting light from the ring crystals catches my eye, and I look up. The gray sky seems to quake, and a low rumble reaches my ears. Releasing Foster's hands and tugging my hood tightly around my head, I beat my wings, rising toward the dome. I reach the ring and peer into Upper Earth as another wave of motion jolts across the realm barrier.

Chapter

2

ANOTHER SHUDDER TREMBLES THROUGH the bedrock separating our realm from Upper Earth.

"It is just the Ulawun volcano rumbling." Foster wraps his arm around my waist. "You know it is common."

"You act as if I have misplaced paranoia."

"I see your unease. You are hardly ever still."

"Can you blame me?" I spin into him. For as much as I believe I made us safer, the same tenets of our existence hold true. We rely on Upper Earth for our wellbeing.

"Sonia thinks you dead, gone. Our realm is safe." He places his hands on my biceps.

"Yes, but if she is set to destroy the upper realm, it will affect us—if lava burns their land and smoke blocks the sun… if earthquakes destroy the bedrock…" With a hard beat of my wings, I approach the dome and place my palm on the cold rock. "If this barrier fails, we are doomed." My breath catches in my lungs, and I fight to expel it.

Foster runs his palms down my arms. "Only once, in the thousands of years of the fae, have Upper Earth's tragedies affected us. Rains flooded their realm for over a year, and our people persevered."

I shake my head. "Those were very dark times. Many of the plants and animals of our realm nearly became extinct. We scrounged for sustenance in our soil, eating the bugs and worms to survive. Many fae died. The judges feel it in their bones. They say the dark times are near again. We have been through so much. How much more are we to bear?"

"Do you not believe the Creator will stop Sonia from destroying Upper Earth? He has done so much to protect His human creations. We were set in this realm to protect humans from the evil spirits below. The ethereal fae and the angels were set in Upper Earth to guard humans there."

"Does the Creator have that power? Much of me believes the Creator is only that, a creator. What the beings do is up to them."

His eyes narrow. "What of the Goddesses? Do you believe they have power to protect us?"

"I believe the Goddesses guide and bestow us with gifts, but I do not know what power the Goddesses possess beyond that."

"Whatever may come, we are safe now. You are safe now. You ensured that Sonia will spare our realm. Let that sink into your psyche. Once you send Terran away, take a period of rest. Walk through the forests, watch the birds, note the flowers, and let the beauty of our land restore your faith."

I look up at the rock above me. *Faith.* That is also not something I wish to think about. "This is spoiling our flight. I do not want to waste our time with you thinking about these things."

Sliding his hands to mine, he grips my fingers. "We need to talk about them. I want to share your burdens."

Forcing a smile, I kiss him. "Race you."

I pull my hands from his and dive. Holding my wings taut against my back, arms straight at my sides, I drop headfirst toward the ocean. The cool wind beats against my face as I eye the churning water rushing toward me. I stretch my arms above my head and plunge into the salty, cold, dark sea. As my body loses momentum, I kick my legs into the darkness, letting the nothingness surround me. I am safe. I am free. *If only I could become a mermaid.* My lungs start to protest, and I look up to catch sight of Foster's dark form. I kick my legs and rise to the surface.

As my head breaches the water, I suck in a breath. "I won."

"I let you win." Foster splashes me.

"This cloak is heavy." Treading water, I release the garment from my shoulders.

He takes it and, rising above the water, wrings it out. "This will do you no good if you do not wear it."

"There is no one about this late." With a kick and a hard beat of my wings, I join him.

We fly to the beach and alight on the sand. "Tell me of news from the castle. It has been almost a week. Surely there is something new."

Tucking my cloak under his arm, he takes my hands. "There is much. Now that the rainy season will be over soon, they seem to be moving forward with many things."

He tells me of my cousin Quinn, now King of my kingdom, and his wife and how their youngling is expected in months. My cousin Princess Gatuika and her fiancé Prince Lowell of Hilbron, the kingdom lying to our east, have set their wedding for the summer solstice, to be held at my palace. Her sisters Makani and Isla continue their school and dote on my parents and my maid Alfreda. The girls' parents still visit, Mother taken for walks in the garden by her sister often.

"But she remains unchanged, not a word has passed her lips since she insisted your things be held in chests," Foster says.

"And Father?" Tears pool in my eyes as I think of Father's crimson beard laced with silver strands.

"He is often with Quinn, busying himself helping with affairs of the kingdom."

"Parents should not lose all their children as my parents have."

Foster wipes a tear from my cheek with his thumb. "I thought we were to escape our challenges for a while."

I step back and wipe my face with my fingers. "Yes, you are right. Tomorrow I will make a picnic, and we will fly someplace exotic to enjoy a meal together."

"I shall like that very much." He clutches my chin and presses his lips to mine.

Even with the pressure in my chest that plagues me when I think of my family, the warmth of Foster's lips against mine, the soft-yet-firm set of his mouth, transports me.

Ending the kiss, he squeezes my hand. "We should let Adam and Nicholas return to their families."

I take my cloak from his arms, wrap it around my shoulders, and raise the hood, shivering as the cold, wet drape touches my skin.

We retrace our path, sweeping over the desert and back through the woods to my cottage. Landing on the fern-covered floor of the forest, Foster takes my hand. We hop to the porch, and I fit my finger on his lips then kiss him quickly.

I listen to the banter inside, Terran complaining about the boring games and Adam grunting in reply. It is past time Terran integrated into our society. That is my fault. I must face my uncertain future.

⚬⚬⚬⚬⚬

"TEA?" BIA, GODDESS OF POWER, *offers a white porcelain cup ringed with purple irises. "Your mother is here."*

I follow her gaze to the far side of the bright green meadow. Flowers of every color dot the field. Three women sit around a table canopied by tree limbs: Artemis, goddess of the hunt; Athena, goddess of wisdom; and Mother.

I blink, and I am before them. Bia lounges on an empty chair.

"Sit, Titania." Athena points a long, thin, golden-nail-tipped finger at the empty chair. "We will be five then."

I study the faces of the goddesses and meet Mother's eyes.

"You are not alive, Titania. You need to accept what is." She pats the empty, tufted seat beside her.

Heart pounding, I suck in a breath and bolt upright.

"Same nightmare?" Terran's voice and the scent of coffee reorient me.

In my cabin. In my woods. In my Kingdom. In my Realm. *You need to accept what is.*

"Yes." Wiping the cold sweat from my brow, I wrap the covers around my waist and cross to the table. "Or a version of it."

"You've never said what the dream is about."

"No contractions." I pour tea into a tin cup.

Terran rolls his eyes. "You have never said what the dream is about, and you *are* deflecting."

"Deflecting?" I raise an eyebrow.

"You are evading the question. Is that acceptable?"

"Yes." I sit opposite him. "I have decided Alemayehu and I will each test you on fae culture and skills, and if you pass, you can go to Rotuga with Alemayehu to join their army."

"Really?" Eyebrows raised, a smile forms on his face. His knee bounces under the table, and for the first time in three months, he appears genuinely excited.

"Maybe the test will be that you must go a whole day without one human term, mannerism, or action."

He raises his arm and holds his wrist in front of his face. "Can we start now?"

"Why did you raise your arm like that?"

"To look at my imaginary watch?" His voice rises in pitch.

"A fae does not have a watch."

Rolling his eyes, he lowers his arm. "Okay, now?"

"If you wish."

"I do wish."

If Terran is only to be with me a few more days, then I mean to take advantage of his help. We clear a large area in front of the cottage, moving rocks from one side, using them to build a divider in the middle to pen goats on the other.

As the last boulders are placed and the sun hangs low in the sky, I sit atop the wall.

"We need to till the ground for a garden tomorrow, and then fashion a fence to hold the goats."

"That"—he smiles—"is going to take a whole day. I thought you said I could leave once I passed the tests."

I lift my water pouch and take a sip. "Alemayehu will not come until the first day of the week, so that will give us another day to finish the projects."

"And that is what you are to do once I am gone? Plant and tend a garden, raise goats?"

"Yes." I gaze into the forest.

"It will not be enough. We are the same. We cannot be satisfied with a simple life."

"You do not know that, and if you admit this to me, then I may never let you leave." I push off the rocks.

"I am to join an army. I will have a purpose. I do not see that you have any now that your research is stalled."

"What if I have served my purpose already and I am meant to enjoy my lack of purpose?" I approach the cottage.

He flits ahead of me and opens the door. "What is your nightmare?"

I bite my lip, wondering whether to further his argument with the admission. "It is of my mother. She is with the Goddesses and tells me to accept what is."

Letting the door swing shut with a bang, Terran jumps to my side. "See? Accepting that you have no purpose is your worst nightmare. We are the same."

Shaking my head, I lift a pot of water onto the stove and stoke the fire. "I do not believe so. I am new to this life, or second life. I will adjust."

Waiting for bathwater to heat, I cut a chunk of bread and gather some meats and cheeses into a basket. Terran does not know what he is talking about. I do not know that I can trust the message from Mother and the Goddesses after they tried to persuade me to abandon my promise to the witches of the trinity. Of course, the women may have known Sonia already had the power of an archangel. *Would I have been happier in the soul realm with them?* No, it was not my time. I will not believe it was.

This stubborn idea pushes me to a deeper quandary. *If I do not trust they had pure intentions, have I lost faith in the Goddesses? In Mother? Or had I cheated death out of selfishness and fear? Did I belong with the Goddesses? Was that their plan for me? Could I serve my people better in the spiritual realm? Should I have stayed dead?* My heart thuds as I think of never touching Foster again. *But you would have your mother.* It is that thought which spurs my belief that Sonia wants her mother. *What other bond, save for that of for a child, could have a larger pull over a being's heart?*

"The water boils. Would you like me to take it to the tub for you?" Terran's whisper brings me from my churning thoughts.

I shake my head and lift the pot from the stove, amazed at his offer of aid. It is the first time he has shown kindness. I remember Hunter's assessment of poor character and disdain for his half-brother. Yet, Alena, another witch of the trinity, sees hope for him. I will continue to withhold judgment yet err on the side of caution. He must remain in Middle Earth. If free, Terran could reveal to Sonia that I still live. It is a risk that he knows I still exist in this realm, but there was no other who could ensure his security in the transition to fae.

Terran's eyebrows shoot up as I enter the cabin, my dress swishing about my legs. "You must have a fancy"— he bites his lip—"event planned for tonight."

"You were about to say date."

"But I did not. What do you call dating? Or a date?"

"If you are dating someone, then you are courting. We do not have a word like date. We would just say we are seeing them or name the activity."

"Thank you."

"You are welcome." Part of me feels guilty that his acting as a fae dampens his personality, but I would guess he may find a way to integrate it once fae life becomes more natural.

"Same boots, same dagger, I see."

"I do not need more than one pair of boots."

Hearing the thud of footsteps on the porch, I check the peephole and swing the door open wide as Timothy, another of my former guards, and Foster remove their cloaks.

"Hello, fair Queen," Timothy says.

"I am not your queen." I take his wrap and fit it on the hook beside the door.

I explain Terran's test, and Timothy expresses nothing but glee at the chance to challenge Terran's ability to act true to fae characteristics.

Foster and I take our leave, descending the steps hand in hand.

"You look beautiful tonight," he says.

Pushing to my toes, I press my lips to his. "Thank you. You look handsome, too."

"Where should we go?"

"How about the northern coast of Lindleton? We may be able to see the Northern Lights."

"Splendid idea. I have never seen them, have you?"

"Yes, although they were faint both times. I hear in winter they are the brightest."

"And if there are no lights, perhaps we can find a polar bear. I would love to see a polar bear."

"A polar bear? You never told me that."

"You still have much to learn about me." He runs a finger down my nose.

We walk to the tree line and leap into the air, whizzing around tree trunks in the deep forest. At the coast, we rise high, flying just feet below the dome separating us from Upper Earth. Thinking of the Northern Lights brings memories of my trips to the lights with my cousins and then my suitor. I shudder when I think of what my life would have been like had I married him.

"You are deep in thought again." Foster squeezes my fingers.

"I am sorry. It is hard not to think of everything that has passed."

"I will help."

He begins to narrate our journey, speaking of the elephants and black and white bears of Chastam, the birds with feathers of every color.

"But this land has no redeeming qualities whatsoever," he says as we pass over the border to Lindleton. "The birds are gray, bears ugly brown. It rains all year long, and the food is bland as mud."

I open my mouth to admonish him, but he lifts a finger.

"Do not say it is not true."

"The coasts are beautiful, vegetation bright green, and water oh-so blue in the late summer."

"When it is not raining. Which is a lot. I mean, we have rainy season, but then it is dry for months. In Lindleton, it rains every day."

I roll my eyes. "That must be an exaggeration. When we vacationed there, it only rained one afternoon."

"You are blessed by the Goddesses in all things. I am sure it was them who gave you the gift of sunshine for your holiday."

Not so in my dreams, I think as we land on a barren plane near the north sea under a remote portal to Upper Earth.

"I see no lights yet." Removing his cloak, he spreads it on the ground. "Should we eat and wait?"

"Yes, we should eat." Pulling his pack closer, he reaches in and produces a bunch of grapes.

He pops one in his mouth then holds one out for me. I take it and, lifting my chin, toss it up and catch it in my mouth as it comes down. I slide off his lap, and we snack on the bread and cheese and sip wine from our flasks. We lie on the cloak, side by side, holding hands, watching for the lights.

After many minutes of silence, he pushes up on one elbow. "What would you have done if Sonia did not come with the dragons? If an occasion for you to fake your death had not presented itself? Would you have wed Mikel?"

Sadness settles in my psyche as I remember the pain my engagement to Mikel caused Foster. I force the thoughts away. I cannot undo the past, all I can do is face my future with hope. "I had to have a bigger army to protect our fae. I knew there would be another attack. The engagement contract gave me a year to wed. I planned to delay the marriage as long as I could, but if I had to honor the contract, I would have."

"But he, his whole family, are so…" His lips contort.

"Pretentious, stuck up, entitled, patriarchal, condescending? I know." Folding my arms across my middle, I sit up. "Why are you asking me this now? I thought we had been over everything."

Sitting up, he leans over his legs. Flying over Lindleton, his family's kingdom, seemed to have brought it all back. "I do not see how you could abandon, or sacrifice your—"

"My morals, my heart?" Taking his hand, I spin to my knees. I duck my head so we are eye to eye as my heart threatens to leap from my body. "I wish you had said this before, let me know you felt this way. I know I hurt you. It broke my heart to do it. That is how I know I love you, but it had to be done. Sonia was coming for me, for my kingdom, and she would not have stopped there. She would have taken our entire realm. I needed a bigger army, and Mikel had the largest one."

Foster turns his head away. "It makes me sick to think… He did not deserve you. None of them did. I hate that you had—"

"Shhh." I cup my hands around his cheeks. "Do not hate them. Yell at me. It was me. I deceived all of them. And believe me, I feel all the shame and guilt that I deserve."

"No." His jaw goes hard. "If they had open minds, would have enough respect for you to honor your truth, you would not have had to go to those lengths."

Running my fingers from his temple to his jaw, I shake my head. "It would not change the fact that I had to face Sonia. It would not alter that I needed to die. Will you ever forgive me? Because if you cannot I fear we cannot ever be truly happy. This, you and I, may be all I can ever give you. I cannot give you a wedding with friends and family to witness. I cannot provide you evenings around the fire with your family jostling our younglings on their knees. I understand if I am not enough—"

"No, love." He plants kisses on my cheeks. "I am so sorry. I did not mean to ruin our evening. You know I want to be with you, however our lives unfold, but it makes me sick to my stomach thinking of how they dismissed you, acted as if they were better than you. They do not deserve to reap the benefits of your sacrifice. I am trying to understand the magnitude of your devotion to this cause. That you would sacrifice every bit of your happiness for it."

"You have done the same. You had no life save from your position as my spy. You came when I called, went as I commanded."

The sides of his lips creep up. "You do not know that. You were off galivanting with Holden, then his brother Brandon, and then your suitors. Perhaps I spent many nights in pubs with pretty maids, danced with them late into the night, took them into my room for a night."

I steel my reaction not knowing if he is trying me. "You are right. I do not know, but for the record, I never liked Brandon, and I never shared anything beyond conversation with the suitors."

"You spent the night with Brandon."

Posting hands to hips, I roll my eyes. "We were fighting goblins." I shudder as I remember the grotesque bodies of the goblins turning bald head over bulging middle in the churning water of the flooded canyon. Dropping to my butt, I hold his gaze. "I sacrificed everything because I had to. There is something inside me that drives me to protect the fae and the humans above us. Do you think I was given the power to blast beams of energy from my palms to entertain or delight? No, the Goddesses granted me the ability to perform remarkable things. I could not waste my gift."

A smile grows on his face as he places his hands on my cheeks. "And this is why I have loved you from the second you stole my quiver and bow. You are the bravest person I know."

I lean in and kiss him, pressing my lips to his.

He answers my kiss with the same intensity, and his arms wind around me. As his lips pull away, he leans his forehead on mine. "I did not mean for this evening to go this way. I am sorry," he whispers.

"Do not be. As you said, we need to speak of these things. If we are to be true partners, you must share your feelings with me."

"What keeps you from saying you will marry me?" Foster asks.

"I am still figuring out my life. It was selfish for me to let you know I still live, to commandeer your nights this way, to entice you to leave your post, your family. We need to make sure we will not make each other miserable."

"The only way I would be miserable is not being with you."

After another long kiss, we decide there will be no lights to see this night and start the journey back to my cabin. I try to imagine my life post-Terran: waking with the light, sipping tea, tending the garden, milking the goats. Perhaps I shall raise sheep and learn to weave. Hunting may take a part of my day. I could add to the small cabin, enclose the bath area. Foster will visit on weekends, and when I feel we are both content, I could say yes to being his wife. He would leave his post, and we could travel or do whatever else we may choose.

The thoughts take a quick backseat as we land on the grass outside the cabin. Loud shouts come from within. Shaking my head, I rush up the steps.

Foster grabs my arm. "One more kiss before our evening ends?"

I open my mouth, and before I can speak, his lips press to mine. I yield to the soft pressure of his skin, savoring the feel of his arms around me, the scent wafting from his frame, the warmth enveloping me.

"The fae do not behave in this manner," Timothy bellows from within.

"Ugh." Foster sighs. "Goddesses, please."

Pressing my finger to his lips, I smile. "It was a wonderful date, thank you."

Hands on my waist, he kisses me again. Warmth spreads through my body, and I never want it to end. Releasing me, he waves me ahead of him.

I enter the cabin to find Terran and Timothy at the table, holding cards. "The fae do not behave in what manner?"

"He was counting the cards," Timothy says.

"I wanted to win. Is not that the point of the game, to win? How was I supposed to know that the fae do not count cards?" Terran's eyes grow wide as if pleading with me.

Unlatching my cloak, I swing it to the hook. "You should always assume if an action is ethically wrong, or even a gray area, that fae, in general, would not pursue it."

"Please do not count this against me. I think I have done really well today," Terran says.

I cut my eyes to Timothy. "Apart from the card incident, how do you judge him?"

Timothy acquiesces that, other than being a swindling mouse, Terran has passed.

He stands. "So, is it decided? I pass?"

"I believe you do," I say.

"Yes." Terran throws his cards on the table. He looks up, his eyes darting between the three of us. "I mean, praise the Goddesses?"

"It is fine, friend." I pat his shoulder. "Congratulations. I am happy that you are ready for fae life. If Alemayehu approves, you will be free of this cabin and forest for good."

"Yes." Terran slaps his leg.

Timothy takes his leave, and I walk outside with Foster as he prepares to go as well.

"I wish you would stay till morning. I have dove eggs." I squeeze his hand as our arms stretch between us.

"Save them till Terran is gone. I will come that very night. Then we shall be free to come and go as we please." Pulling me to him, he kisses me.

I watch Foster, his orange hair reflecting the light from the cabin, until the dark forest takes him. Trapsing back into the cabin, Terran and I prepare for sleep. The next morning, I wake to the bitter smell of coffee brewing. With no disturbing dreams of the Goddesses or Mother, I cross to the slit in the door, relishing the sight of first light causing the hovering fog to glow.

Terran lifts his cup as I join him at the table. "The last day you may have to endure the smell of coffee."

I touch my tin cup to his. "Yes, we will complete the goat pen, and I would like to find a small pasture for sheep."

"Now you are to have sheep, too?"

"I should learn to weave and sew. People cannot swipe clothes from the castle for me forever."

Terran leans forward. "To sew? I thought you said fae females learn to sew from an early age."

"Yes, most do, but with four older brothers, I tended to join in whatever they were doing. After losing them, I spent all my free time studying histories and training to become monarch."

"Being the one who is supposed to assume leadership is tough. My father expected perfection."

"I am sorry your situation did not work out."

One side of his lip curls. "No, you are not, but you should be. If I achieved my goal, the curse would never have been broken. You would never have been dragged into this affair. You would have your kingdom, and the fae would have gone on with their merry little existence with no troubles. Now look what you have. Nothing. Just like me. All because of my brother."

Astonished at his assessment, and taking a minute to process his words, I take a sip of my tea. Under the rule of Sonia and her sons, Thanatos and Theron, the witches would have wiped out the vampire population. The old guard of fae may not have blinked an eye, even welcomed the culling, but many humans would have been harmed to satisfy Sonia's wishes. *Would she have stopped with destruction of the vampires?*

I cut my eyes to him. "Now you call him brother?"

"That is what you question about what I said?"

"I worry that Sonia would have taken innocent lives."

"Unless they were human, you would have no responsibility to intervene. Your life would have proceeded without turmoil. You would still be Queen. The battles with the kobold, goblins, ogres, and dragons would not have happened. So now I ask"—he leans in so our faces are but inches apart—"who is the bad guy, and who is the good guy?"

"All of the Creator's beings should be treated with respect. You were part vampire. What if Sonia killed your mother? What if she sought to end your Earth life?"

Terran bolts up, flinging his chair across the cabin. "She wouldn't do that. Let's just finish the goat pen."

He stomps outside, and I run my palms to the edges of the table. My stomach turns, knowing he is half right and that only I am to blame for my life path. If I had not aided the trinity of witches that first time, much would be different. Maybe many more lives would have been lost. That mattered, even if they were beings of Upper Earth once considered soulless. *And* would *Sonia have stopped with destruction of the vampires, or would she attack the werewolves, elves, and us?* I grip the corners of the table. None of this can be known now. What is, is.

The day passes with few words between me and Terran. I think about what Foster would say about Terran's rant. Likely that he aims to alter my opinion of Sonia and his father, that he is a manipulator and wants me to feel sympathy for his plight, perhaps even sway my opinion of the trinity of witches. I am not blind to the grays of this battle but know I am on the right side of it.

I breach the silence over dinner, inquiring whether Terran is anxious about his move to Rotuga.

"I am used to people disliking me. It will be fine."

"Why do you assume they will not like you? Fae are not like human teens. You are an adult fae, will be a soldier. There is respect attached to that position. If you perform well, contribute, and show leadership aptitude, you could be promoted. You will have comrades, perhaps even friends, and there are plenty of beautiful fae girls in Alemayehu's village. His is the largest in the kingdom."

He peers at me over his soup bowl. "Do they all look like you?"

I cut my eyes away and then back to him. "What do you mean?"

"Well, your stones, or whatever they are on your forehead. You never mentioned them. Do all female fae have those?"

Touching the middle stone on my brow, I chuckle. "I had not thought of that. I apologize. I am the only fae with these decorations that I know of. Before I escaped Lower Earth and Abaddon by exploding one of our rings, my markings were more like Alemayehu's, dark lines and dots, but after reentering Middle Earth, these graced my brow."

"Weird." He lifts his spoon to his lips.

"Yes, they are strange."

The rest of the meal passes in silence, as does the evening, both of us with our noses in books. He inquires about the rings and the crystals required to power their magic. I recite only what is commonly known because the exact crystals and the procedure for activating the rings are secrets known only to the Ring Keepers and monarchs.

"So, you must physically take out the crystals to close the rings?"

"Yes."

"And if they are in place, the rings are open, which is most of the time unless there is an emergency, like someone trying to invade your realm? So, a fae can pass through the ring anytime they wish?"

"Correct, and technically, yes, but rules require you to ask permission of the Ring Keepers before entering Upper Earth. The rings are watched at all times."

He narrows his gaze. "So, you got permission to travel to Upper Earth to help me escape Lower Earth."

"Yes."

"And this is common knowledge?"

"No, my alliance with the witches is known only to a select few believers. We have a Ring Keeper and High Judge who supported the missions."

"Believers?"

"Those who believe in the Creator, the Goddesses, the original teachings."

Leaning forward, he lets his book fall to his lap. "Why am I just learning of this now? How much of what I learned were the original teachings? What do most fae believe?"

I stand and pace to the fire. "Most fae believe we are of the Creator, but many fail to pray to the Goddesses, lack faith that they can direct our paths, that they will protect us. It has been a long time since the great flood, so fae have felt secure for many millennia."

He shakes his head. "The great flood? Like the one in the Bible?"

"Yes, water from above flooded into our portals, and they had to be closed for almost a year. Those that survived the deluges of water were left in a dark world, and thousands died of malnutrition. It is known as the darkest time. Many of the aging fae see signs of the return of a dark time."

"Great, I'm saved from endless darkness to face the threat of endless darkness."

"No. My sole mission, till my dying breath, holds to do all in my power to keep light and water flowing into our realm. That is why whatever information you are keeping from us about your family is so important. It could help us keep Sonia from plunging us all into darkness… All of us, including the Upper Earth realm."

"I'm only nineteen. Family trees weren't high on my priority list."

Crossing the small space, I grip the arms of his chair and lean over. "You were being groomed to be the next High Priest of the Witches. Do not offend me by pretending you were not privy to your family's history. We will see how long you hold out once you are eating earthworms for sustenance."

"You are quite fierce when you try to be."

TRICIA COPELAND

The timbers rumble under my boots and Terran's chair vibrates in my grip. My dishes clank and crash onto the floor, and burning logs spill from the hearth. Dropping to my knees, I crawl toward the fiery wood that bounces toward my trunk as the walls quake around me. I grab the water bucket, douse the embers, and brace myself between the wall and the trunk.

Chapter

3

"I TAKE IT YOU'RE NOT DOING THIS? I miss LA a little bit less now," Terran yells over the pounding of board against board. "I'm guessing there are no building codes here. Is this roof rated for falling trees?"

The knocking subsides to a tremble, and the structure stills. Clutching the side of my cot, I start to stand.

"Get down!" Terran yells.

"Wha—" Before I can get the word out, another rumble jolts through the cabin, sending my legs up and my back to the deck. My lungs seize as my breath catches and shoulder blades sear with pain. I gulp for air as the quake subsides. I sit up to find Terran hunched under the upturned armchair.

He rises. "Earthquakes 101: Protect your head, and don't get up until the aftershock."

"One-oh-one? Aftershock?" I spin to my hands and knees.

"One-oh-one, a basic class and the most important thing to know, and aftershock, the quake after the quake. LA had many earthquakes. You've never been in an earthquake?"

"No. Aubren has not experienced a quake for many generations. Sonia is making good on her promise."

We hold our posts for what seems like eternity until Terran declares the tremble to be finished. Crossing to the bureau, I sweep the broken pottery into a pile. We right all the furniture and clean the floor and hearth. Eyes panning the forest, I note a couple of leaning trees, their roots protruding from the dirt. We were lucky, and I say a silent prayer to the Goddesses that Foster and my family and fae were all so blessed. Heart pounding, I pile dry logs into the fireplace and light the tinder.

"So, is that what you mean when you talk about a believer? That these tragedies of nature are caused by evil beings?"

I spin to face him. "Sonia literally threatened this. These quakes, if they continue and worsen, will degrade the bedrock and collapse our realm. We will be forced to abandon it, and the fae will be no more."

Crossing outside, I suck in the cool, moist air. I shoot to the treetops, scouring for significant holes in the forest. I startle as Terran lands beside me.

I point to the dark dome above. "See? The ring is closed. They will wait till morning to open them."

"All rings in the realm?"

My mind pings with a warning at his question. Now is the time for a lie. "That is protocol."

Motion below catches my eye, and I look down to see a being land on our porch. The fae sheds a hood and swings the cabin door open. The light from the fire illuminates orange hair. *Foster.*

"Titania?" He strides inside.

I drop to the cabin. "I am here."

Closing the distance between us, he wraps his arms around me and squeezes tightly. "You are okay?"

"I am okay. Is everyone at the castle safe?" I cling to him.

Releasing me, he shakes his head. "I do not know. I was with my family. I came to you first."

"Why did you come here first? You must go to them. Make sure everyone is okay. I will come with you. I can stay in the forest. No one will see me."

"What about Terran?"

"Curses." My heart thuds in my chest, and I bolt outside.

Terran sits on the porch, swinging his legs over the edge. "I am right here. Where am I going to go? You have given me no maps."

I press my palms to my ribs as my breath draws in and out, in and out. The need to go to my castle, to each of the villages to see my fae, ensure everyone is safe, strums through my veins like waves pounding the beach.

"Foster, go!"

"Goddesses, you do not have to yell. " He stomps past me. "I was out of wits worried about you, thinking a tree fell on the cabin."

"I am sorry. I am beside myself thinking of my family and fae. I feel frustrated that I cannot help."

"I will go and send word, or come myself, to let you know all is well. The Goddesses will protect them, you will see."

"Thank you, and please forgive me. I did not mean to raise my voice to you."

"I do." He presses his mouth to mine in a hard kiss.

I answer his intensity, clutching his jacket, then push him away. "Go."

He presses his forehead to mine. "Be safe."

"I will."

Raising his hood, he leaps into the air. I watch the dark forest until his form is out of sight. I realize the wood appears blacker than ever before. I sense no movement, see no light reflecting from small eyes, and hear no sounds from the forest. The animals know this is the time for caution as well. After another survey of the trees, I back into the cabin and close the door.

"The Goddesses will protect them? That sounds like a fool's folly. If that's what a believer is, I'm not one. You can't seriously think these mystical beings watch over and protect you." Terran slumps into a chair.

Taking a seat opposite him, I lean on my elbows. "Tell me about the earthquakes. What other precautions did you take?"

He stands and crosses to the bureau holding the dishes. Describing that tall furniture would be tethered to the wall, he reviews how one might stay safe during a quake.

Grabbing a parchment, pen, and ink from the drawer, I start a list. A thud sounds from outside, and the structure creaks. Bracing for another quake, and sensing none, I rise and cross to the door, checking the peephole.

Adam stands, hands on hips. "It is I. Let me in."

I swing the door open. "Is there news from the castle? Is everyone okay?"

Adam reports that no one in the castle was injured, but that the kitchen and library were in shambles. I inquire about the rest of the kingdom, and he indicates that reports are still being gathered. Frustrated at my inability to help, I show Adam the list of earthquake precautions.

"Where will I say I came up with this?"

"It does not matter. Say you noticed the shelves falling and books flying off.."

Adam backs to the door with the list. Noting my black cape beside the door, my mind sparks an idea.

"Can you bring some dark leather?" I ask.

"Of course. How much?"

"Perhaps six palms by six palms and some string to match?"

Even with the late hour, I cannot rest, so I enlist Terran to help me anchor the bureau to the planks behind it and add slim bars of wood across the open shelves.

"There is still nothing you can do to prevent one of those huge trees from crushing you." Terran rests in the chair.

"We have wings, and I have my magic."

"I have never seen your magic. Would it really be helpful in an earthquake? What exactly are you capable of?"

"You are becoming quite testy."

"And you are becoming unhinged. Realizing I am right? That raising goats and sheep is not going to satisfy you?"

"But you, my friend, are becoming more fae every minute. That is three sentences straight without any contractions."

His eyes grow wide. "Ghastly. But I think you may be skirting the topic. Do you have access to your magic or not? Perhaps I could escape through any of the rings any time I want."

I grip the chair back and lean over it. "But now you will never know. Because they will leave the rings closed until the morrow when Alemayehu comes."

"Seriously, show me," he says.

I know it is not a wise use of my magic and pray to the Goddesses I can still wield it. I raise my hand and will the power toward my palm.

It grows green and I smile. "Do you still wish to experience my magic?"

"Hit me."

With a curl of my hand, I sling a small spark of power. It darts across the space, landing in the exact center of his hand.

"Ooooww!" Closing his palm, he wraps the other hand around it.

"Perhaps you need some aloe for that? I did that to myself once. It took two days to heal."

"You are pure evil, woman." Terran waves his injured hand in the air.

I cross to the bureau and slide the jar of salve across the table to him. "But you will not tempt me to use my magic again, will you?"

My pulse races as I watch him treat his wound. Guilt itches at my psyche, but he did ask for it. And now I know I have my magic. But with worry for my fae, I know I will not sleep tonight. I grab a bottle of wine and two glasses and sit kitty corner to Terran, pouring him a drink and then myself.

⚬⚬⚬

SLEEP FINALLY COMES, and my mind buzzes with worry about the state of the kingdom. *It was a small tremor,* I reassure myself. Loud thuds sound on the porch, shaking the tiny structure, and I remind myself to stay present. Today, Alemayehu will test Terran for his readiness to join the Rotuga army.

Rising, I cross to the door and peer through the small opening. Alemayehu stands with a large soldier flanking him. I swing the door open.

"Welcome, friend." I offer my arm.

Locking his palm around my forearm, Alemayehu points to the soldier. "My eldest, Lencho. He will be Terran's superior when he joins our army."

My fingers wrap not halfway around Lencho's bulging arm. I note his broad shoulders and muscled chest and imagine that Alemayehu may have looked much like Lencho when younger. I invite them inside. To my surprise, Terran stands, arms straight against his sides, palms rigid. I raise an eyebrow. *This is new.* I cannot imagine Terran ever showing deference to anyone. I amend my assessment

43

quickly. *Except perhaps to his father or grandmother.* They were, and may still be, the two most powerful witches of Upper Earth, and the only ones who could either elevate or condemn him, sealing his fate.

Terran strides forward, arm raised to greet Alemayehu. "Good to see you, sir, and thank you for coming."

Alemayehu chuckles and takes the boy's arm. "Well, this is a first. Good for you, Terran."

"I am ready to begin the next chapter of my life in this realm. Thank you for the opportunity." Terran extends his arm to Lencho.

Lencho crosses his arms over his bulging chest. "We will see if you are worthy to serve."

Alemayehu describes how they plan to administer the test in three parts with ten challenges in each, including a section on skill, fae culture, and fae history. Lifting tools and weapons from the wall, we file outside, Lencho inquiring about the story we will use for Terran's appearance in their ranks.

Skin colors of the fae in Rotuga range from medium brown, like the feathers of an emu, to almost black, like Alemayehu's. With Terran's light coloring, the story he will tell is that he craves adventure and wishes to experience a different culture. Since his family has many sons to work their farm in Aubren, he traveled to Rotuga to start his own life. Few fae will understand this, as we tend to be inherently bound to our family and land, but it is not completely unheard of. Fae sometimes, although rarely, do venture beyond their birthplaces. The story is akin to

Foster's: a farm boy itching for a different life, spurred to action by the threat of invaders from Lower Earth.

Terran passes the skills tests easily, and Alemayehu asks him to dance.

Terran scoffs, posting his hands to his hips. "If you would like me to dance to hip-hop or rap, then I may oblige you, but I will not do a jig."

"Just show us. A fae not dancing will look odd," Alemayehu says.

"Not all fae can love dancing."

Alemayehu shakes his head. "All fae love music and dancing. You must at least attempt each trial, or you do not pass."

Terran relents, posting his hands to his waist and, lifting his knees one after another, shifts his weight from foot to foot in a bouncing motion.

Alemayehu stifles a chuckle and accepts the attempt.

Terran recounts fae history with few errors.

Although not wholly in support of the plan, Lencho must concede Terran has passed his tests.

Alemayehu assents that Theron is now ready for life in the Rotugan army. Both make it very clear that with a single misstep, Terran will find himself in the dungeon.

I smooth my vest. "Terran is aware of the conditions of his position. I pray he will be an asset to your army and finds happiness in doing such."

"We should all pray to the Goddesses for that. Let us go." Lencho strides toward the door.

Terran's frozen features face Alemayehu then turn to me. "This is real?"

I nod and extend an arm. "Goddesses' speed."

He blinks, and his fingers lock above my wrist. "Thank you."

"Be well, friend." I watch him lift his pack to his shoulders and follow Lencho.

Alemayehu wraps his arms around me. "You will be well?"

"I will be well, friend. Write to me of news."

He pats my back. "I will visit as soon as I can."

"Thank you."

We step out onto the porch, and I watch as, one after another, they jump into the air, rise to the canopy, and slip between the branches. I examine the space around my cabin. With the garden seeds planted and the pen and meadow ready for goats and sheep, the evening spans out as a blank slate. I drop my eyes and, seeing the dead fowl from Terran's archery skills test, scoop them up.

"Well, at least I have you to clean."

I am pulling the meat from a bone with my teeth when I hear bleating sounds outside. I check the forest to find Foster alighting in the center of the stone-ringed enclosure, a small goat under each arm. Adam, Nicholas, and Timothy land beside him, each also carrying an animal under each arm. They release the goats into the pen and herd four sheep into the meadow. Indicating they have another trip to bring supplies, the four fly off.

I fill buckets with water for makeshift troughs, and by the time they return, the goats have cleared their small pen of ferns. Each of the soldiers land on the porch and set boxes atop it. I open the lids to find the first filled with texts on tending animals and farming. The second holds embroidering materials; the third fabrics, string, and sewing implements; and the fourth, parts for a spindle.

They apologize for making their visit short but report the High Council will convene on the issue of earthquakes, and the army is going house to house to educate all in the kingdom.

I thank them for the supplies as they take their leave. Sliding the boxes inside, I search the fabric bin for the leather. Finding none, my spirits dip. I parse through the other spans of fabric, finding them all of light color. These will not satisfy my needs like the dark leather.

I set to work reading the texts on goats and sheep. The next day, I tend the animals, read during the midday heat, eat supper, and then hunt as the light wanes, devouring my texts well into the night. I repeat this the next day but, by the third, realize I have run out of books. I stare at the boxes of sewing materials thinking I may go mad. I never liked these sedentary activities. Recalling how Mother and Abeetha would make me sit for at least an hour a day embroidering handkerchiefs, I shudder.

Where are Adam, Nicholas, and Timothy? Foster often came to visit mid-week. *Where is he, and why have I not at least had* some *communication?* Perhaps the earthquake caused more aftermath than they knew. Tucking these worries away for later, I decide my next task will be enclosing the bathing area.

I fill a pouch with water and start into the forest, determined to build my washing room. Downing trees is slow, but I topple four, dragging them each to my clearing. As the light wanes, I identify another perfect tree, hack at the bark, and then saw into the last small portion until the tree crashes over. Stripping the branches, I tie ropes around the girth and drag the log through the forest. Almost to my pasture, I raise my leg to ford a boulder. Movement catches my eye in the clearing ahead. My heart thuds, and I lower my body, one knee at a time, to the forest floor, balancing the trunk on my back. I hear the footfalls of boots on my porch. Raising my head, I try to make out the person in front of the cabin. Head covered by a hood and body by a long cloak, it is impossible in the dimming light. If only they would spin my direction, perhaps I could catch sight of hair color, but if I can see them, then they may see me as well.

Goddesses. How long will I be stuck hunched under this trunk? Frustrated, I attempt to even out my breaths. It will not do to have a tree rising and falling on the forest floor.

"Coo-oo-oo."

I strain my ears to ensure they have not misheard.

"Coo-oo-oo."

The unmistakable dove's call reaches my ears again. It must be a friend. *Goddesses, please let it be Foster.*

"Here." I lift my face and call out.

I press my hands into the ground, pushing my arms out straight, attempting to stand with the weight of the tree on my back.

The body appears before me. "What are you doing?"

"Adam. Thanks to the Goddesses. Can you help with this trunk?"

"Of course, but Queen, what are you doing?" He hops to the far end and lifts.

"Finishing my bathing area."

"How far have you dragged this?"

"How else would I get them there?" As we near the cabin, I release the trunk, and it thuds atop the stack of others. "Sorry, that was rude. It has been a long day."

"You should have requested a donkey or cart."

Standing straight, I post fists to hips. "Perhaps so, but this is what I did."

He lifts an eyebrow. "Are you well?"

"Oh yes, I am quite fine. My muscles are in top shape. My mind, however…" I point to my temple. "I do not believe I am suited for solitary life. I need things to do."

Adam reaches inside his cloak and produces a bundle of dark leather. "This is for you. There are letters inside for you."

"Thank you." I run my hand over the smooth, supple pelt.

"I am sorry. I cannot stay. But Foster will come tomorrow night."

I retrieve my stack of letters from the table and give them to Adam. As he jumps into the air, I latch the door closed, muscles searing and head pounding from exertion, yet proud of my progress. Pouring water into a cup, I hate to admit Terran may be right. I need purpose, some aim beyond myself. I smooth the black leather over the plane of the table. This may provide the means.

Chapter 4

TEARING INTO A PIECE OF DOVE jerky, I retrieve my shears from the cupboard and measure with my hand the span of my forehead, distances from the edge to my eyes, between my eyes, my nose, my cheeks, my mouth, and my chin. I work until my candle burns low, tucking under and sewing the edges of the masks to fashion a smooth, comfortable interior that fits the form of my face and produces no bumps or scratching. Fitting the first over my face and tying it around the back of my head, I study my image in the small mirror. If I were a youngling, this would be a terrifying sight. Any adult fae will be suspicious.

It serves that I must create a story to explain if I am caught in one of my good deeds. The problem rests that fae seldom are injured beyond natural repairing abilities. A burn or cut heals as if never there. I have not heard of a fae baby born with an aberrant form, although it could be possible. The bumps from the studs on my brow and cheeks lend themselves to that explanation. I could say my family was lost when the ogres attacked, and I have adopted a mission to help where needed. This story strays little from the truth, the difference being that I left my family, more concisely *faked my demise*, in the dragon attack. But the dragons did little damage to the countryside, focusing instead on me and our army, so the ogre narrative fits.

Now, all that lacks is a cause to commit to. It occurs to me that I need not limit my deeds to Aubren. I could fly through the kingdoms until I found somewhere to help. Surely there may be at least one a night to come upon.

I read Foster's letters, and my love for him grows as he provides much detail about the state of my family and our kingdom. I feel hopeful I have found a solution that will make both of us happy. I shall be safe from recognition yet helping where needed. To my surprise, Alemayehu reports that Terran integrates well into their army's ranks.

Body exhausted from dragging logs from the forest, I fall asleep fast and wake dream free and rested. Foster will come this day. Still, nightfall feels many furlongs away, and on the other side of our realm, darkness falls. Eating my bread and cheese with speed, I pack a water pouch, arrows, a mask, and my dark cloak. I start out, and from the edge of the beach, I shoot straight up, beating my wings as hard as possible. Over the long stretch of water, there is no need for hiding, and I dip low to the waves, letting the salt spray splatter my face. I reach the western coast of Borean and catch sight of a pod of whales with their calves.

The midsection of the continent experiences harsh winds, and I decide to focus on the wide plains and perhaps damage caused by the gusts. I hope to find downed trees across roads, fallen onto homes, or blocking water to a village. *You wish for disaster?* My mind pings that this is very wrong. *Only minor devastation,* I amend. *So that I may help.*

I follow ever-increasing gales as night descends on the heart of Borean. Sweeping low above farms, I hunt for anything amiss. Within minutes, I spot a barn with a gaping roof. Hovering above the structure, I slide on my black cloak and mask then drop down to inspect. A large tree rests across the end section of the barn, roof half decimated, and stalls shattered by the heavy trunk.

Alighting near the structure, I tiptoe toward the farmhouse. No light emits from the home, and I stoop low under the windows, listening. I hear no sounds, no signs anyone is awake and assume they have left the cleanup for the morning light. I stride in quick, leaping steps back to the barn where the animals crowd into the good side and planks serve as a temporary enclosure.

One of the sheep bleats a warning, and finding some fresh hay, I placate it into quieting. I stand, hands on hips, deciding what to do with the massive tree. Even if I had an axe or saw, it would take hours to cut the tree and haul it from the barn, not to mention the ruckus that effort would produce. I force my powers to my hand, and my palm grows green.

Testing a theory, I send a stream of energy to the trunk. As the beam hits the bark, smoke rises. I intensify my effort, and the stream of light cuts through the tree, sawing it in half in seconds. I repeat this, sectioning the column into chunks. When finished, I roll the pieces out of the back open section of the barn. Reentering the half structure, I realize there is so much more I could do, rebuild the stalls and walls, repair the roof. This, however, would take hours and fresh planks and timbers.

Feeling guilty for not helping more, I rest in the center of the barn, reenergizing myself for the flight home with bread and cheese. *You have helped enough. Moving the tree would be the hardest job for the farmer. A team could have the barn rebuilt in two days.* I rise, test my wings for strength, and leap into the air. I fly high up over the land as the cool breeze invigorates my travel.

My heart soars as the wind grazes my face. Joy floods my being as I think about the relief I imagine the family experiencing at sunup. *Relief and joy, right? Not fear and confusion. No animals are harmed, and no fae were traumatized by my actions, correct? Yes,* I assure myself. I hope the farmers hail the occurrence as a gift from the Goddesses. *What other explanation would they have?*

Descending to the beach and weaving through my forest, I land on my porch as the light wanes. With little time before dark, I shed my smoke-drenched clothes and dunk them into my bath water as I scrub the grime from the day away. I dress in my one gown and stow the day's tools as darkness takes the forest.

I study the space. *Food? The evening meal? Should I have one prepared for Foster? A good wife would, correct? You are not a wife, but that is what we pretend, right?* That is the aim. All except for the intimacy part, which, by the reaction of his body when we kiss, he wants, although he refuses to share the cot with me until we are wed. Wed by whom, I am not sure. Alemayehu? With Adam, Nicholas, and Timothy to witness. *Can I promise to honor Foster even as I make double-sided concessions? You uphold your promises,* I tell myself. Yet, I know my pledges skirt a line, a boundary between what my soul longs for, a mission, a purpose beyond the norm of simple fae, and Foster's request to stay safely hidden.

It is not just him who wishes me protected. I do as well. Sonia cannot know I live. Hiding keeps my people out of her crosshairs. I count myself disguised in this realm, although that, too, may be a farce. The archangels have exerted power in our realm before, and they could again. My physical disguise may do little to conceal my soul's signature.

Lifting a smoked duck from a hook above the table, I heat it in a pan with vegetables and potatoes. The smell of dinner permeates the cabin, and my mouth waters with hunger as my stomach turns with longing. Wielding my powers for the hours it took to cut the trunk into pieces sapped my energy as fast as hefting an axe.

The clunk of boots upon the wood sounds in my ears, and the cabin shakes under foot. I jump from my chair, smoothing my gown, and jump to the door. Through the peephole, I spy Foster's red-orange hair and swing open the door.

I wrap my arms around him and press my lips to his before his cloak is off.

"Wow." He smiles as I release his mouth. "I should stay away more often."

"No, you should not." Making bug eyes at him, I grab his hand and pull him into the cabin.

"The food smells amazing."

"Come, eat, I am starving."

"I would guess so if you moved all those trees."

"What trees?"

"The five huge trunks beside the porch." He points a finger toward the open door.

Stepping around him to close the panel, I peer outside. "Oh, those. I forgot. They are for the bathing room. I think I may cut a door from the back into the room once I enclose it and build a floor."

"You dragged all those from the forest?"

"It took all day." I pour wine into our two chargers.

"I can imagine." Lifting a glass, the edges of his eyes crease as his smile widens. "To life in your little cabin."

My side ticks with reminder of the day's activity. But to see those eyes every day of my life, I could give up much. I lift my glass and tap it to his.

"To life in my little cabin," I repeat.

We sit at the table, eating the duck. He tells me of today's news from the castle. The High Council has kept their debate about the quakes secret, not wanting to cause panic, but the armies prepare for more damage.

"What is the story for the soldiers?" I ask.

"Quinn told them he wishes them trained before festival season so they may enjoy the summer before the need to prepare for the rainy season."

I sip my wine. "That was smart."

"He has good aptitude for the position." Setting down his mug, he slides his hand across the table. "How are you? Adam mentioned you were out of sorts?"

"I was tired from dragging the logs from the forest."

"What did you do today? Adam said he brought you leather? Did you sew something?"

"Not yet." I do not wish him to worry about my gali-vants. Yet, I do not wish to lie. "Although I am not sure the application is correct. Do you think it will work for the hinges for the door I intend to cut?"

"Metal plates and bolts would hold up better. They are no trouble for me to bring when you need them."

"Oh, good." Standing, I lift our chargers and empty mugs and cross to the sink.

He joins me in my makeshift cleaning station, pour-ing water from the jug to rinse the dishes I scrub with sponge and lye. We carry our chairs to the fire and sit in front of the flames, my muscles welcoming the relief from the heat. Taking my hand, he pulls me into his lap, and I nestle my head on his chest. He smooths my hair and kisses my cheek.

"Do you miss your harp?"

"I do, but I do not wish to dwell on that. Shall we dance?"

"To what music?"

"I can dance and play at the same time." Jumping up, I lift the fiddle.

"I knew I chose my mate well." He stands and claps as I start a tune.

Mate. The word is like the sweetest note from a pluck of a string. Heart warmed, I sashay around him, drawing the bow across the strings. As I hang on the last note, he lifts the instrument from my hands. Setting it on the chair, he wraps his arms around me. I slide mine inside his and snuggle into him, head resting on his shoulder. This could be enough. My eyes wander around the room as we spin in slow circles, imagining returning from a long day of travel to waterfalls, distant rainforests, and glaciers, or a small crib with a babe, a toddler flying around us, giggling with delight.

Lifting my head, I look into his eyes. "Will you stay the night? Please?"

"Of course, love."

I would guess my smile spreads from here to the other side of Middle Earth. "Why the change?"

"I cannot find the strength to leave you." Kissing my hand, he plants kisses up my arm and neck and to my lips.

I melt into him, letting the feel of his skin, the smooth-yet-urgent pressure transport me to another world.

He ends the kiss too soon. "We should sleep." His eyebrows rise.

"I do not believe I can now."

"I could read to you as we try to fall asleep."

"That would be nice."

Dropping my hands, he draws the cloth divider across the room. I shed my gown, tightening my corset and pantaloons that once sat on my waist but now sit on my bony hips, around my middle.

"Ready."

He moves the curtain and fixes it to the wall. Shedding his boots and jacket, he lies on the cot opposite me, his white shirt open to show his structured stomach muscles.

"I rather you beside me. You can pull your bed to my side."

"That would be just as if we were sleeping together, and you know I am making you wait until we are wed."

"Until we are wed or until I agree to marry you?" I push up on an elbow and smile.

Eyes reflecting the dying embers of the fire, he lifts a text from the floor. "History of Rotuga. This should help you sleep."

"You are awful." Huffing, I spin to my back and fold my arms over my middle.

"But you love me anyway."

I turn to look at him. "I do love you."

"And I love you." He opens the cover of the book.

Closing my eyes, I listen to his low, soothing voice. My pulse calms, and I picture Rotuga, the dense rainforests and dry prairies with abundant odd wildlife: the wildebeests, hippopotami, and elephants. I think I should like to ride an elephant, or perhaps a camel, or both.

JOSTLING OF MY BED WAKES ME. I open my eyes to the dark room, thinking it a dream. The table legs across from me clunk on the wood floor, but lately, my dreams only bring me to the green field of the Goddesses and Mother. This must be a nightmare.

"Titania, get under your bed." Foster's voice cuts through my haze.

Hugging my blanket around me, I climb to the floor and spin underneath my cot.

"We should go outside. What if the cabin collapses?" The wood planks bang into my shoulder blades.

"What if a tree falls on us? The cabin will be more protection." Foster's eyes pan around the room. "I cannot believe the cupboard still stands."

"Terran helped me tether it to the wall."

"Terran helped with something." Foster grips the cot legs.

"He was very cordial once he began to think he may get away from here."

"That is concerning."

"I thought so too." I hold tightly to my bed as it attempts to bounce away. "This is a long quake."

Boom, boom, boom. The floor knocks against my back. Rumbling sounds of bedrock shuffling echoes through the air.

"Do not move, there could be—" Foster starts.

"Aftershock, I know. Terran was the one who knew so much about earthquakes, remember?"

"Right. I do not see how you are so calm."

"Kobold, trolls, ogres, dragons, earthquakes … kind of fits my life."

"You believe this is Sonia." His light eyes seem to suck all available light from the space between us.

"I do."

Counting out fifteen minutes, punctuated by a few ripples of movement, I glance up at the ceiling and scoot from underneath my cot.

Foster slides across the floor toward me. "Holy Goddesses. Everything looks okay. Are you okay?"

"Just a few bruises. You?"

"Yes, I am fine. I should get to the castle though." Lifting his jacket, he shoves one hand into a sleeve.

"I will come too." I grab for a pair of pants, now squished to the wall underneath my bed.

"Are you mad? You cannot come."

"I will wear my cloak and hood. It is dark, and I can help." I yank the pants up to my waist.

"Someone will see you, and all your sacrifice could be for nothing. You will just end up hurting those you seek to protect."

"Ugh." I stamp my foot to the floor. "I hate this."

Buttoning his jacket, he winds his palm around my neck. "Just, please, be safe, my love."

Mesmerized by his wide eyes, red lips, and the earthy scent like wild grass in a meadow, I nod. He presses his lips to mine, and the hard push of his skin against mine catches me off guard, but before I can close my eyes, he pulls away, crossing to the door and pulling it behind him with a thud.

My eyes dart around and then back to the door, expecting to see it open again. Crossing to the table, I light a candle. *How does he do that to me? Enchant me, make me forget my aim? You were asleep, disoriented. Him just as much.* Which seems odd. He has never been out of sorts like that before. Always seems so in control. I guess he will go to his family first and make sure they are safe. I could go to the castle, hide behind the tree line of the wood across the meadow, and confirm all is well. At least it will put my mind at ease.

Searching to the bottom of my folded pile of clothing, I slide a mask from under my bed. I dress, check my outfit in the mirror, and cross to the exit, sliding on boots and fitting a blade in each. I drop a hatchet and large blade in my pack and tighten it to my back. Deciding I can find water and food if necessary, I exit the cabin, turning the key in the lock.

I dart down the mountain through the dark forest, focusing on the path in front of me. I fly over the river, following its turns. Finally, I reach the wood beside the castle and slow as I near the clearing. I peer across the meadow, squinting as I try to make out forms in the halls of the castle, all ablaze, light pouring out each window. Although many pass in front of the panes, it is impossible to decipher who they are, but with no soldiers flooding into the structure, I assume all is fine.

Wondering where the epicenter of the quake is, I trace back to the river and shoot up high in order to assess where the damage lies. Villages to the west appear dark, so I assume they have no problems. To the east, near Capitolshire, I detect a flurry of activity: dark bodies weaving around, in, and out of structures like ants on a mound. I circle around the castle and descend to find many of them garbed in the green uniforms of my army. *Drat. Why hadn't I thought to steal a uniform?* A mask under a helmet would be less suspicious than my disguise.

I land behind a barn so I can keep to the shadows. Peeking in windows, I find floors filled with various belongings and wares, fabrics toppled on the floor of the tailor, and ink spilled on the stone in the printer's shop. Seeing no real danger or need, I slink to the outskirts of the village and take to the air again, flying high over the straight between the northern tip of my kingdom and Bedham.

Historically, volcanic activity has plagued a path around our kingdom from the southeast extending north to Bedham and crossing west into Chastam. It would make sense that the quake's center would likely be in one of these areas. I pray Bedham has prepared as our kingdom did for the rumblings. As I fly over the island, I find that clouds have coalesced over the kingdom. I dip lower, discovering, as ash fills my lungs, they are not clouds but smoke plumes wafting up from below. Diving, I fight tearing eyes and focus on a center of light, Bedhamshire, the capitol, consumed in blazes.

Seeing a farm on the outskirts, animals streaming from a barn engulfed in flames, I land in an open space in a line of fae passing water buckets from one to the next. A male fae, face soot black, startles as I relieve him of the weight of the pail.

"Goddesses bless you, friend."

"And you." I lower the pitch of my voice as I hand the fae an empty bucket from the other direction.

It is not half an hour before the flames die under the onslaught of water.

"What started the blaze?" I ask of my neighbor.

"Burning lava, or magma, or whatever the blazes they call it leaked through the ring before they could close it. One minute, I am asleep, and the next, my farm is on fire, animals screeching for help."

"May the Goddesses bless you." I dip my chin and take a step back, hoping for a fast exit.

"You as well. Nice protective attire you have there." He motions to my face.

"I have fought fires before." *Flames of angry dragons, at least.*

"We appreciate your help."

"You are welcome."

As others gather around, I slink through their frames to the back of the group. Seeing towers of smoke to the north, I take to the air. I help douse three other fires before I catch sight of the uniformed soldiers of my army descending. They must have called for support from Aubren. With the growing light nearing dawn, and remembering Foster's warning, I give the soldiers a wide girth, ringing them to the north and circling back to my forest.

Nearing my cabin, I start to worry that Foster returned and found me gone. *What will I say when he finds me dressed as such?* Loosening the tie on my mask, I slide it down to the bottom of my pack as I slow and alight in my clearing. The cabin sits dark, and I exhale in relief that I will not have to explain my smoke-saturated garments. I heat water and again soak my clothes as I wash. The warm water penetrates my muscles, relaxing their taut threads, but my brain spins with possibility.

In two days, I have helped four farms, without detection, without stirring wonder, and the two fae I did speak with noted my attire as appropriate for firefighting, a benefit I had not thought of. I flick my toe above the level of the water. This could indeed work. I will be the masked, firefighting, helper fae.

With growing light, I hang my outfit on the line, taking care to hide the mask under the cloak. Still too wound up to rest, and not knowing when Foster will return, I tiptoe through the forest in search of dove eggs. I find a handful of nests and test their eggs for maturity, harvesting three total for breakfast. Back at the cabin, with waning energy, I crack one and dip bread into it. Tea settles my stomach as I grow restless. *Has Foster flown to Bedham? What other kingdoms were affected, or was the quake limited to one? Did the problem emanate from the dome bedrock as the farmer reported?*

I decide there is no point in pondering on the possibilities, and I begin my chores. With them finished, I begin to dress for another day of anonymous aid. As I slip on my mask, I hear boots on the porch. A look through the slit in the door finds Nicholas's fist raised to knock.

I stow my disguise and pull open the pane. "Is there news? I did not expect you."

"There was much damage to the north. Quinn sent forces there. Quinn and Foster went to report to the High Council after surveying the area. He wanted me to let you know he may be late tonight."

"What happened? Were lives lost?"

He recounts, in part, what I have already seen and adds information about the expanse of the damage. I inquire about other kingdoms, but he has no other information save from Bedham. He lifts a basket, showing me the vegetables he snuck from the kitchen. "These were all I could manage. Foster said you were running low."

"Thank you. I appreciate your time. Are you hungry? Would you like a meal?"

Hoping he will decline, I cross outside. He follows my lead, indicating he must return to the castle, and I bid him goodbye. I dress with haste, happy I know where help is most needed. I glide through the forest and, rising high to the dome, cross the sea to Bedham. Finding fae gathered on a wharf, I help them pull damaged ships from the water, saving as many planks as we can. Several inquire as to my dress, and I pray they think me a male fae. I answer each time that I come from inland, and my aging mother bade me wear protection from the hot lava and flames. This seems to appease all as I guess they have many more worries than an odd fae helper. As the light wanes, I fly home, exhausted yet satisfied and happy. I dine alone, sipping on my one glass of wine in front of the fire, waiting for Foster, but he does not come. As the heat from the flames warms my body, I cannot fight my heavy eyelids and shuffle to the bed, shedding my pants and blouse and sliding under my covers. I wake during the night and contemplate another outing but, hoping Foster will appear any moment, decide against it. It would not do for him to find me gone, and anything I wrote in a note left would be a lie.

⸺⊶⊷⸺

I WAKE TO AN EMPTY CABIN as the first light breaks outside. Thinking Foster will come any time, I cannot leave. I tend to the goats and sheep and set out on a hunt. As I alight at the edge of a meadow, the ground rumbles below me. I shoot to the cabin, slamming the door behind me and rolling under my cot. The quake lasts only seconds, and I slide from my hiding place. *Curse these earthquakes.* I round the cabin to retrieve my cloak and mask from the line. As I stomp back with my outfit, I stop short.

Foster stands on the porch.

I tuck my disguise in my laundry basket and set it on the stairs. I jump to him, planting a kiss on his lips. "I missed you. I was worried."

Foster slides a text from his cloak. "I am sorry I was not able to come last evening. Here is a text on building structures."

"Thank you." I take the book. "Will you come in?"

"I cannot. There is much to do. I am sorry." With a peck to my cheek, he spins away and jumps into the air.

⸻◈⸻

DAY AFTER DAY, I SET OUT on my treks, helping where I can. On this day, it is almost pitch black when I leave the forest and decide to fly north. Sweeping high over Bedham and then swooping low to the sea, I revel in the ocean spray. A flash behind me catches my attention, and I turn to see blazing balls falling from the dome. Rumbling, cracks, and booms sound in my ears. *Another quake?*

I gauge the distance and realize the burning lava rains down over Aubren. Snatching my disguise from my bag and fitting it on, I change course. With a hard beat of my wings, I speed full force toward my kingdom. As I approach the north shore, I note the ring has been closed. Horrified, I take in the view: splotches of glowing fires and wafts of smoke litter the landscape. I charge toward my castle and, seeing it spared, dart to the village. Women dressed in nightclothes carry younglings and bags through the streets as structures burn around them. The men fan out like spokes on a wheel, passing buckets of water from one set of hands to the next.

Finding the end of a short line, I grab a bucket from my neighbor and splash it on the flames. I look up to realize the flaming roof belongs to the tailor's shop—the one my cousins and I frequented for ribbons and festival gowns. I focus on the task, hoisting bucket after bucket from the fae beside me and pitching the water on the fire. After dozens of pails, the flames diminish, and with one more splash, they die.

"Thank the Goddesses." I set the empty pail on the ground with a thud.

"You can say that again," the fae beside me mutters. "Thank you for your help." His hand shoots out.

I keep my chin low. "My pleasure. I should help another."

Head down, I weave through the village, finding another structure afire. We work, handing load after load of water from one set of hands to the next.

"That is the last one. I believe the fire is out." My neighbor hands me a pail.

My fingers brush his as I grip the handle. His gaze lifts and his wide eyes lock on mine. I freeze.

Chapter

5

TAKING IN THE WIDE EYES of the villager, I lower my chin.

"Do I know you? Do you live in the village?" he asks.

"No, I live in the wood."

"You seem familiar."

"I must go. Goddesses blessings." I touch my fingers to the front edge of my hood and, heart thrumming in my chest, spin away.

The look of bafflement in the fae's eyes as they met mine hangs in my memory as I stride away. I must leave Capitolshire. With its proximity to my castle, and the number of times I walked the lanes with my cousins, paraded through the streets celebrating our victories, and hosted the villagers at my castle, there are too many who may recognize my eyes, the unmistakable gold halos surrounding the onyx pupils. Keeping to the shadows, I weave to the south edge of the village and jump into the air. Noting more smoke rising in the south, I speed toward my next project.

I fly high over Westshire, checking that Foster's family's farm is safe. Seeing no fires below, I set my course for the next plume of smoke. Helping drown fires in another shire and three farms, I abandon my mission as light from the kingdom's southern ring grows. I fly north toward my parcel of forest, finding most fires doused and within control. My mind spins, trying to grasp what has passed. My worst fears have come to fruition faster than I could have guessed. I must contact Alemayehu to discover what he knows of the witches' efforts to reconcile Sonia with her family.

More thoughts barrage my brain as I near the cabin. *Is Foster okay? Are my friends well? Have there been other eruptions in the realm? What damage are the earthquakes causing in Upper Earth? How many lives have been lost?* The lack of knowledge eats at my stomach.

⸺◈⸺

"Titania. Titania." My cot jostles.

I push up on one elbow. "Foster, you are here."

He paces the boards beside my bed.

"Masked priestess, dark-hooded angel, golden-eyed goddess, black witch?" Picking my sack from the hook, he empties the contents on the table. "There are tales from here to Borean and back."

"What?"

He lifts the lid on my chest and tosses half my garments out. Dropping to the floor, he reaches under my cot.

My heart races. "What do you speak of?"

"Do not lie to me." He produces a fistful of my dark masks.

I take a deep breath. "I have not lied."

"Omission is the same as a lie. How can I trust you when you are not fully honest with me? How can we have a relationship?"

Tears spring to my eyes, and I jump up. "I was being careful, keeping my distance from people. No one recognized me. I stayed clear of the rings."

"Try. That was all I asked. *Try* to lead a simple life. You have a garden, animals, sewing projects, and a washroom to build." Red-faced, he drops the leather strips. "You know the fae. They talk, they gossip, and we are all the same. You could at least vary your disguise. I may have been thrown off."

Slumping to the floor, I bury my face in my hands, guilt at betraying the one man I am supposed to be faithful and honest with gnawing at my core. "I am sorry. I just wanted to help. Please, forgive me."

I feel his warmth as he drops to the floor in front of me. He wraps his fingers around my wrists and places my hands on his cheeks. "For as angry as I am, for as much as you frustrate me to the realm's end, I love you for all the same reasons."

"I will not deceive you again."

"Your heart is bigger than any fae I know, but you must promise. I must be number one."

I swallow. *That is a lot to ask. The most important thing to me? Before the Goddesses? Before my family? My fae? They are not your fae any longer. You must trust the Goddesses, trust Quinn and your cousins, and trust Alemayehu and the witches.* "I can work on that."

"And I can work on seeing you more."

Biting my lip, I peruse the cabin. "Bread and cheese?"

"When is the last time you ate meat or vegetables?"

"Perhaps two weeks ago?"

His eyes grow large. "We are hunting *now*. You are going to starve yourself."

"I am a witch. We do not need food."

"You wish." Grabbing my hand, he stomps outside.

We down a pheasant and circle back to the cabin, cleaning it and setting it upon a spit.

"I hate having such little information," I say as we wait.

"I have heard of birds that can carry messages on their legs, short notes written on parchment, rolled and attached to their ankles. Perhaps we could train a couple of birds. That way we could get messages to each other if needed."

"I like that idea."

Foster promises to research the carrier birds. We sit in front of the fire, watching juices dripping from the meat, both round-eyed—me from just waking and Foster, I assume, from the weight and wear of his day.

"You are probably not tired, but I am exhausted. Do you mind if I nap? I brought you a new book." Lifting his pack, he hands me a text.

Foster stretches out on his cot.

At the table, with my ink and parchment set out, I watch as he falls asleep. After another few months, Quinn will be more confident, and Foster can train another to take his post. He will be with me day and night. Then I will not feel this angst every moment.

Nerves on edge, I write pages detailing my feelings to Alemayehu. I implore Alemayehu to tell me of news from the witches, how Terran adjusts, and ask ideas for how I may help to resolve the issue with Sonia. I roll the parchment and fit a tie around it.

My mind whirring with ideas, thoughts on actions I cannot risk, I tiptoe out the door and sit on the porch. I listen to the sounds of the forest, the crickets chirping, doves cooing, owls calling. My eyes adjust to the darkness, and I make out small white balls of the goats and sheep huddling together. I say my prayers into the forest, wishing for peace for my family, protection for my people, and patience for myself.

Hearing the door behind me, I turn to see Foster exiting the cabin, my letter to Alemayehu in hand.

"You should not have let me sleep so long."

"It seemed you needed the rest."

He lowers his body to my side. "I must go."

"I know." I take his hand in both of mine.

"It will inquire of some birds. They train them in Borean."

I fight an eye roll. If King Joseph knew the birds were for me, he may teach them to eliminate on the head of their owner. Or to be more precise, would have someone else train them to do it.

"Are you rested enough to fly?"

"Yes, and I will get more sleep in the barracks before morning." He leans toward me and presses his lips to mine.

"I wish you never had to leave."

"And that is just the way I want it." Smiling, he taps my nose. "Stay safe. Do not be reckless."

"I will try. Can you get word to me as to the status of my kingdom and others?"

"I will try." He kisses my forehead.

Standing, he tugs on my fingers, and I mold into his embrace. He squeezes then releases me and jumps into the night. Within three hard beats of wings, he disappears into the black wood.

With renewed dedication, I commit to the tasks before me, tending to my animals and furthering my building project. Speaking with the Goddesses and Mother as if they tarry alongside me, I finish splitting the logs into planks. By the time Foster joins me at dusk, I have three walls built a third of the way to the roof's edge. He commends my progress, and I pester him with questions, trying to ensuré he does not waver in his decision to forgive me.

He kisses my lips. "I do not believe I have the power to stop loving you."

"But I want this to be the right decision for you as well. You are giving up much to be with me."

"I know my mind, and it has always been for you."

I lift my finger. "There were those few months."

Smiling, he presses his mouth to mine. "Neither one of us is perfect. Should we speak of Holden or Mikel?"

I shake my head. "We should not."

He spends the night lying across from my cot.

I stay awake, watching him breathe. I fall asleep wondering how I could be so blessed that this man loves me so unconditionally.

73

THE NEXT DAY, WE HUNT AND GATHER berries and roots from the forest. We picnic on a rock and drink our wine in front of the fire. I cannot picture a better day.

I finish the washroom and the next day take up embroidering. I sew flowers, trees, and the seal of Aubren on handkerchiefs and, with fingers aching with wear, have a stack a foot tall by the time Foster arrives.

When I open the door, I lift my pile. "Look. What do you think?"

Eyes wide, he lifts the top one. "There are so many. You made all of these today?"

"I did."

"What shall you do with them?"

I bite my lip. "Perhaps you could sell them at the market in Capitolshire?"

His brow furrows. "Where shall I say I got them?"

We conjure the story of an aging fae widow, and with little time, he fits the whole bunch in his pack and heads back to the castle.

The next day, I set to sewing and decide to make dolls. By dark, I have ten, and I am excited to hear how the sale of my kerchiefs went.

Hearing footfalls on the porch, I ensure it is Foster. I swing open the door and hold a doll up.

"Do you mean to start the practice of voodoo?"

"What?" I turn the black yarn adorned body to face me. "No. It is a doll."

His eyebrows rise. "Oh."

Dropping the doll to my side, I stomp into the cabin. "They are hideous. I am horrible at making dolls. How did the kerchiefs sell? How much money did I make?"

His shifts his weight between his feet. Then a smile spreads on his face. Shedding his pack, he produces a book.

"I brought you a book of sea creatures."

I look from the cover to him. "Did you buy it with the money from the kerchiefs?"

"Not exactly." He produces the linens.

"No one liked my handkerchiefs?" I slump into a chair.

"I believe they are just different than what most fae are used to."

"Admit it. They look like a ten-year-old made them."

He comforts me, saying that not all fae are meant for detailed work. Insisting most of the dolls are quite nice, he starts to place them in his pack.

With a new idea, I yank them away. "You are not a good liar. I will deliver them in the night as gifts."

"You will give younglings nightmares. I think you should use them to induce pain in Sonia and any other foe you like." He lifts the dark-headed version, shakes it, and lays it on the table. "I must go."

He kisses my forehead and, with a swirl, crosses outside.

I start reading the text, learning of whales, squids, and octopi, but the kerchiefs and dolls hold my attention. Dressing in my disguise, I make for Narielshire, peeking in windows to see where younglings live and leaving a handkerchief and doll at each door. It is a quick jaunt, and I take up my book again.

I wake to a page pasted to my cheek. Cold air pervades the room, and setting the book on the floor, I pull my blanket up to my chin. I light a fire but cannot regain sleep. Giving in, I set to my chores and have finished all by midmorning. I trudge up my steps as my stomach rumbles with hunger.

A shadow encroaches on the clearing, and I raise my eyes to a cloudless sky. I stand, watching, listening, braced to bolt inside and under my bed. The graying light rests overhead, and the forest falls silent. Before me, the lambs huddle into groups, and goats scuttle under the porch. Like a wave rolling to the sand, a symphony of clacking leaf tips passes overhead. The branches whir about and trunks quake. Under me, the porch planks shiver. I race up to the canopy.

I land on a limb just wide enough for the middles of my soles and hug the trunk. Confirming my assumption that the ring above has been closed, I rise above the branches and study the horizon. Clear to the south and east, I take comfort that my family should be safe. As I turn my head, there stands an unnatural glow beyond the northwest horizon. Ducking back under the trees, I shoot to the cabin. I grab my satchel, cloak, and mask, and I take flight, rising high to the dome, then speed toward the growing orange ball.

Passing over Chastam, I pass over the sea lying south of Lindleton. The glowing mass begins to take shape as I approach the southern tip of a strip of land holding Lindleton's capital. Shaped like a boot, the firmament juts out into the body of water. Today, a small island to the south appears as if a giant decided to build a campfire of glowing boulders atop it. Lava steams as it flows into the sea, cooling. Where a village sat perched on a hilltop before, hot, smoldering rock and earth litter the land. Dozens of fae hover above, and fitting on my mask, I join them.

"Was that your home?" I ask.

"No. I live to the north. I am not sure anyone survived."

"Why isn't anyone helping?" Flipping head down, I drop to what must have been a roadbed.

Hot, smoldering rocks, larger than homes, surround me. Heart pounding at the enormity of the devastation, I swallow. *Where should I start?* My breath seizes in my lungs, and I repeat my mantra. *You are in control. Do the next right thing.*

"Hello? Is anyone hurt?"

Hearing my voice as if removed from this body, the words sound absurd. Still, I press on, searching foot by foot, hovering just above the ground, calling out, and listening. Others join in, inspecting collapsed structures, moving beams of shattered homes when possible, searching for survivors. Sweat pools under my mask and cloak, but the barrier protects my skin from the scorching heat of the glowing rocks.

A bugle sounds, and I look up to find soldiers descending. Recognizing the colors of Lindleton, Chastam, and Rotuga, I keep my head down, focused on the rubble, praying for signs of life. Finding remains of a charred cow, bile rises from my stomach. *Could it be possible that none survived?* Rage grows in my core, and I ball my fingers into fists. My palms flame with heat, and looking down, I realize they glow green. This is too much. It cannot continue. I must stop it.

Chapter

6

Releasing a long, slow breath, I grapple with the promise made to Foster. I will not skirt the truth with him again, and I cannot risk being discovered by Sonia. That would make things far worse for the fae. There must be a way. A soldier from Rotuga zooms by. Terran comes to mind, and I wonder if he was sent here. It would be far too much risk. My mind jumps to thoughts of Alemayehu. After spending so much time with the witches, he knows more about magic, the Trinity of Witches, and Sonia than any other in the realm.

I jump into the air and dart up, examining the landscape and dome. Most rings within sight are open, save for one just above. The ring keepers must have decided there is no immediate danger. My eyes drop to the decimated island below. Tragedy could strike again at any moment. I must do something to stop these atrocities, and Alemayehu will be the best person to help figure out how.

Turning southwest, I shed the mask and hood, letting the wind cool my skin. I keep near the dome, hoping to avoid any soldiers enroute to Lindleton but pass none. I fly over the continent, the vast desert with towering dunes and flattened planes stretching out like a brown sea of sand. Further south, jungles ring the coast. I descend to the outskirts of Rotuga's capital where the tree canopy almost conceals the shire. I land on a forest floor coated with ferns. Huge leaves, the size of a youngling fae, hang head high from stalks as big as my thighs. Foreign noises, the call of a bird, I believe, the cheep of something odd, inundate my senses. Fitting the mask on my face and hood over my braids, I skim past huts—mud-caked dwellings thatched with roofs of dried leaves tucked between trees.

I do not dare knock at homes without knowing where Alemayehu lives. Thinking someone in the village may direct me, I head toward what appears to be a brighter spot ahead. Houses lie closer together, trees become less populous, and the path opens into a small clearing. A well stands in the center, and larger structures circle the gathering place. Several fae mill about, and my nerves twitch as I realize, with or without the disguise, I will stand out here. My skin is far too light for this climate.

Seeing two soldiers in uniform, I land a few feet from them.

As one turns to face me, I recognize Alemayehu's son, Lencho.

"Excuse me, can you tell me where I can find Alemayehu?" I ask, praying my disguise will be enough. Even if he recognizes me, Lencho would not react here, would he?

He crosses his arms over his chest. "Depends on who would like to know."

My mind spins. "I am a friend of Foster of Aubren."

His eyes shift from me to his partner and back. "I am Lencho, son of Alemayehu. You have news or perhaps a parchment?"

"No." I shake my head. "I must see him."

Lencho's eyes hold mine. "I will bring him here."

I reach out to grip his arm but think better of it. "Please. This is not a conversation that can be had in public."

"I do not know you. There are tales about a golden-eyed bandit stalking villages and farms. And with those golden eyes, you appear to be that fae."

"A bandit?" I stifle a laugh. "What does this bandit do, and what could I do to a large fae like yourself?"

"They lurk around sites of devastation, muttering incantations. None is sure whether they are hexing the sites or bringing good fortune."

"A magical fae? There are those that believe in such?"

"After the beasts that plagued Aubren, yes. The bandit is said to hail from Aubren."

"If I am this bandit, I bring good fortune, I assure you." *To everyone but myself.* "I mean you or your father no harm, but I must see him. I will go door to door to find him if necessary."

My hands warm as my frustration rises and, seeing a slight tinge of green emanating from my palms, stuff them under my cloak. The day wanes, and Foster will be at my cottage by nightfall. I need to be there when he arrives. Not being a queen proves quite inconvenient.

"Show your face," Lencho demands.

"It is healing from burns. The healer says I should not expose it to air. Salve and this mask protect the skin while it reforms. Please. This is of the utmost importance."

"Wait here." Lencho calls another from the building to watch me and saunters away.

The other two soldiers have no words for me, and I stand there feeling exposed as the number of fae in the area increases. Their eyes dart to me, and I begin to regret my strategy. Perhaps I should have tried finding him on my own, but a masked fae lurking about homes would probably bring more suspicion. It seems my reputation has garnered a sinister tone. I clasp my hands under my cloak, trying to be patient and still. Perhaps black for the cloak and mask was a poor choice. Brown leather would be less jarring.

Movement catches my eye, and I find Lencho's head above those gathered, Alemayehu beside his son. Alemayehu strides straight toward me, extending his arm.

"Greetings, friend. I did not realize you would come today," Alemayehu says.

"It has been too long." I try to keep my tone light.

With a sweeping glance for the many eyeing us, he cocks his head. "Please, come have tea with me at my home."

"It would be most welcome," I say.

He thanks his son, and we retreat from the village center, weaving through the houses to a hut surrounded by tall trees. As Alemayehu closes the door, the stifling air mixed with the scents of cooking spice overwhelms me, and seeing we are alone in the small space, I shed my hood and mask.

"Are you mad? Why would you risk coming here? And dressed as the bandit?"

"Foster said there were rumors, but I did not realize I had magical powers."

"No need to remark on the irony of that." Shaking his head, he hangs a pot of water above the flames. "You should not risk exposure."

"I had to come. I cannot sit by and do nothing while the consequences of these earthquakes and volcanoes ravage our land from above. I went to Lindleton. A whole village is covered with burning rock. We found no survivors."

With a glance and a growing smile, he pours water into a cup and lowers himself to a mat on the floor. "Thank the Goddesses. It took you long enough."

"What? But you kept telling me I should not be involved, that it was too dangerous." I kneel beside him.

"It is. I would never ask, but that does not mean that I do not want you to be."

"I must figure out a way to go to Upper Earth without being discovered. Can you think of anything that would allow me to interact in their realm? I could project my soul as we did prior, but I believe another soul would recognize it, as I did Theron's."

"Yes. You are correct." He rubs his chin, but a crooked smile forms. "I was with the witches often. I heard their incantations, witnessed many spells. I wrote each one down when I returned for the night."

I grab his hands. "You have their spells? A cloaking spell? Do you think it would work? That I could use it?"

"I hope so." Crawling to the edge of the room, his bulging belly nearly sweeping the dirt, he lifts a brightly patterned rug.

From a hole underneath, he lifts a text. I slide in beside him as he opens the cover. He flips to the back, turning the pages, one by one. I note the headings which read: Healing, Light, Heat, Rain, Thunder, Conveyance.

I point at that one, and he shakes his head.

"That is merely moving an object," he whispers.

"I never saw them speak when lifting objects."

"I believe they think the spell for small objects. For large items or many, more power is required."

He continues turning pages, pointing to the titles, which include Wind, Smoke, Fire, Melting, Turning Ice to Steam, Boiling, Transformation of Liquid to Acid, Transformation to a Poison, Closing Skin of a Cut, and Drawing Healing Elements to a Burn.

"How did you witness so many spells?"

"They were training DJ. I was in talks with Hunter and Alena, but I heard his instruction, sometimes from levels away. Our abilities in Upper Earth seem almost magical."

"Do you think we need permission from the High Council?"

"You do not exist, and I know nothing." Turning another sheet, he presses a finger to the text. "Here. Cloaking a Soul."

Grabbing the book, I study the words, estimating the pronunciation. I read them aloud, and Alemayehu suggests edits. I practice until he approves my oration. He coaxes me to shut my eyes, concentrate, summon my magic, and repeat the spell. Crossing my legs in front of me, I draw in a centering breath, imagining DJ sitting before me. My core warms, and I push my magic through every part of my being. My thoughts jump to all the reasons this should not work, but I was able to use their spells to cast my soul even before I had been able to use my magic at will.

This must work. I quiet my mind, center my intentions, and then repeat the words for the spell.

"Holy Goddesses." Alemayehu's words are but a thought floating through my mind.

I think about where I want to go, and in a flash, I am at the ring above Rotuga. I look down on the forest below, and the next instant, I open my eyes to Alemayehu.

"Did it work?"

"You were here, and then you were not."

"I went to the ring as fast as I could think it. You could not see my *physical* body, but how will we know if you could detect my soul?"

"I blinked my eyes, and I had no recollection of what I had been doing the second before. When you reappeared, the memory came back. It was as if you were erased from existence."

I grab his arms. "Then it worked?"

"I believe it did."

"This will work. I can go to the witches and help them with their quest without being detected."

"What will Foster say? He does not like you putting yourself in harm's way."

"I do not know but cannot keep it from him."

"What will you do if he says no?"

"I will try to convince him there is no danger, or not any more than usual. Perhaps less."

He rolls his eyes to the roof as he stands. "That is a stretch."

I lift the book of spells. "Can I take this?"

"It is yours to use."

"Thank you so much." Fitting the text in my bag, I hug him. "May I come here and use your home as a base? That way, someone will know when I come and go from Upper Earth."

"Of course, of course." He replaces the rug over the hiding spot. "I support anything that stops these cursed earthquakes."

"Now, I must go and convince Foster." Peeking out the door, I note the dimming light and fret that Foster will arrive at the cabin before me.

"Godspeed. When will you come again?" Alemayehu asks.

"Tomorrow. If I cannot, I will have a letter delivered." I fit my mask and hood on my head. "Thank you, friend."

Inspecting the area around the doorway, I exit then disappear into the woods behind his house. I gauge my location, shoot up into the canopy, and then rise to the dome. I speed through the air, crossing the vast ocean to the south of Chastam as darkness descends. Almost no light penetrates the high foliage as I enter my woods, and weaving through the trees, I find Foster pacing my porch.

Perhaps sensing motion, his eyes rise to me. A scowl marks his face. This is not good.

"I am sorry to be late." I alight before him.

"Where have you been? I was out of my mind with worry."

"I went to Lindleton." He opens his mouth, and I lift a finger. "But I did not stay. I will explain."

Opening the door, I tug him into the cabin.

"Do you know what I have been through today? I thought that you were gone. Lost to me for real this time," Foster says.

"What? How long have you been here?"

"That is not the point."

He describes how my mother came out of her silent state. She was delirious, yelling and screaming that she could not find me. My father had to tell her I died many months ago. She insisted she had been with me just this morning. Then, for no reason, she quieted. She resumed staring into the fire as she always does as if nothing had happened.

My heart pounds in my chest. "Oh, Foster. This is good news. It means the spell I attempted did indeed work."

Lifting the bottle of wine, I grab two mugs and set them on the table.

He sucks in a deep breath and places his palms on the tabletop. "Spell? Titania, what did you do?"

"It is fine. It is all good. Did you know that in Rotuga they believe the golden-eyed bandit can do magic?"

"You said you would not be the bandit again."

"I just had to find Alemayehu."

"Titania." His voice rises. "I can get Alemayehu to come to you."

"There was no time. I had to see him. And that Mother could not find me means we indeed accomplished what we sought."

"You need to explain. Now."

Pouring wine in the glasses, I urge him to sit. He shakes his head and demands to know everything. I gulp down half the mug full of wine and begin the story with the state of the isle in Lindleton and how I could not sit by and let Sonia ravage our land. His head lobs to and fro, his face growing redder by the second.

"But Alemayehu has all the witches' spells. He has one that cloaks souls. Or, I do." Slouching out of my backpack, I produce the text. "I can recite a spell that cloaks my soul, and it is as if I never existed while my soul is hidden. Alemayehu had no memory of me or the spell I performed until I released it. That must be what put Mother in a state."

"Wait. Your mother can normally see you? Knows where you are?"

I nod. "I told you. I am with her and the Goddesses almost every night in my dreams. I believe she also sees me through them. She must know I am alive somewhere, but when I performed the spell, I disappeared from their sight."

"I think I need that drink now."

I hold his glass out to him.

He downs his wine in one gulp and slouches into a chair. "And you mean to cloak yourself to go aid the witches."

Rounding the table, I kneel beside him. "If you agree. I told you no more secrets, and I mean it. You are the only thing I have left. I will not jeopardize what we have."

"Titania." Resting his forehead in his hands, he rolls his head in his palms. "What am I to do with you?"

I describe how I plan to discover what they are doing to fulfill Sonia's demands and if there may be something I can do to further their cause. I vow that if it is too danger-ous, or I am not needed, I will not aid them.

"And I promise to tell you everything, every day," I say.

"I cannot see you every day. With all that passes, our mid-week visits are challenging."

"I will write letters. Perhaps I can leave them hidden in a secret spot where you can retrieve them easily."

"And what if someone finds them?" he asks.

Pacing away, I lift my arms. "I do not know. All I know is that I cannot let Sonia continue to harm our fae."

"I will get the birds tomorrow. It will be safer."

I do not see how and voice such. He concedes, and we decide to use the carrier birds only in emergencies. He repeats that he hoped I would find contentment with my garden and livestock, and my hearts sinks. I feel as if I have let him down, have not tried hard enough. *How can I ignore the deaths when a spell to allow me to travel with in-visibility lies right at my fingertips?* It is as if the Goddesses provided me with the path. *How am I to close my eyes to these gifts?* If I can save one life, it will have been worth the risk.

We eat the rest of a smoked bird and dip bread in the wine, the lines on Foster's face tight the entire meal. Afterwards, we sit in front of the fire, reading from the spell book. I demonstrate easier spells, lifting a chair from across the room and levitating it to us. Then I repeat the words for the cloaking spell. When I release the magical bond, his eyes are fixed into saucers.

"You truly did not exist for the moment you finished the chant until you appeared again. That was amazing. I would not believe it if I had not experienced it, but how will you convince the witches of your identity if they cannot recognize you?" he asks.

Reading the rest of the spell, I realize one may invite another to know them. I test the skill and Foster, stunned, agrees it worked.

He wraps his arms around me and kisses my head. "I feared you were truly gone today."

"I am sorry. I will try to tell Mother in my dreams so she will not upset everyone. I can imagine it caused the whole family pain."

I say goodbye to Foster and lie on my cot. The time inches by as my mind spins with questions, but one thought at a time, like sand grains dropping from an hourglass, I quiet my brain. My dreams produce terrifying sequences of encounters with Sonia. I awake to my stomach searing as if gutted by a spear the size of a tree trunk and my wings aching as if shredded into straw. Heart racing like a roadrunner tearing across the sand, I sit up and raise my ailerons. Seeing my green wings rise behind me, I run my fingers across the smooth surface. The veins in the membranes pulse under my touch.

Stomach still in my throat, I cross to the wash tub and splash my face with water. Patting it dry, I spin to face the room. *In my cabin. In my realm.*

THE DAY PASSES AS MOLASSES flowing from a bowl, but I have promised Foster I will wait for the birds and intend to keep this pledge.

It is well past dark when Foster arrives with two gray doves tucked in a cage under his cape.

Cooing at the birds, I set them on the floor. My assumption holds that we need do nothing more but tie a note to the bird's ankle, and it will find the way to Foster. I learn there is much more to carrier birds. They must trust you and be willing to be touched and held until they are ready to carry a message. Because Foster housed them for a week then brought them here by foot, they should know their way to the castle, but we will need to test this.

Holding seed out to them, I coax one onto my hand then my arm.

Foster shows me the book of instructions for training the birds, and we skim through it together. Part of me wonders if I should end this strife now. We work so hard to make living apart work when we could be living together. If only I were to agree to marry him, things could be easier.

At least one season. I should give him a season to acclimate and truly decide whether he can leave his family, his post, and his kingdom. This life has been my choice. He must be sure of his.

Turning my face, I kiss his lips.

He responds, pressing his mouth to mine. One hand winds around my neck and the other around my waist. His warmth envelopes me, and we kiss until I am out of breath. I kiss his neck and savor his scent.

"Mmmm." I press my mouth to his again. "I could kiss you forever."

He runs a finger down my nose. "I pray soon you will be able to. What is your plan for saying yes to my marriage proposal? Why do you wait?"

"I told you. We should fully understand what we are committing to. We are not just committing to each other but a lifestyle neither of us could have predicted or perhaps would not have chosen for ourselves."

"You can say it. You believe I will grow to regret the decision to live with you, that I will be miserable and blame you."

"It is a concern. Giving up sharing your life completely with family and friends is not a small thing."

"You worry too much." He kisses me. "I cannot wait to be married to you. I think you wish this issue with Sonia to be resolved first. But what if it never is? You cannot wait for that forever."

I look to the ceiling, blinking away the tears that come too easily. "Perhaps you are right. I have been naïve about her capabilities before, believed that if I just achieve this next task, all will be resolved."

He takes both my hands. "That is why I wish you to make your decision by the winter solstice. Can you give me that?"

Nine months seems a fair compromise. I cannot make him wait forever. I kiss him. "Yes, I will decide by the winter solstice."

With constant nightmares the prior night, I focus my thoughts on Mother and the Goddesses. Still, their presence eludes me as dreams of screeching dragons, spewing volcanoes, and sliding rock pervade my psyche. Waking, I realize many fears about entering Upper Earth haunt my subconscious. I sit on my porch in the morning light, sipping my tea and feeding Messie seeds. Foster finally agreed that we may leave notes under my cot for each other. Although more centered, I crave the release of anxiety that will come once this day is done, for today, I shall see the witches.

Chapter I

AFTER CHORES, I ARRANGE SUPPLIES into my pack, including the book of spells, bread and cheese, my quiver, bow, and some arrows. Wishing for a lighter summer cloak, I fit a mask on my face then my hood over two long braids. I fly over the vast ocean and descend into the jungle surrounding Rotuga's capital. I walk to Alemayehu's home, finding him sipping tea.

"Greetings, friend. Do you take tea outside often?"

"I like the trees, and it is too warm to be inside."

We enter the structure, closing the door and covering the windows for privacy. I lay my mask and cloak on a stool, and we discuss details for my journey into Upper Earth. He thought through more issues than I realized existed, and we decide on a few solutions. His Upper Earth language skills surpass mine, and he produces a list of best practices for speaking so I can blend into their culture. My leg bounces as I recite the terms, ensuring correct pronunciation and questioning meanings.

He lays his palm on my thigh. "You hoped for a faster process?"

"Yes. I want to go now. DJ will know me. I know he will. The book explains that I control who will recognize me. In the words of Upper Earth, I got this."

Urging me to practice on him, I recite the spell then invite him to know me. This works without effort, and I jump to my feet.

"I am ready," I say.

"How will you get into their compound?" he asks.

"I will wait until they come outside?"

"I should send a letter alerting them to expect a visitor." He paces in the small space.

"That could take hours for a reply. I want to go now. I will figure it out."

"You do not know where they are."

I look at him sideways. "Do not pretend you do not know where they are."

"I do not. Their last correspondence was weeks ago. I believe they think it too risky for our style of communication."

"All the more reason for me to go without fanfare." I lift my cloak and spin it to my back.

"What is your name? What will your disguise be? We should test your appearance after entering the ring."

"I remember how Alena and Camille dressed. I will have red hair and blue eyes, and I shall call myself Thessalonia."

"Thessalonia? No one in Upper Earth has such names." He clutches my mask.

"Then it can be shortened to Tessa. DJ always called me T. Why are you being so stubborn?"

"Why are *you* being so reckless? You never were before. Foster will kill me if anything happens to you."

"I am dead. I have nothing to lose." I know it is a lie, but I say it anyway. "And DJ will protect me."

"When you find him. If you can convince him of your identity. If—"

I raise a hand. "No more. I am going."

Snatching my mask from him, I fit it over my face, and lift my hood over my hair. I check the space around his hut. Seeing no one, I dart to the trees. A rustling behind me indicates Alemayehu follows. I shoot up to the dome, and we fly north to the ring near Sardinia. I start to recite the now-memorized incantation.

Alemayehu grips my arm. "Linger beside the ring when you pass through. At least allow me to check your disguise."

"Fine." I tug my arm from his grasp.

Closing my eyes, I think the words for the soul cloaking spell. I open my lids and, checking the horizon again, jump into the air, speeding through the magical barrier between our realm and Upper Earth. The magic of the ring washes over me, and my skin tingles as if thousands of tiny sprites dance over it. I land in the Upper Earth forest and conjure my disguise.

Alemayehu rubs his chin as he circles me. "Okay, you may have this."

I raise my hand to my hip. "I told you I did."

"Don't get snarky with me, young lady."

"Who are you? My dad?"

"Great amount of belligerent teen. I like it."

I bid him goodbye and fly invisibly through the woods to the wall surrounding the witches' compound. I jump to the top of the wall and, seeing no one about, circle the grounds. The space appears devoid of beings, so I make my way to the nearby town. Alighting on the outskirts, I display my disguise and walk into the city center. Villagers greet me, and I reply with "ciao" or "salve," the typical Italian greetings Alemayehu taught me.

Finding the city center lined with shops, I marvel at the trinkets. What Alemayehu has told me is called a café catches my eye. I watch people go in, order, and wait for their drinks to be delivered. Then a pair of men, heads bobbing through the crowds, catches my eye. As they stop in front of the café, one spins to face me, and I recognize the brown mop of hair atop a beautiful dark head. DJ. The luck of the Goddesses is with me today. My pulse races, and I wrap a hand around my satchel strap.

I watch as they enter the café, and DJ exits to the roadside seating area, taking a table. *Even better,* I think as I anticipate the reunion with my friend. His companion Tyler, who waits inside, has not been my favorite person, or I his. I smile, watching DJ fit headphones over his ears and scroll through his phone.

Weaving to his table, I stop beside him. "Hi, I noticed you spoke English."

DJ peers up at me, squinting. "Yeah."

"Thank God." Dropping my satchel to the sidewalk, I slide into the seat beside him. "Finally, something to make this town bearable."

DJ lowers his headphones to his neck. "I'm guessing you're from the US on vacation here?"

"Yes, from LA. I'm Thessalonia." I eek out the contraction with some struggle and extend my hand.

He raises his palm and clasps it around mine. "I'm DJ. Also from LA. Thessalonia? That's some name."

"Yeah, family name." I roll my eyes for effect. "Most of my friends call me Tessa."

Glancing back at the café door, he runs his hands down his thighs. "How long are you here?"

"I have no clue. My dad carts me around all summer while he works. I mean, it's beautiful here, but where are all the people our age?"

"It's mostly retired people. Not many tourists here."

"Lucky me I found you then." I shrug and let my gaze linger on his beautiful brown eyes.

"Did you want a drink or some food? I could get you something if your Italian isn't that good." He points to the restaurant.

"No, that's fine. I just heard you and your friend talking so thought maybe we could hang out. What do you do for fun?"

"Not much, to be honest." DJ slides to the front of his seat.

"The nightlife is seriously lacking here. And where are all the sandy beaches? I was thinking of renting a boat.

Would you like to do that with me?" I wonder if I were a regular fae teen if I could be this confident and forward.

"My friend and I don't have that much time."

"I get it. You hardly know me. I mean, if it makes a difference, my best friends call me T." I hold his gaze, allowing him to recognize my being.

"T? That's dope. I have a friend I call... Oh my God, Titan—"

I press my finger to his wide lips. Leaning in, he wraps his arms around me and squeezes my shoulders, his fingers tight around my biceps. I take in his scent, allowing myself to be engulfed in his warm arms. The tension in my neck eases. He feels like home.

"Wait." He releases me. "You can't be here. It's way too dangerous."

I shake my head and smile. "Soul cloaking spell. And I can control who can recognize me."

"How did you figure that out?"

"Alemayehu recorded all the spells he heard." I tap my ear. "Extrasensory hearing, remember?"

"It's still a big risk being here."

"You do see what is happening, right? The earthquakes? The volcanoes? How do you think that affects my realm? Last week, an entire village was covered in rock before we could close the ring."

He runs fingers through his thick, dark hair. "I know it's crazy. But, T—"

Seeing Tyler exit the café, I press my index finger to his lips. "Why are you with Tyler?"

DJ lowers his head. "Alena, Camille, Hunter, and Jude teamed up, so I'm stuck with Tyler."

I glance at Tyler as he weaves toward us, his thoughts zinging right into my head. *What the…? Dang, this guy has so much game. I leave for two minutes, and he's already got a hot girl beside him. Why can't stuff like that happen to me?*

Hearing his thoughts sparks questions as well as pride. *DJ's got game? I guess I did a good job with my disguise.*

Tyler sets the cups on the table, slides DJ's toward him, and extends a hand. "Hi, I'm Tyler."

"Hi." I fit my palm in Tyler's. "I'm Thessalonia."

"Wow, Thessalonia. What a cool name." He sits across from me.

I lower my sunglasses. "My friends call me Tessa."

Leaning forward, DJ raises his eyebrows. "Tessa is from LA too."

"I heard you speaking in English so thought I would introduce myself. My dad drags me along on his business trips, and this town is seriously boring." I roll my eyes for effect.

"Do you want anything to drink?" Tyler motions to the shop.

"No, I'm fine."

DJ sets his palms on his thighs and bounces his legs. "I told Tessa she should come to our place, that we could give her a tour."

I smile, realizing DJ is going to use his knowledge of my identity to his advantage.

"I'm so excited. DJ says you're staying at the castle at the tip of the island? I saw it from the plane. My dad said no one gets to go there. The owners have it locked down."

Tyler glares at DJ. "We're really not supposed to have guests."

I dip my head over the table. "There's a rumor that a coven of witches owns the castle. People here actually believe in witches."

"I haven't seen a witch," DJ says.

"Do witches look any different than regular people?" I ask. "The maid at my hotel told me vampires live there too. I can't wait to see this place."

Tyler winces. "We can't—"

"Come on, man. The girl's right. There's nothing to do in this town. It won't hurt to give her a tour." Reaching into a pants pocket, DJ draws a piece of paper from a folded leather pouch and lays it on the table. "Come on, let's go."

I bounce up and grab DJ's hand. "Yay! My friends are going to be so jealous."

Tyler looks between us. "You have friends here?"

"They're in Mexico. Can you believe they got to go to Mexico, and I had to come here?" I shake my head, slide a just-conjured mobile phone from my pocket, and snap a selfie of myself and DJ. "I'm posting this. You're totally adorable."

Pressing my lips to DJ's cheek, I'm bombarded with Tyler's torrent of thoughts. *She's holding his hand, kissing him, and sending selfies to her friends, and they've known each other for five minutes? Okay, yeah, he's good looking, but she's sus as hell.*

I file *sus* away with the *game* word to ask about later. "Let's bounce." DJ tugs me toward the exit.

He flags a cab, and we file in the backseat, me between DJ and Tyler. The vehicle lurches forward, and my stomach clenches. I grip the front seat as we speed through the narrow, cobbled lanes. Flying at top speed, yes. Flailing over a rock-ridden road in a metal contraption with a machine whirring from the front and explosive chemicals sloshing in a tank behind me. Not a fan.

Tyler's thoughts escalate to anger. *Are you insane? We can't take her to the compound.*

I realize this thought is probably being projected telepathically to DJ. Tyler's arm feels like a hot water flask beside mine, and his pulse races. I compare it to DJ's and think perhaps we are being too cruel with the scheme. I switch my attention to DJ.

He seems really agitated.

Serves the ass right for being a dick all the time.

My face flushes as I recall my cousins explaining the meaning of the "d" term.

Oh, shit. Sorry. Stream of conscious. Forgot it was you.

"Why don't we rent a boat?" Tyler asks. He taps the driver on the shoulder, telling him to drive to the wharf.

"I can't do boats. I get seasickness," I say.

"No one's at the castle. It'll be fine. Chill." Extending an arm behind me, DJ pats Tyler's back and instructs the driver to stay with the current course.

What is this dude thinking? Tyler rubs his thighs. *He's thinking with the wrong part of his anatomy, that's the problem.*

The driver takes a fast corner, and I sway into Tyler. He smells of sweat, and I try to focus on the breeze from the window. Looking out the front glass, the road speeds toward me like an arrow bound for its target. My stomach lurches. I place my other hand on the seat before me. "Could we walk instead?"

DJ's arm encircles me. "Do you want to stop?"

Nodding, I pray my face is not a ghastly green or pasty white, but that may be in character. "This car is feeling more and more like a boat," I say.

Tyler yells for the driver to stop, and the car veers off the road.

I slide from the car as DJ opens the door. They pay the driver as I sit, head between my legs, fanning my face with my hands and praying my stomach does not empty itself.

Exhaling, Tyler folds his hands behind his neck. "I'm not sure what we're going to do now. It's a long way to walk back to town or to our place."

"I'm sorry. I'm just not used to these twisty roads."

DJ kneels beside me and wraps an arm around me. "We can call a car from our place. They'll drive much slower."

No. No. No. Tyler's frustration rolls from his body in waves.

I stand. "I think we should fly."

Turning toward me, his mouth hangs open. "Can you fly?"

"Yes. Can you?"

Tyler's eyes cut to DJ and back to me. "Is this a joke?"

"It is not." I hold Tyler's stare. In my mind, I extend an invitation for him to know me.

His eyes grow wide, and he stumbles back. "What the hell?"

"Manners, dude. You're talking to a fae queen." DJ bumps his fist to Tyler's arm.

"A former queen, " I say.

"Ugh." Tyler slaps his forehead. "How are you here? Aren't you hiding from Sonia?"

"Shh." I glare at him. "I am using a cloaking spell."

"She's very good at it, isn't she?" DJ's eyebrows shift up.

I point to the trees, and we enter the wood. As we walk, DJ casts a cloaking bubble around us to guard our conversation. Trekking toward the castle, they review their progress on meeting Sonia's demands. Alena, Camille, Hunter, and Jude are searching for a way to find Sonia's son, Thanatos, or more concisely, his soul and bones to merge the two. As they have not had success locating his soul, they now focus on finding his remains. DJ and Tyler have been tasked with retrieving Lilith, as Alemayehu found the fae texts suggesting she is Sonia's mother.

"This is perfect. I can help." I jump a downed tree.

Tyler expresses skepticism that I could be of any use because a secret faction of vampires have guarded Lilith's remains for millennia. As mother of all vampires, her body is their most sacred relic. Some believe if she is destroyed then all vampires will meet the same fate.

"It makes no sense whatsoever. It's so stupid, I can't even wrap my brain around it, but they're almost impossible to track down. Even with Alena's mother's resources, we can't find them. Anne's technology and reach surpasses anyone else's. I think they've sent us on a wild goose chase," Tyler says as he hoists one leg then the other over the tree trunk.

"Alena, Camille, and Hunter found a five-thousand-year-old dagger. Have some faith, if not in yourself, in us, at least. And, dude. These beings aren't stupid. Check your bias. You believe archangels sired the witch lines, giving us our powers, and you won't acknowledge beliefs of other beings?"

"I never said I think we're actually sired by angels. I don't believe in God, the Creator, Heaven, Hell, or whatever. I believe in science. We're born, and we die. The vampires even genetically proved they're nothing more than a sub-species of humans."

"So witches are a sub-species of humans too?" DJ asks.

"And faeries as well," Tyler says.

"Faeries are descended from angels," I say. "And angels have no physical form, thus proving the existence of the Creator."

"Ahhh." Tyler waves his arms above his head. "None of this matters. The point is we need to find the crazy vampires and convince them to give us Lilith. We hand her over to Sonia, who then will probably destroy Lilith and, according to vampire lore, all the vampires with her. Then Sonia will have achieved her goal and stop with the hell-on-earth threats. Or all the crazy weather is because of climate change, and we're doing this for no reason."

My mind races with this alternate outcome of Sonia's reunion with her mother. *How had I not seen* that *scenario?* It would fit an evil scheme of the typical villain my cousins have described from Upper Earth's many hero stories: an arch enemy demanding to be reconciled with a family member, supposedly under the guise of bringing peace, only to turn the tables, achieving their sinister master plan. My nerves twitch with the quandary. *Is delivering Lilith to Sonia the right thing to do? A bond between mother and child is the most sacred of bonds, correct?*

I zip around him and spin so we are eye to eye. "Why are you still with the witches?"

"I'm with the witches until this thing inside me that tells me I need to protect Alena goes away."

"So, you believe that at some point you will fulfill some unknown destiny, and you will be unburdened of your herald duties?"

"Exactly." Jutting his arm up, he steps around me.

"Bundle of joy, isn't he?" DJ asks. He explains that they've been given this task to help them decide whether they wish to continue to hold places with the witches or integrate into human society.

Tyler's head swivels from one side to the other. "That assumes that whatever is tethering us to the trinity will release us upon completion of *this* task."

Pointing out that Sonia demanded to be reconciled, I contend that Sonia wishes to be reunited with her mother. He reports not to care what Sonia does with Lilith once they have delivered her. I wonder how he can be so callous, to not care about the fate of an entire race. I force myself to examine his plight. He had no control over being chosen as a herald, and being linked to a girl he could never have a romantic relationship with would be challenging. Plus, he feels the need to protect his sister, Camille.

Finding the wall, I stop. "What are we telling the guards? The fewer people who know about me, the better."

Tyler rolls his eyes. "You're Tessa, a random chick we picked up in the village. I'm sure it'll be kosher."

I look between my hosts. "And by that, you mean it will *not* be okay?"

"We'll get Hunter to give you clearance. They'll log you in as a visiting witch." DJ holds his phone above his head and wraps his arm around my waist, taking a picture.

He taps the screen, sending the image to Alena, Hunter, and Camille. A call buzzes in, and squeals emanate from the phone's speaker, Alena and Camille greeting me. My heart warms at their gleeful welcome, but my mind pings with the realization that I will never have this with my true family again. Raising my chin, I exhale. This menagerie of beings, coupled with Alemayehu and Foster, must be enough.

We hike back to the castle gate and are greeting by a vampire guard. Stepping out of the small building in front of the tall metal gate, a vampire guard named Will approaches us. "Why are you walking?"

"Someone wanted more exercise." Tyler rolls his eyes.

Will's eyes dart between us. "Hunter said to be expecting a Thessalonia?"

I clutch my satchel and extend my hand. "You can call me Tessa."

Chapter 8

We walk along the drive, flanked by two vampire guards, Will, and another I do not recognize. As we near the castle, I expect the slight tingle of magic produced by the witches inside. When it does not come, I realize DJ was not overstating. No one is here.

Entering through the security room, where only two vampires sit in front of the wall of screens, we wind through the passage to a meeting room we have used many times. I lay my bag on the floor and slide into the plush, tufted, leather chair, rolling up to the oval wood table. Even with so many visits to this compound, the furnishings still surprise me. The jagged, stone walls remind me of my castle. A much larger version than my own, this structure, with its tall rock spires, large round towers, and ground marble floors, seems at odds with the technology laced within it.

DJ taps buttons on a keyboard, and the picture screen on the wall lights up. He opens lists and maps, detailing their research so far.

"We've emailed and called everyone on this list of suspected Guardians of Lilith with no response." DJ lays his palms on the table.

"These beings are not going to respond to electronic messages and phone calls. They will not trust until they see you face to face, are assured that you are who you say you are," I say. "I believe we must approach them."

"Do you remembering the wild vampires I took you to meet?" Tyler asks. "The ones who tried to eat us?"

"I doubt Hunter is asking you to approach a pack of wild vampires without security," I say.

"We'd have guards," DJ replies.

"What if Anne went with us? She was leader of the vampires, was she not?" I ask.

"These are unregistered vampires. They didn't recognize her when she had power. They aren't going to hand Lilith over just because she says to," Tyler says.

"They occupy the same realm you do, are affected by these earthquakes and volcanoes, just like you. I would guess they want Sonia stopped just as much, perhaps even more, than we do. She has threatened to eradicate the vampires. There must be some compromise to be made," I say.

Tyler argues that these vampires have held the secret of Lilith's location for centuries and will not reveal themselves to be Guardians. Further, he questions why they would even speak with us when we have no real clout. I counter that he and DJ are backed by the High Priest of the witches and myself, the highest-ranking fae.

"Are you?" Tyler asks.

"I can be. The High Judge aided us before. He will again." I realize this may be harder than I grasped and pray this will be true.

Perhaps Alemayehu may make up a tale of who is to represent us. He could say he is travelling to Upper Earth to work with the witches.

Over the next hours, we gain Anne's pledge to help where possible, have four bodyguards arranged to travel with us, and make a list of locations to search for the Guardians. We set the schedule to meet each weekday. My knee bounces because I'm eager to set our plan into action, but my stomach reminds me I have been in this realm long enough, so I gather my bag.

I say goodbye to Tyler, and DJ walks me outside.

"I guess I'll take Alemayehu's job of escorting you to the ring," he says as we cross the lawn.

"I do not believe there is danger." I say this as bumps form on my arms. I would rather not be out in the open and pick up my pace.

"At least we can talk without Tyler's commentary."

"I am sad for him. I hope he finds peace. How are you doing?" I stop and spin to face him as we reach the stone wall.

"Better now that you're here. I was so worried about you. I hope you're not too isolated." He grasps my hands.

"I have a few friends who have supported me, and I told Foster."

"Foster. Your boyfriend, right? How'd that go?"

"Not good at first. We are happy now, but I have struggled with being lonely since Terran left."

"Terran?"

"That is what we call Theron. He is with Alemayehu now, in Rotuga's army."

Jumping the wall and landing in the forest, we trek toward the ring. I explain our kingdom system, telling him about Terran's post and how Alemayehu reports Terran is mixing well with the soldiers. DJ inquires about the High Judge, and I describe the High Council and our relationship with Zekiel. We wonder whether Alemayehu may be willing to be Zekiel's representative, and I pledge to ask.

We reach the ring with its shimmering film of magic. He leans over the edge. "I wish I could visit."

"It is not as idyllic as you might imagine. I believe, if I were in Upper Earth, it would be easier to live in such an isolated place. At least I could call or text someone." I tell him about the carrier pigeons we have trained. "I like our plan. I will see you tomorrow, friend."

I extend my arm, and his fingers lock around it.

"Until tomorrow," he says.

Stepping back, I lift my cloak, fold my wings, and then cross my arms over my chest. With a hop, I fall through the ring, the magic pulsing over my skin, and I drop my cloaking spell. I fan my ailerons out, and turn toward Rotuga. It is dark when I arrive at Alemayehu's home, and I sound the call agreed upon.

He motions me inside. "This is good timing. My sons just left for the village."

Opening my pack, I grab my bread and cheese and sit in front of the fire. He scoffs at the meal and sets dish after dish, left from the meal with his family, in front of me. Showing me how to scoop the beans and grains up with leaves, he urges me to try each item. The seasonings, so rich and powerful, taste of pepper and vanilla at the same time.

"This is amazing," I say through a half-stuffed mouth.

"It is better if you eat slowly." He glares at me.

Even with his admonishment, my body craves sustenance, and I continue to shovel bites into my mouth. After a few sips of wine, I begin to recount the day, telling him of DJ and Tyler; the aim of Hunter, Alena, Camille, and Jude; as well as our plan to find the Guardians.

"I believe we must involve Zekiel, get his blessing, blessings of the High Council, and papers to prove such. DJ and I want you to represent the fae." I grip Alemayehu's arms. "We should go to Zekiel tonight. We are ready to start searching for the Guardians tomorrow."

"Child, first, you know fae cannot move this fast. The High Council may need days, if not weeks, to get word to each member of the request, consult among themselves, and then decide whether to support this. Second, I am not a young fae. I cannot fly from one side of a realm to another."

Knowing of Lencho's post, I ask whether he may serve instead. Alemayehu laughs and indicates Lencho is not a good choice, being more action driven than diplomatic. Instead, Alemayehu suggests a younger son, Yonas, may be well suited. Alemayehu leaves to fetch the young fae, and I cross from one side of the small hut to the other, frustrated at the snail's pace of fae life.

Alemayehu must have prepared Yonas for my presence because he greets me without surprise. We sit around the fire, and I repeat my story for him, pleading with him to help bring this request to the High Court and represent the fae in Upper Earth. To my surprise, he agrees with no further persuasion needed. We draft a letter to Zekiel and the High Council, and Yonas leaves with it, bound for Zekiel's home in Lindleton, as soon as the ink dries.

I clutch my hands. "It may take some time for us to locate the Guardians and gain an audience with their leaders. I believe we can still begin our search tomorrow."

"Perhaps you should stay here. With the distance from the village, I never get visitors."

Rising, I lift my pack. "I must go. I have goats, sheep, and a carrier pigeon to care for."

"You will come here each day before you enter Upper Earth and after returning, correct? Pledge to me you will not travel into the Upper Realm without alerting me."

This seems like an unnecessary step, but it is not too far out of the way, and I know Foster will sleep better knowing he has a point of contact. I agree and, wrapping Alemayehu in a hug, say goodbye. The journey home passes quickly with me making a list in my mind of all the tasks required. As soon as I am home, I pen a letter to Foster outlining all that occurred today. I hide it between the clothing stacked under my cot, hoping if Foster comes, he will find it.

⤜∗⤛

I conjure my Thessalonia disguise and repeat my cloaking spell, meeting DJ, Tyler, and four vampire guards at sundown in the forest flanking the compound. I feel anxious without word from the High Council but know they cannot act in less than a day. Our plan is to begin searching for the Guardians in Italy. As we speak, a whirring sound grows from above, as if millions of locusts fill the sky, humming their songs in a rhythmic pattern. The wind picks up, and lights dart across the brush-covered ground.

"The helicopter's here. We should go," Tyler yells above the noise.

My pulse sounds in my ears. "A helicopter? Is that a type of airplane?"

"Yes. They're better than airplanes for short flights," DJ says.

I fold my arms across my middle. "But I can fly."

"We can't. Let's go." Tyler starts toward the direction of the flapping blades.

Trailing them, I wonder if I can ride in such a contraption without having an anxiety attack. We jump the wall, and my heart thuds. Large blades spin above a small metal box no bigger than a car. *You are in control,* I tell myself. In this case, I am not, and I cannot tell my body any different. My lungs fight for breath. As the image of the helicopter goes fuzzy, I exhale. I clench and release fists. If DJ says this will be okay, it is okay. DJ will be my Foster, the indicator that will help me gauge risk. My mind jumps to Alemayehu and how he told me never to ride in the elevators. This is like a flying elevator. No, Alemayehu would not get in a helicopter.

You are going to, my brain insists. I ball my fists and follow, grabbing my hair as it bats around my head and ducking under the spinning blades. Tyler steps onto a beam and then into the cab, and DJ waves me ahead of him. I sit on a bench next to Tyler, and he hands me a pair of round objects—headphones, I pull from my memory. I set them over my ears, and the whirring sound ceases.

"Put on the seatbelt." He lifts a strap from behind me.

He motions to my other side, and I find a matching device. I study the buckle, unsure of how it should fit together. Tyler bumps my arm and, releasing his, demonstrates how they attach.

With the belt tight across my hips and chest, my body heat rises. I feel my hands warm and catch the start of the light green glow of my magic. *Not threatened, not in danger,* I repeat to myself. The color wanes and I exhale.

Tyler's lips move, and I hear his words seconds later. "Cool, eh?"

I cup my hands over the muff-like foam on my ears. He moves a foam rod in front of my mouth and taps on it. The sound echoes through my headphones. Heart racing, I force a smile and lift my thumb. DJ sits to my left, and the vampires squish into the row behind us. DJ lifts his hand and grabs a hook above his head, and looking up, I do the same. A guard closes the door, and the cabin vibrates as the speed of the blades increase. The machine lifts off the ground, and I latch onto DJ's thigh with my free hand. I clench my eyes shut as the helicopter climbs into the sky, swaying one way then the other.

"The lights from the mainland look very cool." DJ's deep voice carries through the headphones.

I open one eye to see the bright lights from the city ahead twinkling like thousands of fireflies. The helicopter dips, and I squeeze my eyes closed again. I imagine sitting in my office, looking out over my meadow at first light, the haze of dew lifting from the grass fronds. The helicopter descends and bounces as it touches down.

"It's over." DJ taps my shoulder.

Rising from the seat, my muscles feel frozen, as if they've sat dormant for years. I force myself to take one step then the next, clutching DJ's hand and jumping to the ground. He tugs me away from the helicopter.

"See? You didn't die." Tyler laughs as he joins us.

As the helicopter takes off, I spin to see a large black vehicle, doors open.

This car rolls much smoother than the cab had yesterday, and I relax on the soft, cushioned seat, watching the buildings float past us. Stopping in a narrow lane, we exit the vehicle onto a cobblestone road. I eye my surroundings, finding most of the buildings fashioned from rock. *At least this feels somewhat familiar.*

We walk on a narrow rock strip between the lane and the buildings, DJ and Tyler flanking me and our guards behind. The lights, motion, and sounds of the city, with varied motors and blaring horns, overwhelm my senses, and I draw in a deep breath. I realize my mistake as the air filters through my nose. Putrid smells of an origin I could not name accost me, and I clap my hands over my face.

Wrapping an arm around me, DJ pulls me toward him. "Welcome to Rome. Amazing buildings but doesn't smell great, especially to sensitive noses."

The scent of coconut oil from his hair products surrounds me, and I release my nose.

"That's not going to get any better, especially where we're going," he says.

As we wind toward the city center, the streets become more crowded. Tyler walks ahead of us as others pass. Music of many kinds drifts from buildings, mixing with laughter and conversation. *This is more like the lifestyle of the fae,* I think, *gathering in the evening with family and friends. A lifestyle I may never have.* We pass an open door, and I catch sight of a room filled with dancers. My heart clenches as I think of the many nights in my courtyard spent in celebration.

Tyler glances at his phone, leading us through the streets. Cars zip through the lanes, and people file in and out of doors like ants on a mound. I am glad for DJ's arm around my back and his familiar scent as I feel flung into a pot of what Alfreda called scrap stew. I center myself by focusing on the back of Tyler's head. Turning into a tunnel between buildings, we start down a stone staircase, the light from the street waning as we switch back and forth, descending into near darkness.

My nostrils twitch as I reach the last flight of steps and register the number of beings packed into the space— vampires, lots of vampires. I draw in a breath, summoning my courage. My hands glow at my sides. DJ and Tyler were right, black is the color of choice for this group, and I am glad leather pants, much like my riding pants, and vest seem in style here. DJ takes my hand as others close in on us, and I clutch Tyler's shirt so I do not lose him.

He weaves through the throngs of vampires, and I close my eyes, trying to block out all my other senses. Much of our plan for finding the Guardians hinges on me picking thoughts from these vampires' brains. DJ and our vampire guards will listen for any conversations of interest, and we have images of suspected Guardians, but it may be unlikely that anything of interest would be said aloud.

Witch seems to be the most prevalent thought as we inch through the crowd, so I assume they do not get many witches here. They do not seem to register me as different, but I realize I may be steeped in DJ's scent. That works in my favor. This many vampires salivating for one fae may not end well for me.

Tyler stops at a long wooden table positioned a few feet from the wall. Behind it, vampires dart about, filling glasses with what I assume from the smell to be strongly fermented drinks. He raises his hand, and a vampire approaches. Tyler points between the six of us, and within seconds, six small glasses are filled with dark liquid.

DJ rests his hand on my hip and leans in, his lips brushing my ear. "I know you can't drink this. Fake it and hand me your glass."

Bumps form on my arms as his warm breath cascades down my neck. I square my shoulders, fighting the urge to shake the sensation from my limbs. I take a glass as Tyler passes them between us and, copying their actions, lift the drink to my lips and throw my head back. My lips tingle as I lower the glass and slip it into DJ's hand. He turns and empties the contents into his mouth.

Tyler raises his glass over his head, and we clink ours to it. This tradition feels familiar, and I realize this may be much like the late-night festivities that occur at the castle. The ones I was whisked away from as a child and avoid as Queen—*avoided*, I amend.

On the far side of the space, people with instruments start a tune. I fight the urge to cup my hands over my ears as a high-pitched squeal emits from a guitar.

Tyler leads us away from the drink counter, and I focus again on catching thoughts of the beings around us. Again, one idea overshadows any other that may have been there before. *Witch? Why is a witch here? Why is a witch with those vampires? Why did those vampires bring a witch? Are they lost?* Impressions veer from surprise to suspicion.

We stop halfway into the space, where the beings pack in so tightly there is no way to progress forward.

"I like this music." Tyler bounces his head with the rhythm of the drums.

Is he daft? Is he trying to fit in? Does he not register the reaction of those around us? I release a slow breath. He is only a witch. He has no extrasensory abilities, and with that drink he just consumed, he cannot be thinking clearly.

I turn to DJ and whisper into his ear, "Are you sensing the tension around us? I think we should leave."

"We're here. Let's see if it settles." He rests his hands on each side of my waist.

"No. You do not understand. We need to go." I lift my face and hold his gaze.

He reaches around me and taps Tyler on the shoulder. Once he turns, DJ ticks his head in the direction of the exit. Tyler scoffs, but after a stern look from DJ, spins to follow us. We shuffle through the crowd to the side wall, retracing our path up the steps. With the flow of beings descending, we scrape against the rough wall to the exit at the top.

"What's going on?" Tyler demands as soon as we reach the sidewalk.

Pressing a finger to my lips, I motion him down the path. I keep my hand on his shoulder, guiding him away from the vampire gathering spot. In two blocks, I spot a break in the buildings and motion us into the narrow lane.

"What's going on?" Tyler asks again.

"We were not going to learn anything. All thoughts were centered on you. A witch in a vampire crowd had them on edge."

"Fu—Ugh." His eyes hold mine as the odd sound passes from his lips. "I hadn't thought of that."

"It's not your fault. Neither did we," DJ says.

"I can hang back and let you scout the place."

I shake my head. "No, the vampires will remember us. We cannot go back there. We will not be trusted."

"Let's call it a night and regroup," DJ says.

"Fine." Tyler kicks at the stone path.

I do not favor the experience of riding in the vehicle or helicopter but realize we need to discuss a new strategy. So, I follow them to the car and then into the helicopter.

My thoughts swirl with everything I witnessed: the boisterous revelry, the busyness, the noise, the cacophony of smells, so many beings packed in a small space, varied ideas swimming through their minds, and the unmistakable ache in my chest at what I may never have. My ribcage strains with the weight of longing for my family and people, to see them happy, to be part of it again. I draw in a breath. In a few hours, I can curl up on my cot and miss them.

I focus on DJ's warmth beside me, on the wind from the blades hitting my face, and it seems as if no time passes until we land on the grass beside the castle.

As we exit the helicopter, DJ wraps his arm around me. "Are you okay?"

Tyler strides past us. "We need to debrief."

Having no idea what a debrief is, I ball my fists and fight flinging an insult at him. I imagine myself posting my hands on my hips and yelling, "You try to get on a helicopter for the first time in your life." *If he is going to be here, can he just be nice?*

"Ignore him." DJ squeezes my shoulder.

I inquire as to the meaning of debriefing, and DJ explains as we follow Tyler inside, winding to the conference room. I take a chair opposite him and adjust my perspective. Yes, DJ is a friend, and Tyler is somewhat of an adversary, but this is also a joint project, so there are going to be differences of opinion, but we still must work as a team. For whatever reason, perhaps because he has been in the witch community longer, I realize Tyler sees himself as our leader.

Folding my hands together, I set them on the table. "I am sorry tonight did not turn out as you planned."

Tyler stretches his neck. "How do you know the vampires wouldn't have trusted us? This was an important night, we had intel on at least ten suspected Guardians who were supposed to be there. We knew what they looked like. We just had to find them."

I release my palms and press them to the tabletop, explaining the thoughts I heard from the vampires we passed.

"It makes sense." DJ rubs his chin. "And don't you think the Guardians especially will be suspicious of witches? They're guarding Lilith for a reason. Various beings have been after her for thousands of years."

Reaching across the table, I hold Tyler's gaze. "I want this mission to be a success. We may have different reasons for wanting this, but I am just as committed. I would not jeopardize it. You are a powerful witch. Perhaps you can be our eyes, and we can be the ones to make contact."

"I could project myself and find them quicker."

"Yes, good idea." I give myself a pat on the back for acknowledging his strengths. "And you and DJ have your secret language, correct? Does that work in your projected form?"

Chapter 9

TIME SPREADS OUT TO MINUTES as I look between Tyler and DJ, waiting for an answer as to whether Tyler has the ability to project his soul and if DJ and Tyler are able to communicate with Tyler in that form.

His head bobbles, and he glances at DJ. "We could work on strengthening that skill."

Releasing my breath, I stretch my legs under the table. It almost seems as if I am back in the King's study in my castle, strategizing with my advisors and generals. It feels familiar and almost comforting. If only it were Father, Grant, and Foster surrounding me. I refocus on my reality as we discuss preparations for the next night.

DJ walks with me to the ring, as on the previous night, apologizing for Tyler's behavior. A slight bit of guilt enters my psyche. I have an easy role because all I need to do is show up and be the backup, the one with enough power to protect DJ from whatever danger may be presented. Funny how we had been focused on protecting me, with my fae blood that is so salivating to vampires, and Tyler, with his rich, honey-like witch smell, and not one vampire recognized me as fae. I wonder how much of that stems from the soul cloaking spell and how much from my proximity to DJ. *Also, why am I so worried about myself or really any of the others? I could burn any being to ashes with a flick of my hand.*

I challenge DJ to think of working with Tyler as a learning experience. For whatever path DJ may take in life, garnering the skill of pairing with challenging personalities will benefit him.

Stopping, he stares at me. "I forget you are a queen sometimes. It's hard to believe you're younger than me but have so much more experience."

"Our lives move at a different pace than humans.'"

"And did I mention how glad I was to have you with us tonight? I was sure one of those vamps was going to out me as a hybrid, but with you there, I felt like we'd be okay no matter what happened."

I cup my hand over my mouth and double over, barely able to contain my laughter.

"What? You think I'm joking? You have skills."

Standing, I grip his arm. "I just—I was thinking the same thing. I was so glad you were there covering my scent. Why did it not occur to me that I was probably the most powerful being in that crowd? It was all so overwhelming."

"I can't believe we were thinking the same way about one another. I totally get it. You have to get used to all the extra sensations." As we reach the ring, he takes my hand. "We'll figure it out. We always do."

"Be nice to Tyler." I glare at him.

"Get something to eat and sleep well."

"I will." I dive into the ring.

⤜◆⤛

Famished and tired, and with the late hour, I check in with Alemayehu with nothing more than a quick greeting and fly home. I greet my bird and supply it seed.

Exhausted, I shed my outer layers and grab a gown from under the cot. A page of parchment falls from the garment. I scoop it up and, flitting to the table, unfold it under the light from the candle.

T,

I hoped to see you tonight. I find I miss you more and more each day. Thank you for your letter. I love hearing about your adventures. It helps me feel closer to you. I did not want to share my news this way but feel it is best you know. Your mother cried for hours this evening. I am not sure which was worse to witness, her crazed outbursts or her quiet sobs. My heart breaks for her. I am not sure if you can control when you see her and the Goddesses, but for her sake, and that of your family, try.

All my love,

F

P.S. I will find time to come tomorrow. I am not sure when. But I will look for a reply.

I slump into the chair and brace my head on my hands. *Mother.* Tears spring to my eyes. I must try harder to commune with her and the Goddesses. I cross to the fireplace and slide some small twigs and grass under the logs. Lighting them, I sit on the floor, watching the flames as they grow, threading themselves around the wood and intertwining with each other. I close my eyes and spread my shoulders, drawing in a long breath. New tears flow from my eyes as I picture mother crying. I hold an image of her with the Goddesses in my mind: the brilliant sunshine, impossibly green meadow, flowers of every color forming a blanket between the trees, branches sheltering a gathering table, the porcelain teacups held by milk-white fingers.

"Mother, do not be sad. I am not gone. I am helping our fae. You may not be able to see me sometimes, but know I am here, where I always will be, in my soul."

I speak to her aloud, telling her everything about our night. I have almost forgotten our strolls in the woods, arms locked together, when I would talk to her about my day, our kingdom, my feelings, fears, and hopes.

Thinking she knows this, I say it aloud anyway. "We will be together again, Mother. I promise. We may not be in these bodies or in this realm. It may not be with arms, but I will hold you again."

Laying my head on the floor, I watch the flames until I fall asleep.

———— ❖ ————

MESSIE WAKES ME WITH HER CHIRPS, and I open my eyes to a near-dark room. Tiny lines of light peek from below the door and around the shutters. I raise my heavy head not remembering sleep at all. I say a silent prayer to the Goddesses Mother received my message and will be at peace. Uncurling my tight legs, I cross the room to Messie and fill her bowl with seed. I light the fire and make tea, willing my mind to engage with the tasks of the day: garden, goats, sheep, Messie, witches.

I leave Foster a letter under my cot, confirm the plan with Alemayehu, who has heard nothing from the High Council, and meet DJ and Tyler on their compound's lawn as the sun sets over the sea. Our destination tonight is the town of Milan, Italy. Tucked south of a vast mountain range, Milan hosts the second largest population center in Italy. I steel my nerves and load into a long, black car DJ calls a limo. We take the vehicle to a small airport where we board an airplane called a jet. The jet's engines sit on the wings on each side, and with the seating area completely enclosed, this craft causes me less anxiety than the helicopter.

Much like Rome, the cobbled streets and stone buildings of Milan feel familiar. Our first stop is an inn where four vampire guards, the witches, and Tyler arrange their tools—computers, screens, candles, and incense. DJ and I confirm our course for the chosen locations and travel down to street level with four vampire guards.

My hand twitches in his as my heart races. Equal parts excitement and panic course through my veins. *What is the worst that could happen?* DJ is a near-invincible vampire-witch hybrid, and I am a fae with the ability to scorch anything to a crisp within seconds. Fire kills vampires, and unless they have an evil archangel on their side, we will persevere. *But,* using my power will draw Sonia, hence the four vampires trailing us.

Leaving the busy lanes of the city, we wind through what appear to be empty buildings to a large, black-sided, barn-like structure. Music thrums from inside, and my nostrils flare. Vampires, lots of them. A line of beings hug the wall, and we walk to the end. I scrutinize the faces, comparing them with my memories of the potential Guardian members. *None look familiar, but the night is early.*

"Come on, let's get a drink." DJ tugs me into the crowd as we enter the building.

Body meshing between dancers, I focus on the mission, blend in, and look for the Guardians. At the bar, DJ orders two shots and club sodas. This time, I pour the sweet liquid down into my mouth, and it burns my throat as if I had drank a healing elixir of my realm. I need the courage and guess the effects will wear off soon. My stomach feels weird, and my psyche pings a warning. *A drink is not a meal,* I reassure myself.

Most stand in groups while a few loiter in front of the musicians. DJ explains this is a warm-up band, performing before the main act appears. Part of me wonders why Guardians would bother coming to a place like this. *Do they seek entertainment, camaraderie, and information, or is this where they pass messages, much like our communication system?* DJ and Tyler have indicated that, much like our paper letters, phone calls and other electronic messages can be overheard, traced, and intercepted, so in-person communication may be favored.

DJ talks about his friends in LA, the ones he knew prior to becoming a witch, what he planned to do after high school, and the life he envisioned for himself. Describing the series of foster homes he grew up in, football games and practices, school schedules, parties, and entertainment they liked, he expresses disbelief at the turn of his life. Taking in each morsel as if learning a new language, I stir my club soda, taking sips every few minutes, and search the crowd.

"Did you have a girlfriend? Or *do* you have a girlfriend?" I chance a more personal question. He knows Foster and I have feelings for each other, so I consider it acceptable subject matter.

He rolls his eyes. "It's a long story."

I lift my eyebrows and glance his way as we move through the crowd. "We have all night."

He explains there was a girl he cared for very much, but she had ended the relationship a few weeks before his dark-side search for his brother.

"I do not understand why you consider it a negative event. You were following your passion."

"I had no idea what was on the other side of that journey, but in that moment, it felt like I had little to stay for."

Setting my drink on a tray as an attendant passes, I rest my hand on his shoulder. "You are courageous, not crazy. Always remember that. Always follow your heart."

His dark brown eyes seem to seep the last light from the room, turning golden as the feathers of a pheasant.

Gaze turning glossy, I study his face. "What is it?"

"Tyler spotted a group coming in the door."

At his words, a loud squeal emits from the front of the space, and I clap my hands over my ears. Lights blare from the stage, changing from pink to purple, blue, green, and then to red. Drumbeats echo against the hard walls, and a light sweeps over the heads of the crowd. Shouts, cheers, and whistles sound out, and the motion of the throngs gathered shifts to the band.

DJ peels my hand from my ear, tucks it into his chest, and leads me in the opposite direction. I force my palm from my other ear to my side. As we fight the tightknit crowd, he whispers the indicators for which Guardians Tyler spotted. We numbered them so we could know who to look for. The vampires he names we think are tenuously related to the Guardians, but a lead is a lead. We turn and weave to the bar, and I spot the five at the end.

Dressed in black leather, each with sleek, dark hair, their complexions glow an eerie color like white swans on a bright night. It is not so much the way they look, others sprinkled throughout the venue have similar dress and coloring, but that each in the group looks the same: their pointed chins tilted up, long noses sitting in perfect symmetry on their faces.

I hold the gaze of a female, and her red eyes seem to course with energy. Diverting my eyes, I squeeze DJ's fingers, hard.

"Ow. What's going on?" Grabbing his arm, he spins to face me.

"They drink human blood?"

His eyes go wide, and the next second, his lips press into mine. Warm and soft, my mouth reacts, lips melding with his, and I can taste his coconut lotion. Words echo in my mind. *Yes, we told you, they are traditional vampires. They saw you react to them. Act like you're drunk.*

My mission brain kicks in. *Stupid, stupid, stupid, where is my mind?* I release his kiss and smile. I let him lead me to the bar. *I did not realize traditional meant drinks human blood. This changes things. Our council has been lenient about working with you because they realize the vampires of today are not like those of long ago, but—*

They probably didn't kill anyone or even drink from an actual human. The red could be red contact lenses, and their faces may be plastered with makeup.

Probably? Could be? Maybe?

Do you want Lilith or not?

Fine. Get me another drink.

He orders two more shots, and we watch as they, heads high and backs straight as tree trunks, walk toward the back of the swaying crowd.

Why would they be so conspicuous? I ask.

Because they can be. Almost no one still believes the Guardians exist, and if they do, it's doubtful anyone in this crowd would know who they are.

I reach out with my mind, attempting to overhear their thoughts. Nothing. I eye the bartender, picking out his thoughts easily. The same holds for every other being near us.

I cannot hear their thoughts.

Throwing his head back and pouring the brown liquid into his mouth, he takes my hand. "They are strong vampires for sure then. Here we go."

I slurp my shot down as he leads me toward them. Testing the waters, he positions me beside the female I traded stares with. Copying his motions, I bounce on my heels to the rhythm of the drum beat. I take sneaking glances at them, trying to decide how to open the conversation.

Feeling warmth spread over my bicep, I turn to meet her eyes and steel my reaction.

Her eyebrows raise. "You have very red hair and not very red eyes."

Swooping my curls over my shoulder, I lift a lock. "It's my natural color."

"You smell like your mate."

Even with my hardest effort, my face flushes. "He's not… We're friends."

One side of her mouth curls. "That kiss would suggest otherwise."

Her words and the manner of her speech remind me of Alfreda, but I refocus. "You and your friends are very beautiful."

After a quick laugh, her chin drops, and her mouth forms a thin line. "We have no idea who you are but know exactly who your friend is. What do you want?"

"Can we speak in a more private place?" I ask.

The male to the left wraps an arm around her waist and leans toward me. "We do not go anywhere with witches. We will walk to the far end of the bar, and you will follow."

I keep my face aimed at the musicians as the vampires peel away. *Did you hear that?*

DJ dips his chin a millimeter. Gripping my waist, he spins me in their direction, and we follow some six feet behind.

The male and female who I talked with stand at the back of their group, and we file in behind.

"We did not know the High Priest's brother had a mate. It is very good information to have."

"She's not mine." DJ's words come from deep in his throat.

"Message received." She glances back, lifting her eyebrows.

"You think you know who we are. What do you want?" the male asks.

"We want to talk to Caesaria," DJ whispers.

"It is not going to happen," he says.

I speak up. "We know what is causing the volcanoes and earthquakes. They are only going to get worse unless someone stops it. You may be the key to ending this evil."

The male vampire scoffs. "Much too biblical for us."

"And your *Mother*"—I draw out the word, so they are sure to hear the title given to Lilith—"is not?"

The female's chin cuts down. "We will ask Caesaria. Meet us here tomorrow night for the answer."

"Thank you." I squelch the urge to curtsey, squeal, curtsey and squeal, or jump for joy.

"Until tomorrow," the male says and takes a step toward the bar.

DJ's arm hooks around me, and we spin in the direction of the exit. One vampire slides in ahead of us, the others on each side. My stomach lurches at their proximity, wondering if they perceive more danger now than before. One to my side speaks into a microphone tucked inside his sleeve, indicating we need a car. Eyes darting around us, I do not dare speak.

This was the plan. Nothing's wrong. I hear DJ's words in my mind.

I would rather know that beforehand, I return.

Sorry.

The vampires corral us outside and into a black limo. The vehicle lurches forward, and we speed through the streets and onto a wider road, one DJ calls a highway. They tell us that Tyler and the witches are enroute to the airport as well.

"That was fast." Still on the edge of my seat, I study our surroundings as we weave around the car in front of us.

"It went well. You did a good job."

I shake my head. "Except for my reaction to their looks."

"We recovered. They probably spotted me before we saw them."

Remembering the kiss, my cheeks warm. "Why did they insist that I was your mate?"

The vampire opposite me rolls his eyes. "You smell like him. It's obvious you drank his blood. I can't tell what type of being you are. You only possess his scent."

"But I did not"—the memory returns—"*before*, I drank your blood *before* I died."

"Did you really forget?" DJ asks.

"Things that happened *before*, I sometimes cannot recall. Everything changed that day." A chill shoots through me as I remember the pain in my spine, Foster and my family kneeling before my pyre. I blink, trying to clear my eyes of the tears threatening to form, and look at DJ. "You did an awesome job, too. Tonight was a success."

"Let's not be too optimistic," the vampire opposite us says. "They allowed you to request a meeting. It's step one of a bajillion."

Chapter 10

Bajillion? I turn the word over in my head.

It's a fictitious number. It means a huge number. DJ's voice sounds in my mind.

Thank you.

I smile my biggest smile at the huge male vampire opposite me. "We had a conversation with one of them within just three days."

I sit, perched on the limo seat, watching the scenery go by.

DJ wraps his hands around mine and leans in. "How are you doing, really?"

Sliding my hands from his grip, I straighten my spine. "I am better. It was very hard. Now, it seems I hardly remember the rainy season or working with Terran. It is as if it were a dream. This feels more like real life."

"Good. I'm glad." DJ squeezes my thigh and relaxes into his seat.

I allow myself to ease into the back cushion as we glide over the highway. On the airplane, Tyler also reacts with cautious optimism after I commend him for excellent research and scouting. We spend the plane ride back to Sardinia planning for the response we may get tomorrow. It is well past midnight when we land, and shouldering my satchel, I take my leave from the airport, zip to the ring, release my cloaking spell as I pass through, and begin the journey to Alemayehu's.

As the adrenaline leaks from my limbs, I tick through the events of the night. My breathing spikes again as I think of the kiss and how I must tell Foster. He will not be happy, especially knowing my history with DJ, but we were playing a part, one that could have meant life or death. Perhaps when Foster retires his post, he and I will travel the realms, solving issues and helping those in need. Maybe we could form a High Council guard with the charter of working with factions of different beings.

Energy almost depleted and psyche spent, but pulse still racing, I land beside Alemayehu's hut and whistle the call we agreed upon. He invites me inside. Wanting to be in front of my fire, curled up and ready for sleep, I decline. He rubs his beard and trades his weight from one foot to the other. My pulse jumps anew, and I ask if there is news from the High Council.

"Come in, eat, and tell me about your night. You look like you may drop dead of hunger within the drop of a grain of sand."

"I do not wish to burden your food stores."

He steps away from the opening, and the scent of herbs and meat wafts around me. My stomach gurgling in my middle, I accept his offer.

As I pick the last bit of meat from its bone, I rest my plate on my lap. "Out with it. What did the council decide?"

"I did not say the council decided anything. Tell me of your night. You still look distraught."

"I thought it a victory." I describe the conversation with the Guardians and end my story with the admission of the kiss with DJ and how the vampires assume he is my mate.

Alemayehu lets out a long, slow whistle and rubs his belly. "Foster will not be happy about that."

"I know he will not, but it was not I who instigated the kiss, and it meant nothing more to either of us than playing the part. Now, tell me your news, or I shall have to torture it from you." I raise my palm and push my magic to my fingertips, causing them to glow green.

Looking to the floor, he moans. "It is not good. While the council agrees Sonia should be stopped, they will not agree to any communication with the Guardians."

I swallow. "None? What if letters are passed and no fae need be present?"

"They will have no relationship with them at all."

"Because of their lifestyle?"

"The fae cannot compromise our principles. No humans are to harmed."

Jumping up, I circle the room. "What if there could be a clause where the Guardians pledge that no humans will ever be used for their blood again?"

"Your choice of language is interesting to me."

"DJ suggested their red eyes and paste-white skin may be contacts and makeup."

Alemayehu rubs his beard. "You were close to them. Were they wearing colored contacts?"

I admit they were not but argue they could be buying human blood. Crossing to a chest, he produces a scroll of parchment. I take it, unrolling the paper and reading the paragraphs entitled A Proclamation from the High Council Regarding the Guardian Vampires.

The last paragraph deflates my hope. It reads:

> While many vampires adopt non-human diets, Guardian vampires have not proved a respect for human life. Therefore, we condemn communication, in any form, with, to, or from a member of the Guardian vampires. Furthermore, agreements of any sort, written or non-written, binding or non-binding, are strictly forbidden. Fae not abiding to these edicts shall be subject to trial by the High Council.

I lift an eyebrow. "So, Yonas cannot aid us, but that does not hinder my attempts. I do not exist. I am dead."

Alemayehu shakes his head. "They will be watching. Zekiel is not naïve."

"I am not conversing with the Guardians. My soul is not present. The vampires report they sense no fae in me.

Only my visage is present. I am not, so I will not be break-
ing the edict. Not that it would matter, because I am dead,
and what can they do to me that I have not already done to
myself willingly? I have excommunicated myself from society, live as a hermit in the wood, barely seeing other fae.
I cannot live with my family, visit them, or communicate
with them. I already suffer their worst punishment save
the taking of my wings. I will never return to fae society,
so the council will never know that I have broken their
proclamation."

"Zekiel will be following me and my family."

Passing him the parchment, I shoulder my satchel.
"I will not involve you or your family any longer. You are
relinquished from your pledge to aid me in this quest."

His soft, wrinkled eyes hold my gaze. "Promise me
you will find another to track your passings into Upper
Earth."

"I will." I wrap my arms around his shoulders and
squeeze tightly.

My chest heaves with loss as I make my way across
the sea to my cabin. I console myself, knowing there will
be a letter from Foster. I still have Foster. Yet, reading the
new letter furthers my feeling of isolation, digging new
trenches into my heart. *Why had I thought that this mission would bring me more joy?* It does, I realize, when I
am with them, but coming home to no one deepens the
chasm between what I have in one version of my life and
what I do not in the other.

Perhaps I should abandon this quest with the witches. They may be able to achieve their goal without me, but

thinking of DJ among those vampires without the protection of my powers turns my stomach. If something happened to him, I would never forgive myself. *What am I to do?* I could go back to my nighttime good deeds, tending my garden and livestock during the day. Yet chances are, one day, I will be discovered.

Messie jumps to my hand and grabs a seed. No. I must be courageous, own my words to Alemayehu. I am dead, and I need not abide by any law but my own.

I grip Foster's letter. Perhaps if he reported Mother had not been well today, I would not have the strength to go on, but she sat silent all day, as she has done for the most part of the past six years. She has received my message. The Goddesses have heard my prayers, and she is at peace.

I take a new sheet of parchment from the drawer and dip my quill in the ink. I will not tell Foster of the kiss or my decision to ignore the High Council's edict in a letter. My foot taps as I decide what to write. Putting the pen tip to the page, I tell him of Messie and how brave she is becoming with me. I express excitement at the plants growing in the garden and how big the baby goats and sheep have become. I stare at the page. He will know this to be a farce and suspect the worst. I crumple the paper and throw it toward the fire.

The ball of parchment only makes it halfway to my goal, and I rise, retrieve it from the floor, and drop it in the fire. Crossing to the table and starting with a new sheet, I try again.

F,

The only thing that could make my day better is if you were here to share it with me. Until we meet again, all my love,

T

I drag my pillow and blanket to the fire. I sit in front of the flames and speak to Mother and the Goddesses about my day, how I will defy the edict, and questioning who should be my contact when I come and go from this realm. Perhaps there need not be anyone. I did promise Alemayehu, but if Foster comes each day, or sends someone, I could just leave a note indicating the time I left. My letter to him each night will serve as proof of my return. I lay my head on my pillow, pull the blanket to my chin, and let sleep take me.

DJ AND I, FLANKED BY OUR FOUR vampire guards, arrive at the venue in Milan just before the main band is set to perform. The wait outside is shorter than the night before, and within minutes, we are at the door. When DJ hands the attendant his payment card, the male returns it with a slip of paper. DJ nods to the gentleman and, taking my hand, leads me inside. Holding the paper beside his thigh, DJ unfolds it. I read the words that indicate we are to meet in a room at the end of the hall to the right of the bar when the main act takes the stage.

We wind through the crowd, finding the narrow passageway. We pass several doors and stop at a door at the end marked as private. The guard in front of us knocks.

The male vampire we spoke with opens the door, leaving a gap only half a body wide. "Only the hybrid and the girl."

DJ tells Will and the other guards to wait in the hall and, hand tight around mine, steps into the room. I follow, grateful Tyler's casting spell allows him to pass through walls and retain his magical abilities. As the door closes behind us, silence envelopes me. With silence, save from DJ's thoughts, and our breaths, now in perfect synchrony, bumps form on my skin. I cannot hear any of their thoughts. I do not like this disadvantage.

A tall, thin, male vampire, one not with the group yesterday, sits behind a large, dark, wood desk in the center of the room. The walls, all black, hold no windows. Red-cushioned wood chairs circle the desk. I recognize the vampires seated from yesterday.

The vampire behind the desk, I recognize him from our Guardian potentials, extends his long fingers toward two empty seats before him. We sit down, me poised at the front of the cushion with knees bent.

"So, you wish to speak with Caesaria?" the vampire before us asks.

"Yes, on behalf of the leadership of the witches," DJ says.

"Are you a package deal?"

My mind attempts to place the phrase but cannot.

"Yes, Tessa is my comrade," DJ says.

The female vampire we spoke with yesterday coughs. "Pet."

My palms warm, and I grip the rungs below me.

The vampire at the desk clears his throat. "Our group is quite important, as you must know. We cannot risk its security. So, speaking of pets, we are not stupid. We can sense your witch friend. So, either they leave or present themselves here in physical form. If neither of those can be achieved, this meeting is over."

I will go. I hear Tyler's voice in my mind. My pulse jumps, realizing we have lost a significant advantage. Still, I have my magic.

"Good." The vampire seated before us coos. His gaze fixes on me. "Now, as to your lineage?"

"Call my brother. He will confirm Tessa's importance in our mission," DJ says.

The vampire's eyebrow peaks. "We do not know what she is or why she is here."

"You haven't shared your names or positions."

"I see your point. So, you, and the witches, believe the recent seismic activity is caused by some evil?" the vampire asks.

"Yes, a new archangel, Sonia, who's in league with Abaddon and Lucifer," DJ says.

Murmurs sound from behind us.

The vampire at the desks shushes them. "Continue."

DJ confirms their suspicions as to Sonia's former identity, explains Sonia's transformation to archangel, and relays her most recent threat. "We believe she wants to be reconciled with her mother."

The vampire leans over the wood panel. "You cannot be serious. You wish to ask us to release our mother to you so that you can reconcile Sonia with Lilith? Sonia has plagued our kind for centuries, nay millennia. Her mission has been to rid the realm of vampires. If we give her Lilith, we are as good as dead."

"We will ensure that does not happen," DJ says.

"How?"

DJ's eyes cut to me, and I sweep the room, searching for an appropriate object. I focus on the gold candleholders on the wall behind the desk.

"I assure you. No one in this room will be harmed unless we are provoked. Do I have permission to demonstrate?" I ask.

"Now I *am* intrigued." The vampire opposite us smiles.

I lift my palms and tense my fingers. They grow green, and I fling two magic pulses to the candleholders. The gold metal turns black and, within a blink, melts to the floor.

He lowers his chin, and his face lengthens. "Impressive. So, you wish to lure her out and destroy her?"

"If that were possible, she would already be dead," I say.

"We can stop any physical form she takes." DJ scoots forward in his seat. "She is a soul, a powerful soul. As souls cannot be destroyed, we wish to sway her from her present course. She has demanded to be reconciled, and we believe giving her Lilith will fulfill this desire."

"You *believe?* That will not be good enough. We will never turn over Lilith on a hunch."

I hold his stare. "If there were one being that could be brought back, who would you choose? Your mother? The Mother? I believe only a child would rank higher."

"We will be honest with you. We are also working to secure her son," DJ says.

"You sound insane," the vampire replies.

"Does it? Are we? In her threat, she said that every time the earth moved, a volcano erupted, we'd be witnessing her power. Just last week, a hundred were killed in southern Italy. Three other earthquakes shook southern Asia this month. Look up the statistics. It's not only highly improbable these are natural occurrences but impossible. There are always signs before these types of events, but the scientists monitoring the areas had no warning. What other proof do you need?" DJ asks.

From behind the desk, the vampire's eyes trace from one side of the room to the other, gauging, I assume, reactions to our plea. I work to read thoughts of each but hear nothing.

He lays his palms on the desktop. "We will take this to Caesaria and our council."

"Thank you." DJ runs his hands down his pants.

Like his brother, this serves as a sign of his unease. I slide to the very edge of the cushion.

"Should we come again tomorrow for your answer?" he asks.

"We will send word to your brother within three days' time," the vampire replies.

I release a breath I had not realized I held. DJ stands and extends his palm to the vampire. To my surprise, the vampire slides his hand into DJ's. I rise and extend my arm. His fingers close around mine for a second, but the cold imprint lingers. *How old must this vampire be?*

DJ and I sidestep our chairs in unison. We back to the door, which is opened by the male vampire who allowed us access. DJ clasps my hand and guides me in front of him. I cross the threshold, the thrumming music once again loud against my eardrums.

Hmmm, my mind hears. *She is probably more powerful than him, yet he protects her as if she were a China doll. Not his mate, my ass.* The aura feels familiar, and I glance back to see the female vampire I spoke with yesterday staring at me. I realize that if I heard this thought, it was intentional. *Why?*

The warm bodies of our vampire guards crowd me as we stride down the hall. *Tyler wants us out of here*, DJ's voice sounds in my mind. I clutch one of his hands while my other holds ready. My mind reels with possibilities. *Would they want me or DJ?* He is half vampire, a hybrid, and most likely impure in their minds, but they know him to be powerful, and I displayed my abilities as well. Anyone who wanted to force their will upon the witch leadership could hold us for leverage.

My heart thrums in my chest, and my skin heats as we inch our way through the crowd. The bodyguards jostle beings from our path, inciting many hard stares and insults. Finally, I see the door ahead, and the vampire before me swings it open, grabs my hand, and zips to the limo before us. Opening the door, he fits his hand on the back of my head, pushing me into the back seat. He jumps in and sits opposite me.

"Was that really needed?" I ask.

"I was told to get you in this car ASAP," he replies.

"I am perfectly capable of getting into a vehicle."

"One second is all it would take to nab you."

Flicking my finger, I shoot a tiny beam at his arm. The skin sizzles and smoke rises from the blackened dot.

"Sh…" Covering the burn, his eyes cut to DJ and back to me.

"And that's how fast I can burn a being alive." I fold my arms over my chest as the vehicle jumps forward. "You do realize that I am also as fast and strong as a vampire."

"Okay." DJ rests his hand on my knee. "Tessa doesn't want to be touched, got it?"

The vampire rubs his hand along the skin of his arm and rolls his shoulder. "Message received."

I turn to DJ. "What was that?"

"I have no idea. Tyler just said to get out fast."

"Really, what could they have done?" I ask.

"My magic can be muted, poisons could incapacitate me. Based on your experience with the strawberry donut, I would guess that poisons may affect you as well."

I bite my lip. "I had not thought of poison darts."

"Darts, powders, airborne poisons, all possibilities."

"But they would not be immune." I unfold my arms, cross one leg over the other, and refold my arms over my chest. "I do not like surprises. I want to be prepared."

DJ reaches across the space, opens a chest, and lifts a clear plastic bottle. "Drink some water. Let's reset. I'm sure Tyler had a good reason."

"Do you think we shared too much?" I twist the top off the bottle.

"We need them to trust us. They will fact check."

"When do we tell them I am fae?"

"I don't know. Maybe we won't have to."

I down half the water and reveal the news of the fae council's proclamation. As I talk, I sense DJ's pulse rising. His foot bounces.

"You should have shared this the first second you got here. We had the whole plane ride, the half hour from the airport. Why would you come if the fae condemned this operation?"

His energy surprises me, and I try to keep my tone even. Explaining my reasoning, my thoughts jump to Foster and that this will be his reaction as well. I refocus on DJ, acknowledging his concern and stating my truth. I am dead, yet I am not. No one could sentence me to a fate worse than that. I am my own judge and jury.

We board the plane with Tyler, the three witches and their guards already occupying seats. We take off without incident, and my breathing evens out. Perhaps I am what the humans call an adrenaline junkie. For as much as my nerves detest constant threat, I cannot fathom a life without it. This fact tells me Theron was right. I cannot live a normal life. It will not be enough. The question remains if Foster can live this life with me.

Chapter
11

Tyler has no more explanation for his reaction than what he calls a gut feeling. He agrees we handled the meeting well, and there is no more to do than wait.

I slump into my chair. "We could pray for an earthquake."

"You're kidding, right? That sounds like something twisted Tyler would say." DJ shakes his head.

Tyler shoves DJ's shoulder.

"Few are hurt during an earthquake, and it could prod the Guardians to take us more seriously, but yes, I am kidding. I think." I admit that after four days straight of scant sleep my brain performance may be affected.

As the night before, I zip to the ring as soon as I exit the plane. Shedding my cloaking spell and passing through the magic film, part of me feels free knowing there is no one I need to report to. No one will admonish me for not realizing the danger I faced. Another half longs to have someone to tell everything to. I rush to my cabin and write it all out on parchment while I eat chunks of bread and cheese.

Messie stands beside my page, pecking at her seeds. Knowing I will tell Foster all, but that it cannot be left in print, I crumple the pages and burn them in the fire. I pace in front of the flames, reading Foster's letter, knowing there must be so much he did not say. A lump forms in my throat. The one thing he asks is that I be careful. All I do is barrel toward danger as if it is sweets waiting for me on Summer Solstice day. *Perhaps I will have to let him go. Is not that what this trial is all about, to see if we can accept each other?*

Is this what I am choosing? My duty to fae and the Goddesses over a mate and family? I wonder if Mother ever had to decide between the two and realize she did. She elected to be with the Goddesses. Her prophecies aid me immensely, and perhaps this is her reward.

It would be foolish for the Guardians to harm me or DJ. They must know there would be swift repercussions. They cannot be mad enough to self-sabotage. So, we have nothing to fear from them unless they plan to nab DJ's whole family, thinking Sonia will want them, too, and the vampires would benefit from handing over a whole package. My mind spins with the many iterations that end with me captured by the Guardians, trapped in Upper Earth.

I stop in front of the hearth. This gets me nowhere. I need sleep. Tomorrow, things will seem better. Dragging my pillow and blanket to the fireplace, I shut my eyes and think of Mother and the Goddesses, asking them to send me wisdom. I think of all they taught me: to have faith, choose love, and sacrifice for the greater good. Perhaps faith stands as my missing component. *Has all not resolved in the past as it should have?*

Yes and no, I decide. In what world is it fair that I lie here alone? Do I deserve happiness as well? Maybe that is my crux. Do I believe myself to be worthy of finding a person who will love me no matter what? After all of my choices, I am not convinced I do, but there is no way to get to the other side other than to go through this, so that is what I shall do.

Sleep finds me chained to a cave wall, tied to a stake, burning in a fire, and sucked dry by dozens of vampires. I open my eyes to find Messie nestled beside me. I coo at her, and she opens her eyes and stands, head swiveling one way then the other. I rise, realizing today represents freedom.

With no obligations save to myself, I take my time with my chores, training Messie, and feeding the goats and sheep. I meander through the woods, hunting half the day and, when hot, walk through the stream scooping handfuls of dirt and mud in search of faerie crosses. I clean my kill and start the fire for dinner. Bathing, I sit on the porch, legs dangling from the edge as the light wanes.

Catching movement in the woods, my heart patters. Equal parts of me dread seeing him and cannot wait to kiss his lips, feel the warmth of his skin, and drink in his scent. I stand as he lands in the clearing.

His face, ringed by orange hair, looks almost angelic. His square jaw and full lips draw me, but my psyche pings a warning. There is much to discuss.

"Why are you standing there looking at me like that?" He jumps to my side.

Fitting his hands on my cheeks, he kisses me. His lips press against mine, and I dive into the feel of his skin, the taste of wine from his breath. He backs me to the wall, and his body meshes with mine. I run my hands through his hair and squeal with delight as he kisses my neck, all worry for the future burning away like embers from a fire.

Finally taking a breath, he runs his hands down my back to my waist. "I missed you."

"I missed you as well."

He smiles and kisses me again. "I liked our letters. I knew we would figure this out."

"I could not wait to be home to read yours." I fit my arms around his waist.

"Do I smell deer?"

"You do. It may be tough. You know I do not favor hunting deer, but there was an older female who looked miserable."

"Always the tender heart." He lays his palm on my chest.

I cannot remember him ever touching me there, and it stirs new sensations. I kiss him and tug him inside the cabin.

Messie squawks and crosses to her cage.

He commends me on her progress and shares that his has not been so fast.

I test the meat and with it not done, cut vegetables and throw them in a pot with some butter.

He arranges the plates, and we sit opposite each other.

His demeanor seems too positive, and I wonder if he did not hear of the edict. I guess it would not be of interest to most fae and perhaps was not shared throughout the kingdoms.

He reaches across the table and wraps his hands around mine. "You are biting your lip. What is wrong?"

"You are not angry with me?"

"Should I be?"

"Did you hear of the edict?" I ask.

"I did."

"And you know I travelled to Upper Earth anyway?"

"I assumed you did. Tell me everything. I want to know your progress."

"But did you talk to Alemayehu?"

His eyebrows shoot up. "No, should I?"

"We should talk."

Standing, I back to the wall. I tell him that Alemayehu cannot support me further.

Rising, Foster crosses to me, touching his finger to my lips. "Why are you worried?"

"You said you did not want me in danger. There is danger."

He holds my stare. "I know there is always danger for you, but I trust you."

We agree that there should be some system of alerting him when I return home. Waiting a whole day is unacceptable to him. My heart soars at his acceptance of my news, and I fling my arms around him. Tears forming, I squeeze him tightly.

Prying my hands from his back, he kisses my cheeks as tears run down them. "Why are you sad?'

"I am not sad. I am relieved. I thought you would be so mad."

"I am concerned for you. I will always worry, but I told you I will support you. And perhaps once you decide to marry me, we can go on these missions together."

"Really?" I swipe the water from my face.

"Of course. Why not? We said we wanted adventure, and your life with the witches is definitely that."

I kiss him hard, my lips pressing into his again and again. I run my hands down his sides, unable to get enough of the humming sensation that pulses through my body.

He catches my hands as they trace up to his neck. "We need to save this for later, love. You have not agreed to be my wife yet. I am still waiting for that."

Expressing that being his wife seems ever more appealing each day, I land another quick peck on his lips. I gather his hands in mine and broach the subject of the kiss with DJ. Explaining that DJ instigated the kiss for the sole purpose of our characters at the club, I reassure Foster that DJ and I harbor no romantic feelings. I wish Foster was not such a soldier and spy. Sometimes he is impossible to read. I hold my breath as I study his face, waiting for a reply.

Rubbing his short beard, he winds a lock of my hair around his finger. "I do not like thinking of another man touching you, much less kissing you, but I trust you."

"It should not happen again."

"Good." He smiles. "Now, is the meat done? I am starving."

"You did not eat with your men? I tasted wine on your lips."

"You know how it is on the last workday of the week at the castle. I could not skip a chance to have a drink with my comrades."

As we eat, the discussion winds from topics of friends and family, training the carrier birds, and what the Guardians may decide to the plan for our Saturday together. As the wine relaxes my muscles, I think of my musings from the prior night. *Why had I doubted Foster?* He has proven his commitment to me over and over again. I shall have more faith in him.

⋘⋙

THE NEXT MORNING AT THE WITCHES' compound, Will greets me at the gate and walks me toward the door. DJ exits and meets us on the lawn.

"I hope you're used to flying by now because we're going to Paris."

I clap my hands together. "They agreed to give us Lilith?"

"No, but I guess Caesaria is quite interested in us, so we're getting a chance to state our case."

Sharing my thoughts on how the Guardians may be swayed, DJ explains how he already created a list of assurances to offer them. Lena, the new Vampire Chancellor, also shares reservations about the decision but has pledged her support with the caveat that the witches monitor Sonia's signature perpetually, pledge to alert them to any anomalies in her movements and power, and do everything they can to stop Sonia should she attempt to destroy Lilith or the vampires.

"How will you keep Sonia from destroying Lilith if Sonia has her?" I wait as DJ opens the back entrance to the compound.

"We searched the library and found a protection spell that's nearly failsafe. It takes a lot of power, but we believe it can be achieved. Hunter is gathering the witches that can perform it. We need twelve witches from Raphael's line, the line of the healers."

"Are they hard to find?"

"Camille, Tyler, and their father are of that line. We should be able to find others who are willing to help."

"This is perfect. It is exactly what we needed."

Tyler approaches us, sidling in close to me and hooking his arm around mine. "I know. It finally looks like we're getting somewhere. Now, we've just got to get the Guardians to agree. Since you're a queen and excellent at knowing how these leaders think, we believe you should write and deliver the pitch."

"The pitch?" I look between DJ and Tyler, suspicious of his new show of affection.

"A pitch is a speech or letter that attempts to convince someone of something," DJ says.

I agree to take on the task, inquiring about timing and reminding them of my eight-hour constraint. They have a plane ready, and we take the car to the airport. I organize my thoughts, and then, with gleaming white paper and a small, ink-filled tool, start writing them down. The instrument they give me feels odd, but I soon adjust. Over ten of the small pages are filled before I am finished. DJ and Tyler review the document, making some suggestions on wording, but have few changes. I read and re-read the speech, hoping to convince Caesaria and whatever council they may have.

We land in two hours of their earth time and speed into the city. With time differences and the curvature of the Earth, the sun sits high in the sky. I note what the people walking by are wearing and attempt to adopt appropriate dress. DJ and Tyler disapprove of my selection, instructing me to dress as I had at the club, in my with black leather pants, boots, and brown leather vest over a white blouse.

The limo leaves us at an inn, and Tyler and the witches travel up to the room while DJ and I, with our four vampire guards, set out to meet Caesaria. At the appointed address, we find the female and male vampire we first spoke with at the club waiting on a corner. With a glance toward us, they turn down a narrow street. We follow them, descending a hill and entering a tunnel under a bridge. Halfway to the other side, they stop and knock on a metal door fit into the stone wall. They stand outside the opening, ushering us in.

I look at DJ who, taking my hand, ducks through the low opening, our four guards fanning out around us as we step into a room ringed by stone. The other vampires follow, closing the door with a blaring clank. The space goes black, and I fight to adjust my eyes. Cool, humid air, with the stench of old cheese, surrounds me.

"You will get used to the darkness." The female vampire holds up a device with a light shining from the top.

She illuminates a slim opening in the black stone wall and starts into it. We follow, our footsteps echoing off the rock. The path descends, and we walk for many moments, my heart racing with apprehension, before the tunnel opens into an amphitheater carved into bedrock. It reminds me of the temple under the witches' compound. I wonder if they attempt to feel closer to their departed ancestors. Searching the walls from another entrance, I find none. Either there is only one way out, or another exit is so obscured it may be almost impossible to find, and if discovered, I wonder if we could open it or a technology I cannot grasp ensures their control over its use.

The female vampire lowers the light source and it goes dark. Fear grips me as I lose sight, and a puff of wind sweeps across my body. On one side, DJ grabs my arm, and one of our vampire guards grabs the other. Motion before us catches my eye, and as my vision adjusts, I find an altar in the center of the space. Behind the long table stand seven beings I assume to be vampires. The center one, hair of onyx black, skin a luminous white, wearing a deep red, slim dress, lights a candle.

Waving us forward, she lifts the candlestick. "Welcome. I am Caesaria."

The guard and DJ release my arms, and we step forward as our vampire guard flank us. I recognize the male vampire to Caesaria's right as the one we spoke with three days ago.

Caesaria lifts the candle, pointing it to our vampire escorts. "These are Claudia and Dimitri, my first and second lieutenants."

She continues introducing us to the generals beside her, beginning with the male to her right, Peter. He smiles a tight, thin-lined smile at us, as do each of the others in turn. Heart pounding in my chest, I realize this is the time, the moment to bear my true nature, or the truest approximation I am willing to provide.

DJ takes a half step forward. "Thank you for meeting with us. I am Derrick James Michaels, half-brother and herald to Hunter Michaels, High Priest of the Witch Lines and Witch of the trinity."

Raising my chin, I move to his side. I release my human disguise and morph into fae form, wings spanning beyond my back, almost every inch my true form save my smooth cheeks and forehead. Silence falls as if every creature before me stopped breathing.

"I am Thessalonia of the fae. I come to you as an ambassador, lending support to the witches' cause."

I blink, and Peter is before me. "Fae may take any form in this realm. How do we know this is your true self? How do we even know you are fae? You may be a witch, garbed in a spell."

Lifting my wrist, I hold it before his blood red lips. "Taste."

He licks his lips and one eyebrow rises as he turns to look at Caesaria. She nods, and before I can react, he snatches my arm and plunges sharp canines into my wrist. My arm aches with the pressure of his bones squeezing mine, and my skin burns with the searing pain of laceration. As he sucks, a drop of blood oozes from the side of his mouth. My skin protests under the strain of his vacuum pull. Seconds lengthens to a minute as I hold his vacant stare.

"Peter!" Caesaria yells.

When he releases my wrist, his eyes close then open wide as if seeing for the first time. "Fae indeed, with a smidge of vampire, but we have already established that she ingested the hybrid's blood."

My conscious ticks as his face contorts at the use of the word hybrid. He is a being. We are all beings.

DJ rips the bottom of his shirt and wraps the scrap around my wrist.

I straighten my spine and raise my head. "Do you have questions, or may I address you and your officers?"

"We will not allow Sonia to be given Lilith," Caesaria says.

"We understand your hesitations, and Lena shared your concerns. However, the witches have found a spell that will ensure Lilith is never harmed." Reviewing Lena's demands and explaining how the witches' plan to implement them, I launch into my pitch. Attempting eye contact with each, I am unable to discern any sentiment from their gazes. Still, I press on.

"I am here because my fae have suffered and continue to experience tragedy at Sonia's hand. We wish to bind together with the beings of Upper Earth to limit her power. We beseech you to aid us in stopping her reign of evil."

Caesaria turns her head to the right and then the left. Pressing a finger on the altar's surface, she starts toward the end, streaming her finger along the stone, each of the generals stepping back to allow her to pass. Rounding the end, she strides toward us.

As she approaches, a smile forms on her face. "Do you know where you are? Why we chose this venue?"

Flitting into each mind, I find them closed.

Beside me, DJ raises and lowers his chin. "I do not."

"About sixty years ago, the witches' held a trial where-in Sonia was charged with unusual cruelty to other be-ings, and let's not mince words"— Caesaria leans toward DJ, mouth almost touching his ear—" vampires."

She steps back, locking her hand behind her back. "The witch council found Sonia guilty and entombed her live body with an unbreakable spell, leaving her atop that altar to be guarded day and night, freezing her for eternity, unable to hurt another again."

My eyes cut to the barren rock slab.

"But Sonia, escaped, yes? So, you see"—Caesaria walks toward one wall, takes three punctuated steps then spins and saunters back—"it's very hard to believe that the witches can really achieve a similar goal, given past perfor-mance. No judgment to the present company, of course."

My thoughts dart to every conceivable reply. Draw-ing in a breath, I summon the Goddesses.

"What if you kept one of Lilith's bones?" I blurt out before I have time to censor my thoughts. *People can live without one of their bones if a bone is broken, right?* "Sonia would still have her mother, but she would not be whole so could not be fully destroyed. Would that satisfy your fears?"

Caesaria's face jerks toward me. "Her tomb has not been breached since it was sealed. We could not desecrate her body."

I note the faces of the generals remain stoic through-out, showing no hint of their leanings. *Does Caesaria hold absolute authority without input from any?* Spinning, she strides toward the altar. In another blink, she is before us.

Her eyes dart from me to DJ. "I had respect for you and your friends. There are few believers left. I see you're passionate about this issue, but now, you just sound desperate. There is nothing more to discuss."

Raising my chin, I draw her gaze. "The body of believers among the fae grows every day. They see what is happening in the realms and fear for the future. If you do not give us Lilith, and Sonia unleashes her fury on the beings of this realm, it is unlikely the Guardians will ever be aided by any."

She leans in, and I can smell the rage leaking from her pores, a mix of acid and rotting meat. "Was that a threat?"

I hold her gaze. "No. It is an opinion. The fae stood as an island for many years. We have faced extinction and thwarted multiple invasions without help from any, but this generation sees a different path, one that crosses realm barriers, and we realize that we may not survive alone. By teaming with groups from Upper Earth, we foster relationships that will benefit all. The we is stronger than the I. I, for one, would rather be a we."

Her lids close to the halfway point as if she may be falling asleep or has been bored to death. "I doubt the fae will open their arms to our sect."

"Perhaps not without stipulations."

She lowers her eyelids.

A sharp gale cuts across my skin, hands clutch my arms, and fingers lock around my ankles. I am heaved over the heads of the Guardian vampires and flung atop the altar before my next breath. *Goddesses, how are these vampires so fast?*

Chapter 12

My head and back hit the stone slab, and pain reverberates through my bones. I fight for breath as my torso seizes. My lungs frozen within my rib cage, my pounding skull spins with the realization that we have vastly underestimated these beings. I suck in a smidge of air and, eyes skimming my surroundings, find DJ pinned by two of the Guardian vampires, our guards also held by two vampires each. Attempting to flex my fingers under the grip of the vampire to my right, I find my hand sits limp. I try to conjure my magic, but my spine and head throb with pain and lungs gasp for air, I have no energy to spend. I focus on the face above me. Caesaria.

Her thin, lined lips form a smile. "Did you think you could be faster than, or even as fast as, us? It is a common mistake. You see, there are no creatures as fast or strong as a vampire whose only sustenance their entire lives has been solely human blood and whose entire lineage for centuries, even millennia, has only consumed human blood."

She traces a line from my shoulder to my wrist, her sharp nail as a knife on my skin. Bending down, she licks the length of blood, sinking her long canines into my wrist. She could kill me with a flick of a finger, but I know that is not her aim. We would all be dead if that were their desire, if they intended to eradicate the knowledge we possess. No, whatever their plan, it is much worse. My mind jumps to the most horrific scenario, and I shut it out. *Think of an out, Titania. Rest until your magic returns.*

"Leave her alone!" DJ shouts.

"We guessed that may be your reaction." Looking from him to me, Caesaria purses her lips. "He does love you, you know, but it will ensure that he will fulfill the pledges to us. We will hold you until we decide whether there is a deal to be made that may benefit our faction."

A whoosh of motion lands me upright. Held by a Guardian vampire at each arm, head swimming and throbbing with each heartbeat, I contract my thigh muscles, willing them to hold weight. They slack under the pressure.

"Do you want to start a war with the fae?" DJ asks. "A day in Upper Earth, and she will lose her wings along with the ability to return home. There may be a hundred of you, but there are thousands of fae, and they will come for their own. You may be strong, but they can fly, they can become invisible, and they can take any form they wish. I cannot believe you would risk bringing that war to your people. If you need reassurance that we will fulfill our side of the bargain, take me. I am half-brother to the High Priest of the Witches. I am his only breathing family save his mother. I make a far better hostage."

I focus on DJ's blurred form, screaming no in my mind. None of this can be happening. *How could we have been so naïve, overconfident, and blindsided?*

Caesaria's head cuts from me to him. "So it shall be."

Their cold clutches release me, and I fall to the rock floor. Pushing up, I spot DJ across from me, two Guardians holding each arm. *Curses! Oh, Goddesses!* Sucking in a deep breath, I concentrate on my core.

The ground jolts under my knees, a screech emanating from the stone. A low rumble follows, and sand pelts my skin.

Caesaria's head jolts one way then the other. "What was that?"

Louder grumblings from the bedrock sound around us, and I press my palms to the rock, bracing for another quake. The stone floor shakes, bouncing up and down as if Sonia herself may be pounding her fist upon the foundation below.

"What is that?" Caesaria yells.

With a whirl, Claudia approaches, lifting a mobile phone to Caesaria's face. "At least four quakes in this hemisphere: Iceland, Cape Verde, Italy, and Turkey. The tectonic plate is shifting."

I study the image on the screen, small pictures of blurred flames dotting a map of the continents. My eyes pan the space as larger chunks of rock break and drop from the cave ceiling.

I cut my gaze to DJ. *Now. We run now.*

No, you run.

No. We go together. I insist.

RUN, NOW! His booming voice fills my skull.

I lock on his gaze and dip my chin. Pressing against the rock below me with all my might, I shoot into the air, beating my wings as never before. I swirl around the Guardians and zip into the narrow passageway. Dirt and rocks rain down, scraping my skin as I speed through the tunnel. I retrace our steps, exiting to the street, a cacophony of horns blaring, alarms screeching, and flickering lights greeting me. Our four vampire guards encircle me as I double over.

Will scoops me up and starts to run, the city's chaos blurring before my eyes. Bile rises in my throat, and I fight the need to vomit, clamping my jaw closed and burying my face in his chest. I breathe in, a tinge of iron and salt mixed with his musky animal scent, focusing on that one sensation. *How was DJ now a hostage of the Guardians, and why did I wish for an earthquake?*

This was not the time for questions, but I had no idea how we were going to get out of Paris. I had to get to a ring, now. I need to see to my people. I fight maintaining my thought train as the bouncing of Will's body sends thuds of pain through my head.

I cinch my eyes shut against the throbbing sensation. The next thing I know, I am being lowered into a cushioned seat, Will snapping a seatbelt around me.

Opening my eyes, a blurry Tyler forms before me. "I have to get home."

"Are you kidding? Do you see what's happening? You freakin' doomed us. All planes are grounded," Tyler yells. "All of Europe and Asia is braced for tsunamis."

I move my head from one side to the other. "Take me to a ring, please."

"Drink." Will thrusts his arm before me, blood dripping from a slice on his wrist. "We can't get you there. You'll have to get yourself there. Drink my blood so you will heal."

I press my lips to his skin, sucking in the red liquid, my mind attempting to block on the significance yet my mouth and throat protesting with the acrid taste. As I drink, my vision clears and pulse slows. I release my lock on Will's arm.

"Thank you."

Wiping my mouth with the back of my arm, and noting the skin sealing over Caesaria's wound, I straighten my back and gaze out the window. The vehicle curves around and climbs over rubble in our path, jostling my body on the seat.

Chest tightening as if strings of a corset synch around my middle, I process the information on the screen and Tyler's words. *Earthquakes, volcanoes, tsunamis…*

I press my finger to the seatbelt latch. "I have to go, *now.*"

I do not care that Tyler may be left to deal with DJ's capture. *Why had I listened to him, accepted his order to abandon him so easily?* My eyes lock on Tyler. *Did he know how strong the Guardians are?* Lena, as Vampire Chancellor, must have known, yet she sent us to them anyway. *Did she have other motives? Were they trying to infiltrate the Guardians for their own agenda?*

"Stop!" I yell.

None of that matters right now. I do not care that anyone will see me, that all of Paris may see me. Besides, who would be paying attention to a flying fae in chaos like this? Flinging the door open, I jump from the vehicle and shoot into the sky. The closest ring is not minutes away, but the hollow is black, no crystals glow from their posts.

"Goddesses," I whisper.

Beating my wings as hard as I can, I break west. The span over the water seems as if it takes centuries, but finally, I reach land and blast toward the closest ring. Six crystals still glow, but as I watch, the light from one dies. I pour all energy into my flight, skirting through the ring with only three crystals in position. The magic flits across my skin like feathers on the breeze. I plaster myself to the dome wall.

Breathing hard, I offer a silent prayer to the Goddesses. Faces of loved ones, Father, Mother, Alfreda, Foster, Quinn, Gatuika, Makani, and Isla, flip through my mind. *Think, Titania.* I calculate and prioritize, deciding to go east to Alemayehu first, where a group of flame images hovered on the Upper Earth map. Crossing the ocean, I swoop low over the western coast of Rotuga to find villages teeming with piers of smoke and billows of dust. Further west on the horizon, great pillars of black span the sky.

My mind goes blank and will turns to a torrent of energy sweeping through my veins. I beat my wings hard, breathing in and out, filling my lungs and emptying them again. I sweep around the dark smoke towers to Alemayehu's village. Dropping below the canopy of limbs, the wind dies, and my crunchy landing on a bed of leaves serves as the only sound to reach my ears. I zip through the trees to Alemayehu's hut.

On my call, he opens the door. I fling my arms around him, squeezing as hard as I can.

"Do not be dramatic." He pats my back. "It will take a bit more than a few lava floods to kill this fae."

"The devastation is… I cannot even think it right now. I must get home, but I wanted to make sure you were safe. Is everyone—"

Motion catches my eye, and I look over Alemayehu's shoulder to find Yonas seated before the fire.

"Good, you are well. Is Lencho unhurt too?"

"Titania." Alemayehu exhales. "Sit down."

"What is wrong?" I ball my fists at my sides.

"Terran, or Theron, is gone. He escaped through the ring."

A knot, as if someone has twisted my windpipe upon itself, forms in my chest. I drop to my knees and raise my gaze to Alemayehu. "Someone saw him go through a ring?"

Alemayehu raises his palm to his son. "Yonas saw him. He escaped just before they closed the ring."

"There was such chaos." Yonas drops his gaze.

"Curses, today could not get any worse. Were any others hurt?"

"All others are well." Alemayehu grabs a flat bread cake from a plate beside the fire. "Take this. Eat it."

"I had vampire blood, I will be fine."

Alemayehu raises an eyebrow. "Are you okay?"

Pressing my palms to the sand, I rise. "No. Nothing is okay. They tried to take me, and DJ sacrificed himself for my release, but I cannot think of that now. I must know that my loved ones are safe."

"How can we help?" Alemayehu asks.

"Get word to the witches of Theron's escape." I slip through the door into the darkness.

I run from the hut, cut into the forest, and jump into the air. Time seems to stand still and rush toward me all at the same time as my eyes adjust to the dimming light, darker black splotches barely visible against the night sky. As I sweep down over the ocean west of Hilbron, the water spreads out like a lake. My psyche shuts out the signs of violence I know lie ahead.

I speed to Bedham, finding the capital deserted save for chickens, pigs, horses, and livestock of every sort running about the lanes as if they are the landlords. My brain files a check mark beside an item on the list: My cousins' parents are safe. Rising into the air, I cut south. My, or Aubren's, castle lies far enough inland that it may serve as refuge for those that dwell along the north shores, but my body sets its course for my home as if a bird drawn to roost. I will not sleep until I know they are well.

Darting through the forest, I land in the top of a tree on the outskirts of the meadow. Half a dozen tents line the grass below, six more in varying stages of completeness. Soldiers work in teams, pounding stakes into the ground and hoisting canvas atop high poles. I survey the faces, finding Quinn tugging a rope beside Timothy, and smile, my heart warming at the site of my cousin working beside his countrymen just as I would. I spot Adam and Nicholas and hunt for Foster's head of orange hair.

A group lugs a tent canvas to the grass not six feet from my tree, and I retreat into the forest. I am somewhat aware that my brain allows my psyche only certain realizations. Panic and fear can be reserved for later in front of my fire when it is just me and the Goddesses. With foliage blocking a good view, I give up finding Foster and weave to our secret spot at the riverbank. I leave the signal that I have returned and set off for my cabin.

The wood holds an eerie feel, as if all life has been sucked from its crevices. They know. They know something is coming. Sonia's face flashes through my thoughts. She is coming, perhaps coming for me very soon. I lost hold of my cloaking spell the second the Guardians grabbed me, and even if, by some stroke of luck, I were not detected, Theron will find her and spill all our secrets. He will tell her of our guesses at who she requires. Then she will find the Guardians, and DJ, and all of us will be doomed.

A door opens in my mind. DJ is in grave danger. Hunter could best Sonia, but DJ… My breath catches in my throat. I cut skyward, straight toward the ring. I must warn Tyler and Hunter myself. Praying my time in Middle Earth has been enough to afford me another span of time above, I look up. The dome looms black overhead. I peer into the darkness. Each ring from here to Borean has been shut. Perhaps every opening in the entire realm is sealed.

I swoop west, trying to figure out a way to get anyone to open a ring. Alemayehu could say the witches contacted him and have figured out a way to stop Sonia, that a representative must be sent. When the ring is charged, I could slip through with Yonas. The other half of my brain yells, screams, at the top of its lungs. *It will be your death, not a faked death, a real death, if Sonia discovers you live. And how much will Foster be hurt then? Knowing you could have prevented his loss?*

It does not matter. I must warn them Theron escaped. The witches must know. Everything they have worked for, we have worked for, these past four months could be in jeopardy. If Theron does not go to Sonia, he could find the Guardians, twist their leanings, ensure they never give up Lilith or DJ.

Dipping into Rotuga's forest, I do not bother with the call at Alemayehu's and pound on his door. Wide-eyed, he swings the panel open. I trudge in and latch the door behind me, finding Lencho and Yonas sitting around the fire.

"All is well. Everyone is fine. I could not find Foster but assume he is busy managing the chaos. I am sorry to bother you again, but we must get word to the witches that Theron escaped. Can you get Zekiel to open a ring?"

Alemayehu says that this was just their discussion, but Zekiel cannot know we harbored Theron.

"You are right. But are you mad? Theron could be with Sonia, or at the witches' compound as we speak." I relay my idea of the story we could tell Zekiel to get him to open a ring.

"The witches have security. Theron will not be able to breach their barriers. We would deceive Zekiel in this way? What if he learned of our treachery?"

"Are you sure the compound is safe? DJ is not even at the compound. The Guardians have him. If Theron convinces them we are the bad guys, they could kill him.

Hunter was quite clear about how dangerous Theron may be. If Sonia finds out I am alive, all fae will be in jeopardy as well. Never mind. I will search every ring until I find one open." I start toward the door.

Alemayehu grabs my arm. "Rest. Sleep. If the pattern is followed, the rings will open at daybreak."

I do not want to stop. I cannot stop. For if I stop, if I go back and wait, I will witness that giant wave break across our shores, destroy our beaches, ravage our coasts, flood the entirety of Bedham with almost certainty. I will sit in front of my fire with no way to help anyone.

My body suddenly a heavy blob of exhaustion, I exhale. "May I stay here? Just for a few hours? I will leave before first light."

"Titania, Titania."

Alemayehu's dark round eyes greet me. I push up on one arm. He holds a mug of tea under my nose, and my nostrils flare at the surge of mint sucked into my lungs. I sit up and take the cup, wrapping my fingers around the warm surface.

"Are the rings open?" I ask.

"Not yet."

Sitting, I accept bread and eggs then stand and stretch. We exchange hugs, and I take my leave, bound for Aubren. For as much as my nerves twitch for DJ's safety, my heart and body long to be held by Foster. I realize I may not see him, but I hope for a letter at least, something to reassure me all is well.

Before setting course for Aubren, I check the ring above Alemayehu's village, finding it closed. Nearing my homeland, I prepare for the worst. I swoop down to find the beaches littered with seaweed, trees flattened hectares inland, half my forest decimated by the rush and then recession of water. My heart aches for the animals, and I land before entering my clearing. What a horrible farmer I make, abandoning my herds when they must have been frightened beyond belief.

I hike into the clearing to see the goats huddled together in the corner of the pen, the sheep ringing them. As I approach, they rouse, bucking and crawling over each other for attention. Picking up the grain bucket, I fill their troughs. I replace their water pails with fresh cool draws from the pump inside.

Messie coos from her cage, and I set seeds on a plate for her. Crossing the room, I hunch on the floor, reaching under my bed, searching for a letter from Foster. My hand finds a folded page, and I snatch it out.

Dearest,
I found your signal and hoped to find you here although I am not sure why. With the tragedies surrounding us, I cannot wait but will try to return in the morning.
Yours Always,
F

I cannot sit waiting for him knowing the threat looming in Upper Earth. I leave a note indicating I will return before nightfall and swoop up to the canopy. I watch until each crystal in the ring above is placed and the barrier glistens with magic. Waiting another hour to avoid detection, I shoot to the dome, evoke my cloaking spell, and slide through the humming seam.

With Theron free, I cannot know if the cloaking spell matters, but I will not risk detection when there is a slim chance that Theron has done nothing with his knowledge. Perhaps he will decide to carve out a life for himself away from Sonia and his brothers.

I pass high over Asia, across the Mediterranean Sea to Sardinia. Landing in the forest, I trek to the wall and ring around to the guard station.

Will runs out to greet me, wrapping me in a big hug. "You survived. You still have your wings."

To have this huge, six-hundred-year-old vampire gather me in his arms overwhelms my sentiments, and tears form in my eyes. I squeeze him hard. "I survived, friend. I am still fae. What of DJ?"

"Let us get into the compound."

The gate rolls open, and we stroll down the walk. He describes that they have not heard from the Guardians. I inquire as to whether Hunter will travel back to Europe. Will describes that the trinity has not been notified as they are in Lower Earth trying to find the remains of Sonia's son, who is also Hunter's father, Thanatos.

"Tyler will be most grateful you are here to tell them about what happened yesterday." Will opens the door, sliding back to allow me to enter.

"I am sure he will. I have many words for Tyler and, unfortunately, some bad news of my own."

Chapter 13

Weaving through the security room, I march down the hall to the conference room. Tyler sits, head in hands, staring at a blank screen.

"Have you slept?" I ask, squelching my urge to pummel him.

The sight of him brings all my questions to the surface. *Why did I give into DJ's insistence so easily? Did Tyler know how strong the Guardians were? Did Lena send us into a trap? Were we bait in a plot to expose the Guardians?*

He tilts his head, one eyebrow raised. "Have you?"

"A few hours. After the blood wore off, I ran out of energy." I slide into the seat beside him, locking my fingers around the cushion. Throwing accusations will do no good, and I have my own guilt to carry. "Will said they briefed you on what happened with the Guardians?"

"Yes." He covers his face with his hands. "I still haven't reached Hunter. He's going to kill me."

"How did this happen, Tyler?"

"I had no idea they were so powerful. None of us did." He slides his palms to the tabletop.

"What about Lena? Do you think she knew?"

He indicates that they do not know who to trust at this point.

I stare at the wall. "I cannot believe I left him there. I did not want to. That is not me. I never leave one of my own."

"If he told you to, you probably had little choice. I'm surprised it worked on you, but I guess you're more like us than we realized."

"What does that mean?"

He reminds me that DJ descends from the Michaels line of witches, a line blessed with power and authority. One byproduct of their magic is the ability to bend another's will to their own.

"I've never seen DJ exert that power, but it's in his nature. It's not something they have complete control over," he says.

"That sounds very dangerous."

"It's how Sonia and Thanatos got so many to follow them."

"It makes sense now." I suck in a breath. "Do you want to hear more bad news?"

Turning his head, he stares at me. "There's more?"

I bite my lip and nod. "Theron escaped."

"What the?" Jumping up, he leans over me, nostrils flaring. "You sat here, blaming me for DJ getting kidnapped, and you let Theron escape? Please tell me he's still in Middle Earth at least."

Rising, I ball my fists as my skin burns under my fingers. "I did not *let* Theron escape. The chaos caused by the earthquakes gave him an opportunity, the diversion he needed, to slip through a ring."

Huffing, Tyler runs a hand through his hair. "So he's in this realm? Our realm? With the ability to do anything? Contact Sonia? Find his father? How much does Theron know about what we're attempting?"

Informing him that Theron only knows that we are trying to find a way to appease Sonia, I point out that I am in just as much danger as they are.

Tyler sits back down, and his leg bounces with such ferocity I believe he may take flight any second.

"I cannot stay. Get word to Alemayehu if we hear from the Guardians."

"No. I'm not facing Hunter alone. We're supposed to be a team."

I place my hand on my hip. I do not like it, but he is right. Retaking my seat, I sit in silence, but inactivity is not my strong suit. I prompt Tyler to think of strategies for what we will do if the Guardians turn us down, if they decide to hold DJ indefinitely, or if they agree to give us Lilith. We fashion reasons why Lena may have deceived us and what could be done to learn of her true intentions. All these suppositions and plans are just that though. We cannot know what the future will be or our best course of action. Still, it soothes me to have my brain focused on anything besides DJ being harmed and Sonia coming for my fae.

Buzzing brings me out of my worry, and I note the image of Hunter's face on the screen. Tyler sways his head from one side to the other, indicating it is time to face the music. As he explains what happened in Paris, Hunter's face transforms from pale sand to wine red. Behind him, Alena paces, and Camille's cheeks turn ashen. When I divulge my news, Alena stops and glares at me. I believe if daggers could shoot through her eyes and travel through the phone waves, I would be dead.

Hunter runs his hands down his pant legs. "We knew there would be risks. You did your best. Titania, I'm glad you're safe. We'll talk to Anne to find out what she may know and wait for the Guardians to contact us. They won't be stupid enough to hurt DJ."

Hunter asks whether I would have any inkling of what Theron may do or where he may go. I guess he may find his mother. She seems like a woman who would be very industrious, given her ties to the witch and vampire elites. He might search out Sonia, but I could not guess whether he would aid her or, out of revenge, plot her demise.

"He told me that we were the same," I say. "That we both needed purpose."

"But what goal would be most compelling to Theron?" Tyler asks.

"To take back what he believes is rightfully his. Which means the target is on my back," Hunter says.

"If it *is* on your back, then we're all in the crosshairs." Tyler rests his forehead in his palm.

"All we can do is beef up security," Hunter replies.

Hunter ends the call, and I wait for Tyler to respond.

He stands and rolls his head. "That wasn't so bad. I mean, I wanted to know if I was cut out for this life, and now I know I'm not. If they kick me out, then I have my answer."

"Did you still feel beholden to the trinity?"

"God, yes." He leans over the chair, gripping the cushion top.

⬥

CREAKING WOOD AND FOOTSTEPS rouse me, and I jerk a blade from my boot and jump to my feet.

"Titania." Foster extends his hands.

"Oh, Goddesses." Dropping the blade, I rush into his arms. I squeeze his chest, sucking in his scent as if breathing for the first time. Running my fingers down his arms, I draw back, raking my eyes from his head to boot tips. "You are well? Is everyone okay?"

I press my lips to his and run my hands through his hair. He reacts, winding his strong fingers around my back and down to my waist. I kiss him until I cannot breathe.

"I am well." He hugs me close, brushing his lips to my ear. "Many are displaced, but no fae were lost."

"That is a miracle."

"The ring keepers are faster to close the rings now."

I tell him about the Guardians, how they rejected our request, and how they took DJ, leaving out my almost capture. Because Theron's escape and my good outcome overshadow the small detail, I decide it can be left out. Withholding the information may be somewhat selfish, but I also would contend that it is merciful. Foster does not need to know how close I came to never seeing him again now that I am standing before him. If I did tell him, I fear he will ask me not to go back again. That, I could not do.

I describe how I made it through the rings when the quakes struck and, biting my lip, of Theron's escape.

His eyes go wide. "Theron escaped to Upper Earth? Where he may tell Sonia that you are not dead?"

Closing my eyes, I nod.

He clutches my face. "We will run away. We will go now. We will hide in the darkest, most remote part of this realm."

I wrap my hands around his. "I have to go back to Upper Earth. I must help the witches get DJ back."

"No, tell me you are not."

"I can use my cloaking spell. She cannot find me. It may be safer than being in this realm."

He circles the small space. "Where were you last night?"

"I slept at Alemayehu's then returned to Upper Earth to warn the witches of Theron's escape."

"You slept?"

"Yes. I know I should have done more, but I could not."

He fits his hand behind my neck, pulling me to him and kissing me. Sensing his urgency, my lips react, pressing to his mouth again and again.

Out of breath finally, I rest my forehead on his. "What was that?"

"I am happy."

I study his eyes, the creases at the edges and wide stare, a sparkle of excitement evident. "About what? That I did not help? That I could be discovered by Sonia at any moment?"

"That you did not help." Stepping back, he takes both my hands in his. "I have been waiting for you to learn to take care of yourself. Do you know how hard it is to watch someone you love work and work without regard for their own health?"

"I wanted to give to my people. I needed to be their leader."

"I know you did." He raises my hands and kisses them. "But you do not need to now and you trusted others to help your people."

I shake my head. "You give me far too much credit. I was so tired I could not do more."

"You would have before. I saw you, again and again, pressing on even when you looked as if you would drop any second."

I cup my hand around his cheek. "This is twice you have surprised me in one week."

Ducking down, he studies my face. "I hope in a good way."

"Yes, in a very good way." I wrap my arms around his neck and squeeze, knowing he will be a good choice for me when I am ready to make it. Releasing him, I kiss his cheek.

⁕

AT FIRST LIGHT THE NEXT MORNING, I travel to the witches' compound on the island of Sardinia. With little to do but wait for the Guardians to contact us, we spar in the weapons room. I do not want to deplete too much energy, so we make our way to the library. Having only seen the space for a few brief moments, I take in the expanse of the room.

Rows of bookshelves span out like wheel spokes from the center space where a large wood desk resides. Beyond the shelves, staircases spiral up from each side of the room to a balcony lined with more bookshelves.

Tyler shows me the texts cataloging Sonia's activities through the centuries. I am not sure I want to know more of her exploits as my demise teeters on a wire. I choose a book from the shelf describing the witch lines and study the powers of each, Michael's, the leaders; Uriel's, the keepers of knowledge, to which Alena belongs; Gabriel's, the messengers, to which Jude belongs; and lastly, Raphael's, the healers, to which Camille and Tyler belong.

Tyler's phone buzzes, and he looks at the screen. "Holy"—he glances my way—"Goddesses." Jumping up, he motions me to follow him. For once, he does not take the elevator, and we jog down the stairwell to the ground level. Winding to the security office, we find Will and the other guards huddled around a screen.

The monitor displays an image of the gate, a long black limousine parked outside. All windows of the vehicle are open, revealing Dimitri in the driver's seat, Claudia to his left, and Peter and Caesaria in the back.

Will taps on another screen which comes to life showing another view of the vehicle. DJ sits facing Peter and Caesaria.

Relief washes over me at the sight of his olive skin, brown eyes, and fuzzy dark hair.

Tyler turns and grabs my shoulders. "Maybe that prayer about the earthquake worked after all."

The vampires start their inspection of the vehicle, and after long minutes that tick by with agonizingly slow speed, I believe a pie cooling in the sun would have faster results, Dimitri guides the car through the gate to the front entrance.

Will and six vampire guards surround the vehicle. With our prior experience with the Guardians, we would prefer to meet them outside, but with Sonia as a palpable threat, Will and his team escort them into the front hall.

Tyler and I stand in the center of the black marble floor, waiting as the vampires file in.

Smiling, DJ crosses the space to stand beside me.

I fight the urge to throw my arms around him.

"Thank you for returning our friend," Tyler says.

"We would like to negotiate a compromise." Caesaria steps a pace in front of the others. "Are you able to do that?"

Tyler locks his hands together behind his back.

I want to grab his arms and pin them to his sides. *Keep your hands free.*

After a slight glance at me, he releases his hands. "Any binding contract would need to be reviewed by the high priests and priestesses, but we're authorized to negotiate on behalf of the witches."

She lifts an eyebrow. "We are going to need more than just the witches. If you want us to give you Lilith, we are going to need a treaty signed by *all* the beings."

My heart thuds in my chest. *An agreement of all beings? That may be next to impossible.* I look to DJ. *Do you know their terms?*

They told me nothing. His rich voice seeps into my mind.

Tyler invites them into a parlor to the right, a long rectangular room with a wall of windows facing the front meadow. Velvet tufted chairs and couches sit grouped around thick rugs.

"This conversation will not be long if you will not agree to items that are nonnegotiable. We give you Lilith, minus one rib." Her eyes cut to me. "We are afforded the same protections from the witches as the registered vampires, peace treaties are drawn with the other beings, and all agree to help protect our ranks should Sonia or any other foe threaten us."

I fold my arms over my middle. "How many of the other beings would you require to join this agreement?"

She lifts her chin. "It should include all the major sects of beings: the registered vampires, the witches, werewolves, elves, and fae, including the ethereal fae."

"The ethereal fae will never join. They cut themselves off from this realm over a century ago. They have no stake in the fate of Upper, Middle, or Lower Earth," I say.

"We can omit the ethereal fae."

"The Middle Earth fae will not sign without some provisions as to the Guardians' behavior toward humans."

"What if the relationship is consensual?" Caesaria asks.

Not understanding the term, I turn to DJ.

He clears his throat. "Meaning that the human is a willing donor."

I look to the floor and back at Caesaria, praying we can convince all the groups to agree. "I believe the fae will pledge their help if you promise that no human will be harmed or their blood consumed without their consent."

Caesaria opens her bag and lifts a stack of papers from inside. "This is the written version of our agreement. Please review, make amendments, and return to me. We can discuss particulars via phone or email, both are listed in the document. If it is acceptable to us, and after each sect signs the document, we will release Lilith, *minus a rib*, to you."

Chapter 14

Tyler approaches Caesaria, taking the agreement document from her outstretched hands. After a nod to each of us, she pivots on her heels and walks towards the exit.

Will opens the door, and the Guardians peel off, one by one, following her outside.

As soon as the doors close behind the Guardians' backs, I fling my arms around DJ and squeeze his shoulders.

"You're suffocating me."

Releasing him, I fit my hands on his biceps. "Are you unharmed?"

"Yes. I'm fine. They treated me perfectly."

"That's half our problems solved." Tyler hoists the document.

"Half?" DJ looks between us.

"She'll tell you." Tyler turns and starts toward the interior of the building.

Following him, I admit that we lost Theron and that he slipped through a ring into Upper Earth.

"Holy"—DJ's eyes hold mine—"Goddesses. I'm assuming Hunter and Alena know?"

Tyler stops and spins around. "Of course, duh. It's been two days which means he's lost his wings by now. Hopefully, that was a painful process. Either way, Sonia may know Titania is not dead and that we're looking for Lilith and Thanatos. So basically, we're all sitting ducks."

"But Hunter said something about beefing up security. I am not sure what that is but—"

"Oh, shit. You should call your brother," Tyler says.

DJ's phone is out of battery charge, so he uses Tylers's phone to call Hunter. Including Tyler and me in a video chat, DJ is convincing about his wellbeing, summarizes our meeting with the Guardians, and turns the conversation to Theron. DJ stresses that no energy should be spared in tracking him down.

Hunter explains that they have dispatched witches who specialize in monitoring for and finding souls to each of the compounds. As of yet, no hint of Theron's signature has been detected.

"He's probably using the same soul cloaking spell Titania used," Tyler says.

"And what of your search for our father?" DJ asks.

Hunter summarizes his frustration at their pace and admits that he may enter Lower Earth with Alena and Camille.

With Theron able to pass through the realms, I wonder whether that is a good move, but if we cannot get all of the sects to agree to the Guardians' terms, we need something to give to Sonia. Ending the call, we wind to the conference room and lay the Guardians' agreement document on the table.

The words centered at the top of the page read *A Treaty of Beings*. Bumps form on my arms, and my forehead chills. My heart races in my chest and veins thrum with the speed of blood pumped through my body. *Could this really happen, that all beings would pledge to bind together to protect each other?*

My mind bounces to the next thoughts. *But what of the humans? The fae will not consent to any agreement they believe threatens the humans, and will the pact, a contract effectively binding all non-human beings to each other, endanger humans?*

I stand behind DJ and Tyler, reading over their shoulders. My thoughts stick on her words, threatened by *any* other foe. I mentally pinch myself. This could happen. We have a good chance of convincing the sects to agree to these terms. *Why would they not all want a treaty that binds them to protect the others?* Then we will have Lilith.

——◆◆◆——

IT TAKES A WEEK FOR THE WITCHES, alongside the vampire council serving the registered vampires, to craft a document to send to the Guardians. It surprises me that the witches work with Lena, who I suspect used us to out the Guardians, but when I weigh Sonia's devastating acts versus a possible misalignment of goals, I would probably come to the same decision. I tend to my garden, goats, and sheep, waiting each day for news from DJ. Foster and I spend every evening together and, by the end of the week, have Messie trained to take a message to Foster's quarters at the castle.

In another week, news finally comes that Caesaria and the Guardians accept the terms of the agreement. The registered vampires, represented by the Vampire Council, and its head, Lena the Chancellor, are the first group of beings to ratify the document.

Two weeks after Beltane, I receive the document and deliver it to Alemayehu. He and Yonas agree to take it to the High Council. I hate that I will not be able to help sway the council, but Alemayehu, Yonas, and I strategize and practice speeches to aid the cause. DJ, Tyler, and I will take the document to each of the other sects in the coming days, so I am happy to have diversions from waiting.

"The Elves do not like the Fae." Foster paces my floor the night before I am set to travel with DJ and Tyler to present the document to them. "How long has it been since a fae has even talked to an elf? They have always been jealous that we have our own realm."

"I think that envy died with the flood." I slide before him and take his hands. "You are more fretful than I."

"It is the peace. For two weeks, we have had no rumblings. I hate the feeling of waiting for something bad to happen, knowing it will, but not knowing when."

Rising to my toes, I kiss his lips. "Do I ever fail?"

"No, you do not, but this is completely out of your control."

"We will or we will not succeed. If we do not, we will find another way."

"How can you be so calm?" He kisses the inside of my wrist.

"We cannot both fall apart."

DJ, Tyler, and I fly to an island grouping near the North Sea known to them as the Faroe Islands, one of which holds a settlement of elves and the gathering place of the Elf High Council. Lena helped arrange the meeting, and we follow her direction to the location, winding along curved roads over a barren land. Snow covers most of the land that appears devoid of vegetation, much like the tundra of Willhelm.

We stop at a trail leading to a waterfall in the distance, and Tyler points to the landmark denoting that our destination lies behind the falls. We hike towards the falls on a well-worn but empty path. Tyler consults his phone and guides us behind the water. I watch my footing as we shuffle along a ledge not three feet wide, water pouring in deluges on our left, carrying melting snow to the sea. Tyler flanks right, disappearing into the rock wall, and we follow him into a crevice scarcely a body wide.

The rock walls reach high above my head, and the closed space, the graze of the rock along my limbs, begins to grate my nerves. I take slow, deep breaths, letting the slice of blue sky above reassure me there is a way out. Tyler turns left, out of my sight, and I follow DJ in the same direction. Within steps, the passage opens to a small room, empty save for several dark openings.

Three tall beings, each at least seven feet with long white hair, file in from the center tunnel.

The first approaches Tyler, extending his arm. "I am Edrym, leader of the elves."

"I am Tyler, High Priest and herald of the trinity of witches." Tyler locks arms with Edrym in the traditional greeting of a warrior.

I imagine that Tyler must feel proud to be sought out first, and DJ steps forward to greet Edrym after Tyler. The other two elves are introduced as first and second officers to Edrym. As the elves, like the vampires, witches, and werewolves, enjoy the use of modern technologies of Upper Earth, the documents had already been sent, and our visit serves to relay the need for such a treaty as we believed that information may be too sensitive to be shared widely.

DJ summarizes our recent experience with Sonia, detailing the need for obtaining Lilith's remains from the Guardians. I watch the elves' faces, each so similar with long noses; high cheekbones; tall, pointed ears; and red lips set upon fair, almost pure-white, skin. Their bodies make no movement, their flowing white robes, hanging still over their shoulders, gathered tight to their waists and draping down to cover their feet.

As DJ finishes his speech, Edrym paces down our line to me and stops. "The Elves have little interaction with most other beings, much like the fae. We have no need for protection as our powers limit threats from other sects. Why would we sign such a document when it potentially opens us to more vulnerability if we are required to aid other beings? Are the fae really going to sign this document?"

"I believe they will. Our land has been ravaged by the quakes and volcanoes of the past months. Sonia brought a series of beings to Middle Earth, killing many fae."

He raises his chin. "Yes, Queen Titania. We have heard of that battle. Her attacks seemed very specific until the earthquakes of late."

A lump forms in my throat at the sound of my name. "That is why the fae seek unity. Sonia cannot be allowed to exert power in this manner."

Fitting his fingertips together, Edrym strolls to Tyler and spins to face him. "We will sign the document."

My heart feels like hundreds of tiny butterflies alight in it. Four additional elves, same coloring and style of dress, file from the center passage in the far wall, the first carrying a stack of white pages. Edrym produces a seal from one of his robe pockets, signs his name, and seals the document with the Crest of the Elves.

I want to jump for joy but wait with patience as we bid them goodbye and trace back through the passage, along the ledge, over the trail, and to the car.

As we slide inside, Tyler lets out a whoop. "I could kiss everyone in this car right now. Titania, it's a real shame you can't eat here, because tonight, we're having a celebration dinner."

My thoughts jump to celebrations at my castle, and I think how nice it would be to stay with them and partake in the revelry.

"Slow down." DJ swats Tyler's leg. "You might want to save the big party for after we hand over Lilith. There are two more sects to convince to sign."

I part with them at the airport, opting to slip through the ring over northeastern Europe into Willhelm, eager to hear of Alemayehu's and Yonas's progress. Scents of meat and sweet root drift from the top opening as I approach their hut. I signal to them, and Alemayehu greets me, inviting me inside to share the meal with them. Accepting appreciatively, I sit down on a woven grass mat.

As much as I want to, I do not ask of the news from the council while we eat, choosing to ask of the village and wellbeing of their fae after the recent traumas. They report all are healed and many buildings already reconstructed. I help clean the pots and plates, and we sit around the fire drinking tea.

Alemayehu looks from me to Yonas and releases a long sigh. "The High Council is convening the entirety of the judges as well as the monarchs tomorrow. They do not believe this is a decision seven can make for the entire realm given it will be the armies of the kingdoms called to fight should an event arise."

I want to scream and stomp my feet like a youngling set on staying up past their bedtime. *No, no, no.* Reigning in my annoyance, I ask if they will require all to agree. Alemayehu's answer stands as the only pillar of hope I see as a path to getting a signature from the fae. Seven of the nine monarchs and, thankfully, only seventy-five percent of the judges, must agree. I tick through the list of monarchs in my mind. Borean has not experienced the quakes or volcanoes save small rumbles on their western coast. Willhelm also has been spared save small occurrences on the southern border. Lindleton's monarch King Hector favors isolationism as does King Joseph of Borean.

King Luther... I do not know what to think of him. Well, yes, I do, but none of the phrases running through my brain are nice after he stripped Holden from my life, sent another son to woo me, and refused to aid our kingdom time and time again. The man seems as unpredictable as a firecracker set in a cart bouncing along a rock-strewn lane in the midday sun. However, being a people who rely on fishing trades, I would guess his kingdom suffers much from the aftermath of the tsunami that hit our shores. If only Hector and Joseph vote no, we will have the approval needed. I cling to the strand of hope like a block cleaner at the top of a tower.

❖

THE NEXT DAY, I TRAVEL WITH DJ and Tyler to northern Canada to meet with the werewolf leadership. The hierarchy works much differently from that of the fae who have adopted somewhat of a democratic system, although the judges, as well as the monarch positions, are passed from father to son. The werewolves have a Grand Alpha Aldrich who has absolute authority. We have been told he will make decisions with advice from his first and second officers.

We are to meet the three in a clearing deep in a forest, the treetops of which reach higher than any in Aubren. Wide branches hang in rungs all the way to the tallest point. The forest floor is blanketed with brown needles shed from towering plants and cushion my steps.

The wood quiets, and hairs on my arms rise as a new scent registers. Low growls sound around us, and we freeze. I pan the dark space sheltered from the sun by the dense limbs. Studying each crevice, I land on a pair of amber eyes and find a blank snout under them.

DJ grabs my hand, and I hold my other hand up, palm out. "We are DJ, Tyler, and Thessalonia. We are here to talk about the treaty."

At an unheard signal, a pack of wolves emerge from the trees, surrounding our group.

We've heard of your powers, a vampire-witch hybrid, a herald witch, and a fae who can perform magic. A gruff, low voice sounds in my mind. *We'll not meet in our human forms. I am Aldrich, Grand Alpha. I know you can read our thoughts, so we'll converse in this manner.*

My heart races. Werewolves and vampires, being traditional enemies, have much to fear from each other. A pack of wolves is faster than a vampire and can tear their limbs from their bodies. I speak aloud to our group, informing them that the wolves will remain in that form.

"Can they understand us?" Tyler asks.

DJ squeezes my hand. *I thought he was prepared for this.*

I thought I was. I wasn't prepared for them to be actual wolves, Tyler replies.

"Do you have questions or concerns about the agreement?" I ask aloud.

I don't see that we have a choice. If all other beings sign the treaty and we do not, our packs are at risk. The vampires will have the upper hand. We don't appreciate being forced into this agreement. A low growl emits from Aldrich's teeth-bared jaw.

"It was not our intent to force your hand. We requested that the Guardians give us Lilith to appease the archangel Sonia, and these are their terms. They are sacrificing much in giving up their matriarch." I hold my breath, awaiting a response.

Sonia threatens our lands as well, and we appreciate the sacrifice. We have signed the treaty.

The wolf to his right inches forward, bowing her head and shaking a satchel from her neck. I kneel in front of her, thanking her for the document. Tyler inspects the agreement, and seeing Aldrich's signature, we thank the wolves for their comradeship.

We ask that the vampires with you don't hunt in our lands, Aldrich says.

"They will respect those wishes," I say, glancing at Will and the other guards behind us.

The wolves back away in unison, blending into the dark forest, disappearing with no more than the sound of rushing wind in their wake.

Part of me is numb, frozen to my spot. This really could work. Now, only the fae can block the path to procuring Lilith. Odd, since we have the most to lose. If Upper Earth's bedrock is destroyed, our realm will collapse.

Will circles in front of us. "Has a freezing spell been cast that I missed?"

I look to DJ then Tyler.

He smiles. "This isn't going to fail. They gave us this little side mission, thinking we would never accomplish it, and we're crushing it."

DJ huffs. "They didn't think we'd fail."

Tyler raises his hands to his hips. "They totally did."

"I do not fail," I say. "Now, I should see what progress the fae are making in their decision."

"They'll sign the agreement, right?" Tyler asks.

"I pray they do."

"What do you mean? Is there a chance they won't? How sure are you that they will? Please, tell us you're more sure than not."

"I wish I could, but I cannot."

"Fifty-fifty at least?" Tyler asks.

I raise my chin. "Yes, a couple of the monarchs are stubborn but also proud. If they do not agree, and the destruction continues, then they will be viewed negatively."

"And they'll change their minds, the fae will sign the document, and we'll get Lilith. Maybe not as soon as we thought, but we'll get her." Tyler claps his hands together. "A win for team misfits."

"Dude." DJ slaps Tyler's shoulder. "We're not misfits."

"What are misfits?" I ask.

"People who don't fit with others. There's Alena and Hunter, Camille and Jude, and then us." Tyler motions between the two of them. "Late joiners who don't know what we want to do with our lives."

"Speak for yourself." DJ grips his pack straps. "I'm not wasting my powers. I'm in."

"Good for you." Will offers an arm to DJ. "Now can we get out of this wolf-infested forest?"

I say goodbye and, flying to the nearest ring, slip through the magic barrier and head straight to Alemaye-hu's hut. It is empty, and I busy myself with building a fire and heating water for tea. I straighten and restraighten the mats and blankets, sweep the floor, and then rake the clearing.

"What are you doing?" I jump at the sound of Lencho's voice.

"Waiting. Is there news?"

"None."

"That cannot be good."

"That is my thought." He rubs his beard. "Did they find Terran? Or Theron, or whoever he is?"

"No."

"Do you think he is dead?"

"No, he is a survivor. It would be painful to lose his wings, but he will enjoy the benefits of lightened gravity and higher oxygen content for a while."

"Perhaps I should make a meal. It is getting late."

"I can help with that." I rest the rake on the hut wall.

We work together to prepare a small deer and some roots and vegetables. Sipping tea, we soon give in and pour mugs of wine to pass the time. Darkness falls over the forest, and I stare into the fire. I think of my life, how DJ is so sure of his path. When I ask myself what is next, only one thing seems sure: Foster.

"Ho, ho," a voice calls from outside.

Lencho jumps to his feet, and I follow him outside. I study Alemayehu and Yonas, seeing only exhaustion in their eyes.

I hold Alemayehu's gaze. "Out with it, friend. If it is not good news, say it, and we will pour more wine."

Yonas lifts his satchel over his head and sets it on the ground between us. "It is there. Zekiel signed and sealed it."

"Oh, Goddesses." I fling my arms around him, jumping and hugging him at the same time.

When I release Yonas, Alemayehu wraps me in an embrace, patting my back.

"You did it, friend. Thank you," I whisper.

"*We* did it."

My legs bounce as we sit around the fire, eating and hearing stories from the council meeting. As I expected, Hector and Joseph would not approve of signing the document, but each of the rest of the monarchs did. Ninety percent of the judges voted in favor. Excited to share news of the werewolves and celebrate the victory with Foster, I leave them to drink the wine and set my course for home.

All my nerves tingle as the wind washes over my body. I think about what Quinn and my cousins must be thinking about the events of late and wish I could share this happiness with them. Gatuika's wedding will be held in six weeks. At least I can watch from a perch in the wood, see her happiness. Perhaps this is not the life I would have chosen, but after months of wondering whether I could truly be happy, I finally feel that I can.

I swoop in over Aubren, circling high above the castle. Light glows from almost every window, and the faint tune of a violin reaches my ears. I let a few tears escape my eye before I brush my cheeks and turn my thoughts to all that I have. I have my cabin, goats, sheep, bird, and I have Foster. Diving down into the woods, I swoop around the trees to my porch.

It is not but a few minutes, as I am tossing seed to Messie, that I hear a rap on the door.

"Titania." Foster's voice sounds loud and clear through the wood panel. I swing the door open, and he stomps in. "Please tell me the wolves agreed. I know we thought that the fae would be the most challenging, but now that they have ratified the document, I thought of so many reasons the wolves would not be in favor of the pact."

I press my fingers together, holding them to my lips. "You are right. They did not like the agreement."

"Oh, Goddesses." His hands rake through his hair. "What will—"

"But they signed!" I shriek.

"What? You…?" A huge smile forms on his face. "That was terrible."

Leaning over, he scoops me up by my middle and flings me over his shoulder. He spins around, and I laugh and yell, telling him to put me down or I shall faint from dizziness. As our giggles turn to uncontrollable laughter, he sets me on the plank floor.

"We did it." I smile at him.

"We did it." He kisses my lips.

I lay back on the logs, arms splayed out above my head, feeling as if I can finally breathe, like the vacuum on my lungs has finally been released, the seal broken on the barrel of wine so the scent can finally take on a life of its own, my life.

Rising to one elbow, I kiss his cheek. "I love you."

He turns to face me. "And I love you. So, what now?"

"Tonight, we dance and sing, and tomorrow, I shall take the document to the witches, and we will deliver it to the Guardians. And then it shall be done."

We take turns on the fiddle and make our own music for our dance until we have no energy left. Then we lie in front of the hearth, holding each other. I drift to sleep in his arms, his scent infusing my being, knowing this is right. We are right.

A LETTER WAITS BESIDE ME when I wake.

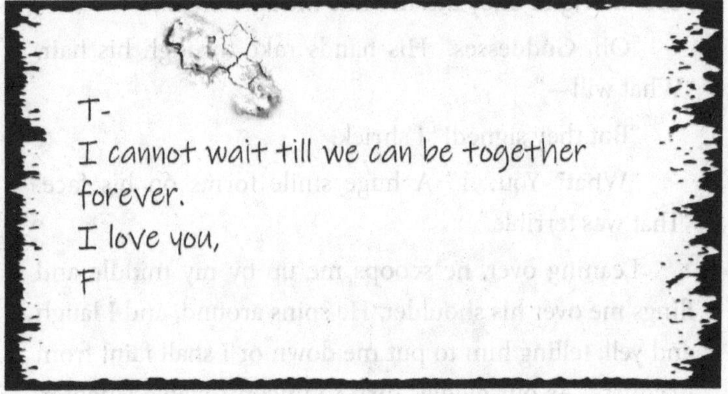

I press the page to my chest, thanking the Goddesses once again for giving me this amazing partner. I bound up, eager to get to DJ and Tyler. I rush through my chores and fly to Lindleton, drawing my cloaking spell as I pass through the tingling magic of the ring. This sun has not reached a quarter of the way through the sky as I approach the gate. Will greets me, but I am too excited to walk with him over the lawn, choosing to fly to the entrance.

DJ and Tyler exit as I land on the drive. Will zips to us, and I pan their faces.

"Out with it, T," Tyler says.

I sling my satchel from my back and hold it high above my head. "It is done. They signed. We have all the sects in agreement."

"Whoop." Tyler throws his arms around, raising them and bringing down again as he walks in circles.

DJ wraps his arms around my middle, spinning me around. The guards file from the compound, congratulating us. DJ slides his phone from his pocket, calling his brother, giving him the news. Within minutes, DJ gets a return call with directions to meet Caesaria and her Guardian team in Milan.

"Okay, people," Tyler calls out above the competing conversations. "We actually shouldn't be celebrating yet. The Guardians have to make good on their promise. Let's pray they haven't changed their minds."

It never occurred to me that they might rescind their offer. *They would not, right?* For if they did, they must know that every one of the other sects would come for them, and I would be leading the charge.

In an hour's time, we board a flight bound for Milan. I am thankful there will be no repeat of visiting the chamber below Paris. I hug my bag to my chest as we touch down on the airstrip hugging the mountains. The plane glides into a hangar as the sun paints orange swaths on the hills beyond. We drive to the same club, parking in the back and entering through a small door set in the corner of the back side. Entering the office where we first met Caesaria by a side door, we round the wood desk, waiting for the Guardians. Tyler's foot taps, and I grab his hand. Tilting his head to each side, he shakes his shoulders.

I lean toward him. "All will be well. You did a good job."

"That's what I'm hoping for."

On my other side, DJ squeezes my palm, and I smile at him. I will miss seeing my friend every day but realize that I may visit any time. Perhaps I will even get a mobile phone to tuck in a tree stump in the wood beside the ring. That way I may reach him whenever I want. *Why not? I am not bound by the rules of the fae now.*

The door centered behind the desk opens, and Caesaria, Claudia, Dmitri, and the generals glide in, their motion fluid as water on a hillside.

Caesaria approaches, lifting an eyebrow. "You have another."

"This is Tyler," DJ introduces our friend.

Caesaria locks arms with him and drops her hands to her sides. "I am told you have news for me."

"Yes." I produce the documents from my bag, laying them one by one on the desktop. "Each of the sects you required have agreed to the terms. All have pledged their peace and to aid in defense in the case of any attack."

Each of the Guardians gathered inspect each page of every document, running their hands over the signatures and seals, sniffing each for scents of the beings. The form a ring, conferring in tones so quiet I cannot make out their words. My fingers tingle, my whole body craving a release as seconds flow into each other. Tension wafts from every pore of Tyler's skin, and I cut my eyes to DJ. He winks and smiles at me, ever the confident and calm presence.

Motion catches my eye, and Caesaria's chin rises. Her team fans out, forming a line in front of us. Lifting a document from the end, she piles them, one by one, atop the others, cradling them in one arm. My heart thuds in my chest, thinking she either means to burn them to ash or seal them away, preserving them for all eternity as Lilith has been.

"We have inspected the documents and believe them to be authentic and true. We will call with directions for retrieving Lilith's remains tomorrow."

"Thank you." DJ extends his hand.

They lock arms, and she steps before me and offers her hand

"You are a mystery. Just a simple fae who can do magic. I do not believe it, but you have earned my respect, Thessalonia of the Fae."

"And you mine. Be well."

"Until we meet again." She smiles and releases my arm.

Bidding Tyler farewell, she folds both arms around the contracts and exits through the back door. With only nods to us, the others follow. Relief washes over me, and I exhale a long breath. We retrace our steps back to the vehicles and climb inside. Little is said on the drive to the hangars, and the air feels as if it is filled with sand. Tyler's foot bounces, and DJ's finger taps on the doorframe.

"What are we waiting for?" I whisper.

"The car to blow up, a sinkhole to open up under the vehicle, flood, famine, fire, mass destruction…" Tyler huffs.

"Seriously, I think we can celebrate."

DJ shakes his head. "Not till we are back safe at the compound. Not until we have Lilith's body."

"Do you think the Guardians would sabotage us? They would be decimated by the other sects."

"More Biblical things have happened already," Tyler says.

Chapter 15

Heart pounding in my chest, I land beside the ring as the first light dawns above, harken my cloaking spell, and slip through the ring, alighting in the ferns nearby. I am to wait here until someone comes with word that Lilith will be delivered. My eyes feel as though sandpaper scrapes the surface each time I blink. Foster could not come to me last night, so I cleaned and paced till late. When I did lie down, I could not settle.

Waiting, I task myself with challenges. *How fast can I zip to the treetop? How far can I throw a rock?* I should have asked DJ to leave me a phone. At least then I could know what was going on. I gauge the sky as I circle the ring for the billionth time. I will need to leave midday before the sun starts its descent to the horizon. I build tiny houses with sticks, topping the roofs with blades of grass. I braid and re-braid my hair. I gather vines and weave them into a circle, fitting flowers and twigs with berries between the strips, and place it on my head. I drink water from my flask as the midday heat swelters around me.

I am stripping my boots from my feet as a crackle reaches my ears. I freeze, panning the forest only with the movement of my eyes. I have not ever seen another being in this wood, but one can never be too careful.

The next instant, DJ's form appears across the ring.

"Thank the Goddesses."

DJ chuckles, then perhaps in reaction to my hard stare, covers his mouth and clears his throat. "I'm sorry. What are you wearing?"

"A crown." Lifting the creation from my head, I hold it out. "I am now queen of this forest. Would you like to be king with me?"

"I would love to be king with you."

I zip to him. "Seriously, DJ. Could you not leave a note, give me a phone, send a message via carrier bird? I have been waiting since before sunrise."

"Carrier bird? Isn't the term carrier pigeon?"

"I know not what carrier pigeons are, but I have a carrier bird, and her name is Messie. She is very good at getting messages to people."

"Chill, okay? We'll get you a phone."

"Really?"

"Yes, really." He widens his eyes. "Do you want to know if we got Lilith or not?"

"Yes." I slap his arm. "For Goddesses sake, tell me you have her."

"We have her. She is safe in the compound."

"That is amazing." I fling my arms around him, squeezing him tightly. "We did it."

"We did." Releasing me, he grabs my hands. "Everyone is at the castle. We're throwing a big party. Will you come?"

I scrunch my face. "I am sorry, friend. I cannot come today. I promised to do something once this was finished. I will come soon, though. Perhaps after you deliver Lilith to Sonia. Then we will have a celebration together."

"Really? Please? Are you sure you have to go now?"

"I will see you soon. Please tell Tyler congratulations again, and give my regards to Alena, Camille, and Hunter."

"I will, T." Pulling me towards him, he wraps his arms around my back. "Be safe."

"I will, friend."

Stepping back, he offers his arm. "Until we meet again."

I wrap my fingers around his broad muscle. "Until we meet again."

I leap into the air and fold my wings, dropping into Middle Earth. The ring zings my skin with magic as if it knows there is a shift. I spread my wings and pan my eyes over the land below, my home, with the oceans lapping the north shore and green mountains rising above the beach. It will soon be safe once again. My next thought is of Foster and the promise I made to myself.

Thinking it odd now that the time is here I feel no reservation. Perhaps it is the adrenaline coursing through my veins. It is midday, and even though I know Foster will come at nightfall, I cannot wait one more minute. I descend nearly to the sand and enter the forest, weaving through the trees and rising with the mountain to the cabin. I land on the stoop with a thud and, producing the key, enter and latch the door. Shedding my cloak, I let it fall to the floor. *Who has time for tidiness in a moment like this?* Crossing to the cabinet, I coo at Messie.

"Hi, pretty. Ready to do an important job?" Opening a drawer, I take out a sheet of parchment.

I remove the cap from the ink bottle and dip the quill in. Holding the tip over the page, I bite my lip. I do not wish to cause him angst. *Do not overthink this.*

Pressing the quill down, I write two lines. *It is finished. Come to me?*

Drawing my blade from my boot, I cut the page into a strip, roll it, and then fit twine around it. I cross to the cage and address Messie.

"Hi, sweets." I free the latch and wait for her to hop to my hand.

Moving to the table, I let her jump to the wood top. I fix the scroll on her leg. With a twitter, she steps to my hand. I cross the room, flip the latch, and open the door.

Lifting the bird, I whisper, "To the castle."

Messie cocks her head, lifts her beak, and with a swift flap, flits up. Rising over the rooftop, she heads east and, in seconds, disappears into the trees. Having an hour or more to wait, I skip inside and start water for a bath. I shed my shoes and place the cloak on the hook then jump around the room, tidying up, and slide my trunk from under the bed.

What to wear? The only dress I have, the velvet green one, will have to do. I hold it above the steam, letting the warm, wet air loose the creases. Water hot, I fill the tub and scrub my skin. With a towel around my body, I tip-toe inside and slide into the crushed fabric. I tighten the strings on my back and lean down to peer into the small mirror. Loosing my curls, I swish my hair along my back. I smooth them with a brush, letting ringlets fall across my shoulders. If only Alfreda or my cousins were here to do my curls, share in my joy. I set the brush on its shelf. It will not do to linger on these thoughts. Today is to be one of the happiest days of my life, Goddesses willing.

I pin the hair in front on top of my head and form a braid down the center. Then, I scrub my teeth with mint and put on water for tea. Or perhaps we should have wine. Opening the shutter an inch, I peer out the window. It is hours till midday. I should be hungry, as I have not eaten in over half a day, but my stomach feels as if tiny butterflies bat the sides with their wings.

With another quick look in the mirror and a pat to my bare neck, I lift the lid of my chest. I dig down to the bottom where my faerie cross necklace lies. My brothers will be here in spirit as well. I link the ends and straighten the rock between my bones. A thud sounds from outside, and the dwelling shudders. Heart pounding anew, I skip to the window and peek through the slit.

Strawberry blond eyebrows protrude from under his hood, and I swing open the door.

"What has happened?" He locks his hands around my biceps.

"It's finished. The vampires released Lilith's remains to the witches."

Scooping me up, he spins me around. "You did it."

He stops, and I slide down till we are eye to eye. "We did it. I just hope it works."

"It will work."

Releasing me, he takes my hands. "I am so proud of you."

"I told you I would find a way." Squeezing his fingers, I swing our arms between us.

"I always knew you would do it. I told you as much." He rests his forehead on mine.

I press my lips to his. The feel of his skin on mine, the warmth of his mouth, his hands winding around my waist, my body pressed against his sets every nerve on edge, and I never want the sensation to end. Gripping his hair, I take a breath. "Ask me."

He stares into my eyes. "Ask you?"

I nod. "Ask me."

His hands follow the curves of my body as he drops to one knee. He looks up at me, smile spread wide across his face. Eyes filling with tears, he lifts my hand. "Titania Alphaeus, daughter of King Oberon Alphaeus, will you do me the honor of becoming my wife?"

Kneeling, I kiss his lips. "Yes, I will marry you."

"Thank the Goddesses! You have made me the happiest fae in the realm!" He presses his lips to mine.

I run my hands through his hair, cherishing the feel of his soft locks. "I love you and cannot wait to start our lives together."

My mind pushes back the thought that we can have no family to witness our marriage. Alemayehu, Adam,

Nicholas, and Timothy will have to do. I wish for only happy sentiments to rule this day.

He stands and, tugging my hands, pulls me to him. "When shall it be? Tonight? We can have Alemayehu officiate and Adam, Nicholas, or Timothy to witness."

"That is fast. I would like a dress and time to pick some flowers for my hair."

"I can look in the village for a gown for you."

"And who will you say it is for?" Stepping from his embrace, I plant my hands on my hips.

"I do not know. A young maiden from the country with not enough funds for a dress?"

"I guess a soldier with your rank may do such."

"Or the shopkeeper will think I took liberties before the nuptials."

I swat his arm. "Foster of Westshire, the scandal you would cause. I am not sure I could trust you to even pick a good-looking garment."

"I do have a sister. I try and pay attention."

"I would like a white dress."

"Then you shall have it." He kisses my forehead. "Whatever you desire shall be yours. I will announce my retirement today, and we shall travel the world together."

I lean into him, savoring his scent. To wake with him every day, to hold him any hour, seems like a dream that would never come true. But it is.

"I hate to leave you, but I should get back to the castle. I have much to prepare."

"Perhaps you should give them a few weeks to get used to the idea of you leaving. What will you tell your family?" I intertwine my fingers with his.

"That I am to go on holiday, see the entire realm."

"I hope that you will not regret this."

"Never." Smiling, he kisses me.

My lips tingle under the pressure, and I wrap my arms around his middle. Kissing me repeatedly, he backs me to the wall. He plants kisses down my neck, and I run my hands over his hips and down his thighs. I am breathless when he releases me.

"I need to get back."

Opening my eyes, I get my bearings. "Fog."

"Yeah, my brain is a bit fuzzy, too." He tucks a strand of hair behind my ear.

"No, there is fog."

"What do you mean?" Releasing me, he spins to face the forest. "Oh, Goddesses."

"This is strange." I cross to the edge of the porch. "The air is warm. What would cause the fog?"

"I will investigate."

Grabbing his arm, I shake my head. "We will go together."

I retrieve my coat and mask from inside, and we dart up the mountain and land at the top of the tallest tree.

"It is coming from the west." Foster eyes the skyline.

"It is moving fast."

"I should get to the castle."

"I will follow and wait in the wood."

Staying just under the canopy, we zip around the trunks. Even with our speed, the fog rolls in below us quickly enough to engulf the ground in a thick soup of haze. Only twenty feet up, our sight distance drops. At the edge of the wood bordering the castle property, Foster slows and disappears into the cloud.

I descend and land beside him. "I will wait here."

"I will come if there is news. Or at the least send Adam, Nicholas, or Timothy." He steps into the field.

Tugging on his jacket, I pull him toward me. "Not so fast."

I kiss his lips and run my finger across his forehead. "I will see you tonight if not before."

"Yes." His eyes sparkle even with the low light. He raises his brows. "Fiancé."

"I like the sound of that." I kiss him again. "Hurry back to me."

"I love you."

"I love you."

I watch his form disappear into the fog. Weaving through the trees, I find the stream and follow as it meanders south, jumping boulders from side to side. After a while, I cut back, retracing my steps north. The fog becomes so thick I can only see five feet. Stopping, I look up. The curtain of darkness surrounds me. The quiet seeps into my psyche, and I realize not even a single bird calls. Whatever the cause of the odd weather pattern, even the animals feel it.

Jumping into the air, I alight in the top of a tree. With the thick fog and my disguise, I chance getting a better vantage point and beat my wings until I am above the low cloud. The top spire is all I can see to the east. To the west, dark dots fill the sky. Small splotches at first, they grow larger on the horizon.

I retake my hiding place in the treetop to wait. *Should I call out? Warn Foster?* They could be birds for all I know, confused and looking for a place to roost. I wait, hunched on a branch, eyes and ears piqued for any change from above. Finally, I see them: gray, blurred shadows pass over. I count them: five, ten, twenty, over fifty… *Could they be cranes? Why so many?* Waiting till I see no more, I chance rising above the trees.

My breath catches in my lungs as the forms solidify. Fae, at least a hundred, bearing the light green colors of Hilbron, ring the castle spire. *What is Luther doing?*

I shoot down into the fog, descending nearly to the forest floor and, not caring who may see me now, ring the meadow to the orchard. Seeing my troops filing from the barracks, armor on their chests, arrows across their backs, and swords in hand, bile rises in my throat. I zip to the armory and huddle under the overhang of the roof.

"Is Luther mad? Why would he surround our castle?" I hear a voice inside.

"King Quinn must be dumbfounded," another answers.

The sound of footfalls trails away, and I peek into the room to find the soldiers gone. A few suits of armor hang on hooks, and after checking around the corner, I duck inside. I fit the breastplate over my shoulders and helmet on my head. The eye shield I hope almost covers my mask. Trying the swords, I take the heaviest one and follow the sound of voices to the courtyard. Head hung, I weave through the crowd to stand behind the front row. I spy Foster huddled with General Kane, Grant, and Quinn.

Quinn. My heart pounds in my chest at seeing my cousin again, now clad in armor. He rubs the back of his neck and nods as Kane addresses him. With the noise of the soldiers, I cannot make out their words, and with Kane's mustache and beard, it is hard for me to read his lips. Quinn nods and takes a step back. He motions to the bugler who snaps into position, raises the instrument, and sounds the call for visiting dignitaries.

Is King Luther of Hilbron with his troops, or did he send one of his brothers per usual? Did he see the fog and take the opportunity? But to do what? My stomach flips end to end.

A small battalion descends through the fog, and King Luther is unmistakable in the lead. I glance at Quinn who strides out into the center of the courtyard flanked by Grant and Kane. Foster follows close behind. Fitting the bow over my head, I hold my sword tight in my hand, my other arm taut at my side, fist balled. I bend my knees and stretch, readying for what may come.

A soldier to my right nudges me. "Cannot say that I have seen a kilt like that before. Is this what all the young fae are wearing now?"

Face flaming with heat, I look down at my green velvet skirt protruding from the armor. *Frog tails.* I had forgotten about my outfit.

I clear my throat and attempt a deep voice. "Do you know anything about this? Was King Luther expected?"

"No, and I heard he has his whole army waiting above the fog. Quinn ordered all the troops to the castle."

"What can Luther want?"

"Our kingdom if I was a betting man. That Luther is slimy as a snail. Never trusted him." The solider spits in the dirt. "The way he disrespected Queen Titania, the Goddesses bless her soul, over and over again. It was a crime."

My heart issues a thud. *Luther take my kingdom? That snake. The High Council will not stand for it, will they? Not in all fae history has a kingdom tried to take another.* "That would be mad. Our army is four times the size of theirs."

"You ever seen fog like this? Something is amiss." The old soldier rubs his beard and pans his eyes to the sky thick with dense white fog.

I refocus on Quinn as King Luther and his guards land in front of him. Quinn extends his arm to the visiting ruler, but Luther's arms remain at his side, a clear sign of disrespect.

Quinn motions to the hall behind him. His mouth moves, but I cannot make out his words.

A hush falls over the crowd.

"I am sure you know my army waits above the fog." Luther's voice echoes around the courtyard. "This is not a cordial visit. I am here to claim my birthright in entirety."

I hold my breath. *Curses, the old soldier is right.*

Quinn steps forward and posts his hands on his hips. "I am monarch of Aubren, rightful ruler of this land, passed this by our great, late Queen Titania, Goddesses bless her soul, and therefore rightful heir to the throne. This has even been sanctified by her father and the kingdom's advisors and judges. Surely you know our army is four times larger than yours."

"Ho." The soldiers around me chant in unison, stomping their javelins to the rock underfoot.

I keep my eyes trained on Luther and Quinn.

Luther raises an eyebrow and chuckles. "Titania's rule was a mockery. You are son to a distant cousin of Titania's father. Your father was not the first son, which is why he still lives, as do you. Surrender, and I will reunite this continent as the original Kingdom of Primus. Fight, and we both lose many soldiers."

My head pounds, and blood burns in my veins.

Quinn lowers his arms. "The High Council will not stand for this."

"Do you see the High Council? Do they have an army to stop me? Every able-bodied fae in my kingdom waits just beyond the border, ready to fight with my soldiers. I would guess that will make for a fairer battle."

"And you think my fae will not fight for their kingdom? Stand against a greedy, arrogant ruler? You do not deserve to call yourself fae."

"Ho." The soldiers around me issue their affirmation.

"I am restoring this land to its original form. You think I will be deterred by weak insults after staging this invasion?"

My fingers tingle. I could end this right now, strike Luther down where he stands, and I will if needed.

"What is wrong with your hands?" The soldier on my left stares, wide eyed.

Seeing my fingers glowing green, I release a long slow breath and draw in my powers. "A rash, I believe."

Movement catches my eye, and looking up, I see Quinn take a step back. "If you will not return to your country and wait for the High Council to convene on the issue, then we will have no choice but to defend our kingdom from takeover."

"Ho." The battle cry grows in intensity, and the rows of soldiers inch toward the gathering of rulers.

Yes. My heart soars when I hear the strong words from Quinn's lips. Still, a hard pit grows in my stomach as if I have swallowed rocks, and my hands warm anew. *Dare I reveal myself to prevent the bloodshed that is sure to come? I have no choice. I will not see my countrymen die in a senseless battle. I cannot let my kingdom be consumed by a power-hungry ogre.*

Luther lifts his arm, and a strong gale sweeps through the courtyard, taking the fog with it. I look up to see the sky covered with fae bearing the light green uniforms of Hilbron. There must be at least five hundred. I slip into the first line of soldiers and meet Foster's wide gaze. He shakes his head and mouths no.

Smiling, Luther lowers his arm and extends a palm. "Please, order your army to defend your rule, family, and countrymen."

"Not without provocation."

"So be it." Luther raises his fist and shouts, "For Primus!"

A wave of arrows descends from the sky, and the soldiers around me crowd toward the castle walls, lifting their bows and shooting into the sky. Luther's army is too high up, and the arrows fall with the others. Crammed against the wall opposite where Luther and Quinn stood, I sweep the space, seeing many tugging arrows from limbs.

Hearing a bugle, I realize Quinn must be signaling the soldiers called from the rest of the kingdom to fight. *How many fae will be lost?* I cannot stand by and see both armies slaughtered. I slide my helmet from my head.

"Goddesses be." The soldier beside me goes white.

"Let me through." I raise my sword in the air, hand and arm glowing green.

"It is Titania."

"She has come to save us."

"All hail, Queen Titania."

Shouts ring out as the troops step aside for me to pass.

I raise my chin and approach the leaders: Quinn, flanked by Grant and Kane, and Luther by his guards. They form a line in front of Luther as I approach.

The troops fall silent.

Looking to Quinn, my heart breaks when I see his pained expression. "Sorry, cousin."

My eyes cut to Luther, and my powers thrum anew. Hands pulsing with green light, I point my sword at him.

"Go home, Luther. You are not worthy to call yourself a steward of this land let alone your own. Go back to your kingdom to face the council's judgment."

He pushes through the line of soldiers and approaches. One side of his mouth rises as he smiles.

"I always knew you were a demon, evil spawn from a witch's womb, and now you have sided with the evils of the deep and have taken their forms."

"No." I draw in my power and hold out my bow. "I am flesh and blood, still of this realm. My soul was protected, and the Goddesses preserved my body."

"Perhaps it is as you say. If you are but fae, how is a single girl to defend her countrymen against an entire army?"

Fitting my bow over my head, I hold up my palm. It glows green with the energy stored under my skin. I shoot a beam at a nearby tree and it bursts into flames. Gasps echo through the space. I take a deep breath and refocus on Luther.

"Because I am a magical fae, gifted by the Goddesses. While I do not prefer to use my power against a fae, if you continue with your attack, I will have no choice but to end you and all those who attempt to take our kingdom."

CRACK!

A loud boom like a lightning strike sounds, and a bright burst of white light beams materialize above. With a sizzle, the streams of light coalesce into the figure of a woman.

Sonia.

"So, you live." Her gray, glowing form is before me in the blink of an eye. "I knew something was afoot. The witches were making much more headway than I could have guessed."

My stomach turns with fear, but I straighten my spine. "This is none of your concern. The witches have what you want. Go to them. You have no power here."

She leans in, her breath hot on my face. "Are you sure, sweetness? Are you missing some slight nuance in the laws of spirits? In most cases, I have no power in your realm because the fae are true and just-souled beings, but what of your estranged counterpart from Hilbron? He seems to have suspended his sanctity."

Heart thudding in my chest, my breath catches. I swallow bile. "You only have the power that beings give you."

Throwing back her head, she laughs, a sinister, high-shrilled cackle. "And Luther and all those who follow him have bestowed quite a bit of power for some time now. Perhaps—"

Her arm flails out, and black shards of metal, hundreds of knife blades, shoot from her fingers. I follow their trajectory and jump into the air. The daggers pierce my flesh, sending sharp pains through my nerves, but my eyes are only on one fae, Foster.

Landing beside his limp form, I see metal shards dug inches deep into his chest, blood already streaming from the wounds, and my mind screams. *Why wasn't he wearing armor like the rest of the soldiers?* I fall to my knees and cradle his pale face in my hands, run my hands down his arms, and squeeze his cold fingers.

"Foster." I kiss his sweat-drenched forehead, the taste of salt coating my mouth.

His eyes open. "Titania, I—" Mouth falling slack, his gaze freezes.

"NO!" I pound my fists on his blood-coated tunic.

I press my ear to his chest and wait. Nothing. His ribs hold their station. I find his sternum, pumping it hard with my palms. I lean in, my ear hovering above his ashen nose. I fit my mouth over his cold lips, forcing air into his windpipe. I watch, I wait. Nothing.

This cannot be my life. Foster is not dead.

I bury my face in his shoulder. "Foster, breathe! Breathe for me. Breathe for us…"

"Titania, let him go in peace."

I glance up as a hand swipes down his face, closing the lids over his blue eyes.

"NO!" I shake my head as tears flood my vision, feeling as though I'll break into pieces if I move even an inch.

Fingers lock around my arms. "Titania, he is gone."

"No." I press my red-stained hands to the stone below me and push up.

Standing, I note the imprint of my palms on the rock. His time in this realm is not over. It cannot be. He still has so much to do. We have our wedding… My throat seizes. I fold my hands over my ribs as they tighten around my lungs. *Breathe in, breathe out. I will take him to the witches, and they will restore him.*

Lifting my head, I see a shadow lengthen in front of me. Eyes thick with water, I turn to face her.

Her smile chills my soul. "I was going to say perhaps a demonstration was appropriate, but you get the picture. Now your mate is dead, and you have no one to blame but yourself."

I face Foster. Arms like lead, I pull the dagger from his belt and place his right hand over his heart. I fix his left around his sword and cross one arm over the other.

My blurry gaze finds Luther. "You did this. Your greed and malice gave this evil creature the power she wanted in this realm."

Motion catches my eye, and I turn to see her hand rise.

"No." I fling a ball of energy at her.

It lands in the middle of her back just as the daggers emerge from her fingers. The blades shoot into the crowd, and soldiers jump into the air to miss the sharp metal stakes.

Face white, King Luther falls to his knees. "Goddesses, forgive me."

Seeing Sonia straightening her back, I refocus on my enemy. "Leave this realm and never return."

"You are not more powerful than me."

"We will find out."

Conjuring my magic, I wield another energy stream at her. As the glowing power source hits its mark, her face contorts, but the next second, her hands rise, and dark metal flies from her fingers. Realizing I have got to get her away from my soldiers, I fashion a wave of energy and shoot it toward her. She goes sailing high over the castle turret, Luther's army fleeing from her path. I jump into the air in pursuit. Praying all below have taken shelter, that my family is sequestered in safety, I fling beam after beam of my magic at her. She counters, forcing dagger after dagger from her fingertips in the short seconds between shocks.

I dodge most of them, but one scrapes my thigh, making a deep gash.

My energy wanes, but fueled by anger and grief, I pour my all into the blasts. As we battle, her energy appears to weaken, and at last, I force her to the ring above.

As she approaches the magic film, she spins to face me. "Why not send me back to Sheol? Oh, that is right, you do not have the power to contain me, and now that I know you still breathe air as a mortal being, your realm will not be spared."

Palm up, ready to defend against any further attack, I answer, "The witches have your mother. They are ready to deliver her to you."

She throws her head back and cackles. "You believe I wish to have my mother? The only reason I would want Lilith is to watch her burn. That selfish, lonely woman bore those beasts, defended them. She and my damned half siblings have been my enemies since the first drop of witch's blood they spilled."

Rage grows within me, and I throw out my hands, sending a deluge of energy that slams into her chest, flinging her sparking body through the ring. One by one, the crystals powering the ring pop and drop from their settings, and the ring goes dark. I do not care. All my work, the last six weeks spent trekking the globe in search of the Guardians, forming relationships with the vampires, elves, and wolves, has been for naught. Again, I am left with nothing. Foster is gone.

Foster is gone.

My wings go slack.

Chapter 16

Humming grows in my ears, and my heart beats as the thrumming of a hummingbird. *Foster is gone.* My grief sizzles through my nerves. I swallow, wanting to fold my wings flat to my back, plunge into the sea, and never surface, but I have Foster's family, my family, my kingdom, and the realm to think of. Leaving them now would be the most selfish thing I could do. *Have I not learned anything from the last months of galivanting with the witches, bringing all the factions of the Upper Earth together? For what?*

Wings spread wide, I make big, sweeping circles, dreading what I must face next. *Titania, do not do this to yourself. You cannot predict the future. You could not have known Sonia did not care for her mother.*

I should have done as Foster suggested and stayed near my cabin, planting gardens, tending sheep, and making clothing. This day may have come anyway. King Luther would still have marched on my kingdom, drawing Sonia to this realm, I would still be here, and Foster would still be with the Goddesses. Water fills my eyes as pain grows in my chest. My breaths become ragged. *One minute.* I suck in air. *You have one minute to fall apart, and then you must tend to your people.*

Drawing breath in and out, I make one large circle over my castle, assessing the situation. In the distance, I see dots growing smaller and guess they represent Luther's army retreating home. I pray Quinn has Luther in our dungeon. Below, I see hundreds of faces raised to the sky. I swallow, praying no other lives have been lost this day.

I land in the middle of the courtyard to large, staring eyes. Two guards hold Luther, and the others follow my path to Foster.

Quinn, Gatuika and Lowell, Makani, Isla, and my parents stand at his head.

Gatuika, tears in her eyes, runs to me. She wraps her arms around my middle. "It is true. You are alive."

"I am alive."

Makani and Isla join our bundle. It is all I can do to contain sobs, half for joy and half for grief. They release me, and I see Father guide Mother toward us, Alfreda close behind.

Father drops to one knee. "My daughter, my Queen, you have saved our realm once again."

"Quinn is still our monarch."

I take Mother's hand, searching her eyes for any awareness. Kissing her fingers, I release her and hug Alfreda.

"Goddesses be, you will be the death of me, child," she whispers into my ear.

Finding no words, I squeeze her shoulders.

She releases me and, pulling a bandage from her pocket, wraps it around my leg. "Promise you will go the healer as soon as this is finished."

I wave her off and cross to Quinn, taking his hand. "Thank you for tending our kingdom when I could not."

"Your kingdom."

I shake my head. "We will see. That is for another day."

Gatuika holds out a bouquet of flowers, all wildflowers from the meadow, and dropping to my knees, I place them on Foster's chest. Adam, Nicholas, and Timothy kneel around me.

"You could have taken him to the witches. They would have restored him for me."

Adam takes my hand. "Foster would not have wanted that. He is with the Goddesses now, and you will join him when it is your time."

I raise my chin. If it were my time, the Goddesses would have let Sonia best me. I stand and spin to face the soldiers gathered. "You all must have many questions. I am sorry I had to deceive you into believing I had passed. I hoped to spare this realm from Sonia's wrath. You have witnessed her power today. All of your questions will be satisfied, and those responsible for granting her power here will be questioned."

I glance at Luther, then Quinn, then my family, and then train my eyes on the soldiers before me. "But this day, we will honor one of the most true soldiers this kingdom has known. This night, we will celebrate the life of"—my voice catches in my throat, and I swallow—"Foster of Westshire."

"Ho." The soldiers stomp their feet to the stone.

Fighting sobs that gather in my chest, I cross to Quinn, asking about Foster's family.

Quinn says they have been summoned.

I kneel beside Foster, cradling his head in my lap as the soldiers come to honor him, laying flowers, wreaths, and blades around him. The crowd parts, and his parents and Nissi come forward. Seeing the grief in their faces, tears form anew. I stroke Foster's hair, his beautiful orange locks soft in my fingers.

His mother, water streaming down her face, drops to her knees and takes his hand, kissing it over and over.

Nissi, eyes red, now almost half a foot taller than last I saw her, fits a doll in his arm.

Matthew stands stoic, one hand around Nissi's shoulders and the other tight around a sickle. He lays the tool on his son's chest beside the sword. Tears form in his lids as he nods to me.

I lift my eyes to see the sky blazing orange. Foster is with the Goddesses.

Resting his head on a bed of flowers, I stand. "This night, we honor a true, brave fae, one who served this kingdom with all his heart. He has kept my family safe and ensured the security of this kingdom and the realm. To Foster!"

"To Foster!" the soldiers bellow.

Torches are lit, and his bed, made of logs twined together at each joint, is laid down beside him. I help lift his body atop it and place the flowers and gifts around him. Tears stream down my face as we heave the bed to my shoulders, Foster's father, Adam, Grant, Nicholas and Timothy doing the same. My eyes trace back to Luther, the guards' hands tightly around his arms, leading him behind us. He will witness every second of the grief he caused.

Hiking to the meadow, we set Foster on the ground.

I pluck flowers and, kneeling beside him, weave a crown. Putting it atop his head, I kiss his lips. I lay my hands on his chest and then my cheek. Linking my fingers in his, I find his skin has grown cold and his hands rigid. I lean up to whisper in his ear, "I will find you. I promise this. The Goddesses will care for you until then." Kissing his cheek, I let my tears flow freely.

Warm hands envelop my shoulders. "You must let him go."

I turn to find Alemayehu before me and bury my face in his chest. "I cannot. I cannot go on without him."

"You will find a way. The Goddesses will grant you the power, and I will be here every second you need me."

"You are as much a father to me as my own flesh and blood." Releasing him, I nod to Quinn, and they lift Foster's bed to the uprights, resting him there. Alemayehu hands me a burning torch, and I pass it to Foster's father. Cheeks covered in tears, with his wife's and Nissi's faces buried in his side, he touches it to the bed of greens. The leaves catch, sending up black smoke. Part of me wishes to appeal to the Goddesses, the witches, or whatever power that may be to bring him back to me this very second, but Adam is right. Foster would not want that. He is with the Goddesses now.

I stand there, eyes trained on the pyre until the last ember dies.

"Titania, you must come away." Alfreda's voice sounds like she is a hundred hectares away. She wraps a blanket around my shoulders. "You must drink, eat, and tend to your wound. The others await your leave."

Cutting my eyes to the side, I realize only Alemayehu, Luther, and the guards remain. Nodding, I grasp the cloth, pulling it tightly around me.

Alemayehu squeezes my shoulders.

Glancing towards the castle, my mind wrestles with the other events of the day. The witches must be warned that Sonia knows they hold Lilith, and something must be done with Luther.

I run my hand down Alemayehu's arm and grip his hand. "Can you, or one of your sons, warn the witches about Sonia? I do not have the energy this night, and they should know soon."

"Of course we will. This very night. I pledge to you."

"Thank you, friend. This will be a weight taken from my shoulders."

He bids me farewell, and Alfreda leads me through the meadow, the guards holding Luther paces behind us. I hold out one hand so the grasses graze my palm, my heart aching as if a chasm may open up and engulf it any second. In the orchard, I look up into the limbs, water pooling in my eyes, remembering the first day Foster and I met, how I stole his bow and told him to leave me alone. Tears stream down my cheeks, and my feet trudge through the grass as if they are weighed down with the heaviest stones of the land. I force my legs to move as we cross into the garden, summer flowers of pinks and purples turning shades of orange as they catch the light of the torches.

At the doors, I stop and spin to face the guards flanking Luther. "Take him to the dungeon. Give him a meal and water."

Luther's eyes do not leave the ground as the guards urge him forward into the hall.

"We must get you to the healer." Alfreda tugs my arm.

My mouth feels like sandpaper and my limbs like limp branches. "I will meet you there."

"If you think I am leaving you alone for a single second, you are sorely misguided." Tucking her shoulder under my arm, she guides me down the hall. I glance around the corridor, dimly lit with torches, wondering where everyone is.

"They said to bring you to the study once you saw the healer," Alfreda says as if guessing my question.

"I would not blame them if they expelled me to Willhelm."

"Are you mad? Quinn is itching to hand over the crown."

"It cannot be done just like that." I hobble on my now-throbbing leg. "I cannot imagine anyone holds me in high regard."

"Again, do you not realize what you have done today? And that every one of your soldiers and those of Hilbron witnessed it? You expelled an evil being from our realm after that wretch of a snake, Luther, drew her here. You are a hero to this kingdom and all of Middle Earth. All want you to rule."

I wrap my palm around the door pull as we reach the healer's room. "I am not sure I can be much good to them. Foster is gone. We were to be married. We promised such this very day minutes before Luther arrived."

"There will be none of that talk. You can, and you will, retake your rightful place." She pushes the door open.

———

AN HOUR LATER, AFTER TEA laced with strong liquor, my wound cleaned, and promises made not to put weight on the leg for two days, Alfreda leads me, hobbling on one crutch, to the King's study. Inside, I find Quinn, Abeetha swollen with child, Father, Mother, Gatuika, Lowell, Makani, Isla, Grant, and General Kane gathered around the table.

I sit beside Father and look at Quinn. "There is much you should know. There is much the whole realm should know."

Father clears his throat. "I have shared all I know of Sonia."

"Thank you, Father." I pat his hand. "What I have done, I have done to protect all of you. It was never my plan to return, but I could not let hundreds die in battle or allow Sonia to pluck off our soldiers by the score." An image of Foster's limp body bounces through my mind, and my chest constricts. "The magic I use does not come from evil but from the Goddesses. I pray you will forgive me. I will answer any question you, or the High Council, or anyone asks. I do not expect anything. If you want me here, I will stay. If you rather I go, I will respect your wishes. I faked my death so Sonia would stop unleashing beasts on

233

our land. Now that she knows I am alive, we are in danger again. I am most sorry for that. I have been working these past months with the witches, vampires, elves, and werewolves to reunite her with her family. We failed to deliver what she wanted, but there are others still working to appease her."

Quinn shifts forward in his seat. "Appease her? Why not send her to Sheol? Is she not pure evil?"

"I believe she is, but she is an archangel and cannot be unmade." I push to stand. "I will pen a statement to our people, the kingdoms, and the High Council to be sent in the morning."

"And what of Luther?" asks Quinn.

"You are monarch. You must decide."

"I do not wish to be monarch. This is your kingdom, Titania. You should retake your crown."

"That is a question for all to consider. I do not want to lead a people who do not want me."

"Word has spread through the countryside that you saved our kingdom from Luther's army and of your victory over the dark angel," Grant says.

"Still, we should poll the advisors and seek guidance from the High Council as to the monarchy and Luther's fate." My hand quakes, and I press my palm to the worn wood. "I will go if it be acceptable to you, Quinn."

Isla races to me and wraps her arms around my waist. "Please, do not leave us again."

Tears flood my eyes, and I kiss her head. "Foster and others brought news of you."

I lift my hand to Gatuika as she approaches. "I am glad I will be here for your wedding."

"I promise neither Lowell nor I knew of Luther's plan." She glances from me to her fiancé.

Dropping to one knee, he kisses my palm. "I promise on my very life, I knew nothing of my brother's ideas."

"I believe you." I survey the group, overwhelmed by the love they show for me, guilt gnawing at my stomach. "This is not my home. I should go."

As Lowell rises, Isla leans into my side. "Please stay. Sleep with me tonight."

"This shall always be your home." Father's eyes cut to Quinn.

"You are most welcome here," Quinn says.

"You need rest." Alfreda wraps an arm around my waist. "I will gather you some clothes and bring them to Isla's room."

"I still have my big bed." Isla's arm replaces Alfreda's.

The group of us proceed down the now-dark corridor to the guest wing. Each of them offer sentiments of gladness for my return and say goodnight. In Isla's room, she and Makani help me wash and get into a gown. The fabric feels so soft on my skin it is as if a feather hugs my body. We lie in the bed, Isla to one side and Makani on the other, blankets pulled to our chins.

"Where were you?" Isla whispers.

"Shh. That is for tomorrow." Makani grips my hand.

I lie there looking at the ceiling, letting the weight of the day descend upon my limbs. *Oh, Goddesses, how to move forward without the one person I could not lose?* I cry into the pillow, my chest heaving sobs. Isla and Makani wrap their bodies around me, and somehow, sleep takes me.

***

WAKING TO A NEAR-DARK ROOM, I struggle to get my bearings. I look up at the stone ceiling above me, and the flood of memories from the previous day deluges my psyche. I cinch my eyes shut, willing the images to the form of a nightmare. Opening my lids again, the blocked ceiling remains. If I were in my cabin, perhaps I could pretend yesterday did not happen. I cut my eyes around the room. The shutters are drawn, and soft light glows from the fireplace.

My cousins ring the flames, talking in soft whispers.

"She will explain, and they will believe. There are many who witnessed yesterday's events and heard the words of the dark angel," Gatuika says.

"How will she recover after losing Foster?" Makani's eyes cut to me.

Ignoring the twitch in my side, I push up on one arm. "You and the Goddesses shall be my strength."

"Titania." Isla flits to me and squeezes my shoulders. "Thank you for not leaving again."

"As long as I draw breath, I shall remain with you." I kiss her forehead.

"Here is your breakfast." Makani lifts a tray from the table and crosses to me.

My stomach turns at the sight of the pastries. *What a wretch I am to be here when Foster is… I swallow. You cannot fall apart. There is much to be done.*

"I shall need pen and paper. Have we any news from Hilbron or the High Council?"

"I believe all await your statement. Quinn said he can speak with you as soon as you are ready." Makani sets the food in front of me.

Taking a deep breath, I force a bite into my mouth. The girls prompt me to take more. My middle aches after an amount that equals less than half my meal, and I move the tray to my side. It is odd. I feel I do not know what to do next. In my cabin, I would have already been dressed in the day's clothes because they were the same as my night-clothes. My next chore would be bringing in water. I look to the table where a fresh bowl sits.

"We had your trunks brought in." Isla flits to the corner.

Tears spring to my eyes. "You kept my trunks?"

"How could we bear to part with them?" Makani lifts a lid. "I believe riding pants and a vest will do nicely."

Standing, I hobble behind the screen and change into the clothes they hand me.

They open the shutters to a day half gone.

My heart issues a strange thud, but I push on. Parchment and pen sit on the table, and I start to craft my story. How Sonia brought monster after monster to our land, and the only way to stop her onslaught was to leave our realm. How the witches restored my soul to my body, and how I have been working with them to stop her reign of terror. How I could not stand by and let Luther and his army destroy peace in our kingdom, and how Luther's greed and deceit drew and powered Sonia. I explain that my magic expelled her from this realm, but she may come again.

I lift the sheet. "It may not be perfect, but it will give the answers needed. Have copies sent to the High Council, each kingdom, and each shire."

"Right away." Isla's smile widens as she curtsies.

"Do not do that. I will take it to the printers. Sorry, old habits still linger."

"But I want to be your helper. I never want to leave your side."

"We shall do it together, then." Standing, I grab my crutch and hook my arm in hers.

"Umm, Titania." Makani points to her head. "Perhaps I could fix your hair?"

Releasing Isla and crossing to the dressing table, I bend down to look into her mirror. My hair splays about in every direction. I take a seat, and Isla and Makani work on each side of my head, pulling the tangles and smoothing my locks. It is painstaking to sit there, doing nothing, as it leaves me time to think, a place I do not want to be in. I make a list in my mind of all I must do: talk with the advisors, generals, Quinn, Father, and the High Council. Finally, the girls fit my curls atop my head and pronounce they have finished.

"Now you look like a proper queen." Isla smiles.

"I am not a queen, merely your cousin." I squeeze her hand. "Let us go get this printed."

Upon exit, I find two guards flanking Isla's door. "Why are you here?"

"King Quinn sent us. We are at your service," one replies.

"I do not need guards."

"You may change your mind when you see the crowds gathered around the castle," the guard says.

"Crowds?"

"They await just outside the wall but for a glimpse of you," the guard says.

My brain spins. I have hoped to pen my bulletin and go about checking the items off my list. Addressing throngs of people had not been on my agenda.

Makani clutches my arm. "You do not have the outfit for addressing your people. You need a gown."

I cannot address them without more answers. I hold the page out to the guards. "Have this printed and posted."

Turning, I march toward the study and find Quinn and Father there.

"Throngs of fae await a statement." I cross my arms over my chest.

"Await *your* statement. There are many rumors." Quinn stands.

"You are King, you must address them."

"Perhaps we should address them together," Quinn says.

"What more is there to tell? I am posting my statement for all to read. Their lives will go on, unchanged."

Quinn crosses his arms over his chest. "They want you as their leader. They have heard what happened yesterday and feel that you can safeguard them better than any other."

"I am not here to take your place. Honestly, I would love to go back to my cabin in the wood." *And sit there and stare at the fire, never leaving that hearth again, the place where I lay with Foster, curled into him. But I could just feel his warmth one more time. He is there. In my cabin. The cabin I could return to if not for the four cousins before me.*

"We are beyond that point." Father hobbles toward me. "Titania, your people want you and they need you, and Quinn wants nothing other than to be with his bride and child when it is born."

I look to Quinn. "And you have no reservations? You truly wish to have your simple life back?"

"It is probably hard for you to understand. You were raised to rule. I have never wanted this. I do so to honor you and your father and will be most happy to relinquish my post."

"I need assurances from the advisors, the generals, the High Council, and all the other monarchs that they honor my position. I will not fight for it again."

As the day lingers on, my statement is posted and sent, and I meet with all groups: the advisors, generals, and judges of our kingdom. Quinn repeats his wish to resign to all, and I admit to myself if I cannot be in my cabin in front of the fire dreaming of Foster's arms around me, I need the weight that will come with the title. *What would I be without it? What would I do except grieve for my betrothed?* I am not sure I could survive without a post, but I will not force myself upon them. I wish to give them time to think, ponder, and perhaps await what may come from the High Council. It is not be assured they will find me suitable to rule.

As we conclude the last meeting, Grant approaches. "Something must be done about those gathered around the castle. Their numbers grow by the minute, and the road through the shire is filled. Some have come from very far, and night will fall in a few hours. You must go to them."

"What am I to say that I have not already said?" I clutch my throat, nerves pricking, at the thought of facing my people after my horrid deception.

"They want to see you in the flesh, be assured you are not some figment of the imagination."

And my people are not the only ones to deserve amends. I must speak with my family and those closest to me, ones I need to make personal amends to, but Grant is right, I cannot leave my fae standing there as darkness falls.

"I am guessing a wave from the castle will not be enough."

"No, it will not."

"Will you come with me?"

"I will bring Adam, Nicholas, and Timothy, too."

I clutch his arm. "Find others. They mourn their friend."

He holds my gaze. "And what of your mourning?"

"My mourning must wait. I cannot even… It is too much." Chest cinching into my lungs, I release him. "I owe you an apology for my absence and trickery."

"Adam said he, Nicholas, and Timothy helped you these past months."

Guilt spreading through my nerves like weighted sandbags, I lower my head. "Yes, but I could not risk involving you. As Fae at Arms, you needed to be untouchable if scandal erupted."

"I grieved your loss, but I do not slight you for your actions. You were trying to protect your people. Everyone will understand that."

"I pray they do."

He dips his chin. "Wait here. I will get some guards to accompany us to greet your people."

Quinn exits the study with Father.

My heart thuds irregularly. The heartbreak at the pain I caused my cousins, Father, and Alfreda reopens like an old sinkhole in my chest.

"I am to see the people waiting outside the castle. Will you join me?"

Quinn shakes his head. "They wish to see you, Titania, and I have not seen my wife all day. We will join you for dinner."

I look to Father, hoping for some reassurance that I have not ruined everything. "And you, Father?"

"I should rest before dinner. We will see you there."

Standing alone, looking out the window at the crowds of fae lining the street, I wring my hands. *What if they wish to throw tomatoes or worse?* I would be most angry at a queen who faked her death and had people mourn her only to reappear months later. I would not want her as leader of anything. *Except that you prevented a battle that could have cost many lives.*

Two guards and Grant escort me from the castle. Walking beside him, fists balled at my sides, my breaths become shallow as noise from the crowd grows. I bat my eyelashes, quelling the tears that come with my next thought. *You are okay, and you are in control.* Foster's words play through my mind. I am not really okay. I have never been and never will be okay. Control is a farce, a state of mind created to help us feel safe. My lungs seize. I force a breath out. *You are always in danger. That is a constant. That is your control.*

Where these oddly calming thoughts come from, I do not know. Releasing my fingers, I imagine it is Foster beside me, the eternal voice of calm and reason.

As we approach the first line, I raise my chin. *What can I say save I am sorry? I did not mean for the story to unfold this way. I will do better.*

"Titania." A young girl runs toward me. "My doll is named after you. See? I sewed stones on her forehead."

"So sorry, Highness." A woman wraps her arm around the child. "We are so excited to see you well."

Tears welling in my lids, I clutch her arm. "It is I who am privileged to see you."

Fae hold out their hands to squeeze mine as the crowd parts, and we weave through the throngs. My heart bursts with joy at each touch, and the part of my soul that has ached for my people these past months overflowers with the love I sense. Water overflows my lids, and I do not stop it.

These are my people. These are my breath, my heartbeat, my life.

It is almost dark when we reach the town square, and fae still stretch as far as the eye can see.

I jump up atop the well. "Fae of Aubren, your compassion truly blesses me. You have read my statement and now know my truth. I am sorry to have left you in that manner. For as long as I hold breath, I will never abandon you again. I pray you forgive me. We should all pray to the Goddesses for strength to face what may come, but I know, if we are united, we shall prevail."

"All hail Queen Titania." The cheers go up again and again.

I raise my hand, calling for quiet. "I bid you goodnight. Please, return to your homes, hug your families, and hold those close that are dear. Blessed be."

"Blessed be," the crowd echoes.

I jump to the cobblestone and, flanked by Grant, greet each fae we pass. Many take to the air, and the streets empty. With blessings from so many, it is dark by the time we reach the castle.

"I believe I have missed dinner," I say.

"You missed a lot of things." Grant nudges my arm, but his face holds no smile.

Tears flood my eyes anew. "I am sorry, I—"

He slaps his leg. "I jest. You are too serious. I am just glad to know how Adam and the others survived your loss. They seemed too okay with it. I could not understand how. My wife says I did not smile all rainy season."

"Again, I am sorry." I lift my skirt as we climb the castle steps.

"Go be with your family. They have much to be grateful for this night."

"As do I." I kiss his cheek. "Thank you for safeguarding my kingdom."

He bows. "I will serve you until my dying breath."

I breach the castle doors to find Alfreda running down the hall. "There you are! Goddesses be, child, you must tell me when you go out. You have missed dinner. Your family gathers in your parents' chamber."

Linking my arm in hers, I take the plate of food. "Thank you for this. Please join us."

She kisses my cheek. "I would not have it any other way."

I lean my head on her shoulder. "I am very sorry for leaving you. I hope you know that I would never have done that if it were not required. I was trying to keep everyone safe."

She kisses my temple. "I know, dearie. You do not owe me an apology. I am just glad you are back safe."

Spinning, I take her hand. "Thank you, Alfreda. Thank you so much for taking care of my family. I do not know what I would do without you."

We weave to my parents' chamber where I find Makani playing the harp. They ask me to play as she ends her tune, and I sit in front of the fire as I have so many times before. My heart fills with gladness at seeing how our family has grown with the addition of my cousins, Quinn, and Abeetha and their daughter. I pray they brought my parents joy these last months.

As they say goodnight, I wait beside Mother to speak with her and Father. He hobbles toward us, and I note his labored breath and slow gait. Even with the complications it brings, I am glad to be back.

Home.

Father clutches the arms of the chair and rests upon the cushion. "It is good to have you back."

"It is good to be back." I grip his hand and take Mother's.

Since her gaze stays trained on the flames, I look to him. "I owe you a huge apology. I could not alert you to my plan. You could not know that I lived. If something happened and a scandal ensued, you needed to be removed from the information. I could not risk any of my family knowing the truth."

Father pats my hand. "I know, dear. You would not hurt us on purpose."

Water forms in my lids. "But I have hurt you, and I am very sorry."

His eyes cut to Mother. "Her fits were terrible."

"I heard from"—I swallow, not wanting to say Foster's name—"my guards. In my dreams, we saw each other many times. There is much to tell, and I will tell you all."

Chapter

17

I HOLD FATHER'S GAZE. I *will* share everything, but not today. Too many of my fondest memories of Foster are held in the past months, and I cannot open that box. I suck in a breath and gather the courage to look forward.

"I will rise to monarch again if the fae of this kingdom and the High Council affirm they wish me to rule. But what of Hilbron? Who will run their kingdom and take their spot on the High Council? King Luther cannot be allowed to serve. Is there anyone in their family we would trust?"

"You are right. Fae do not attack without provocation. Luther proved he is not worthy, and I do not trust Brandon or Holden. Lowell will be implicated as well."

"I am not sure we can know whether or not any of his brothers knew and did not stop him or whether Luther did not share his plans with them. It seems like there must have been someone, or multiple generals or advisors, backing him. Sonia said they had fueled her power for some time. Gatuika assured me that Lowell was unaware. He pledged such himself, but I have not been here. Do you believe Lowell to be trustworthy?"

"I have not seen anything that makes me distrust him."

I rise and pace to the far wall. "So, Lowell could rule in Luther's place?"

"I would not be surprised if the High Council ships them all to exile in Willhelm."

"We can speak as to Lowell's character. I would think that Holden's in-laws in Lindleton would do the same for him."

"But could we? Do we know beyond any doubt that Lowell had no knowledge of Luther's plans?"

"Luther opposed my rule from the beginning. That is not a secret. I guess we cannot know Lowell's involvement fully. Brandon attempted to woo me. Foster…" I steel my breath at how easily his name passes my lips. As if he is still here. "Foster overheard that Luther hoped to have Brandon marry me, thinking I would meet an untimely death."

Father strokes his beard. "It is too bad Foster is not here to witness to such."

My rib cage tightens as tears fill my eyes.

Father dips his head. "I am sorry. That was callus. The words slipped my lips before I realized what I was saying."

"No." Clenching my hands together, I straighten my back. "I must accept that he is gone." I bat my eyes, shake my head, bite my tongue, and look to the ceiling, trying to stave off the onslaught of tears. I swipe the water from my cheeks and cross to Father.

"You cared deeply for him."

Sitting on the hearth before him, I nod. "We were to be married, had just pledged so not minutes before Luther's troops arrived."

"I am so sorry." He leans forward and wraps his arms around me.

Half of me wants to stay in Father's arms forever, cry until I have no more tears, but I wriggle from his embrace. "There is much to do. We must send directions to every judge in each region."

"All your fae adore you. You will be monarch again."

I raise my chin. "The judge of the southern ring holds no love for me, and we do not know how the other monarchs will react."

"What other fae would go to such lengths for his or her people?"

"I would expect any monarch would."

Father shifts to the edge of his seat. "Luther proved he would not. He risked many lives attempting to take Aubren."

I rise. "I guess you are right. I should sleep. There will likely be news from the High Council in the morning, and the judges will poll the people of their regions. It will be a long day."

"The first ever election in Middle Earth."

My lungs fill, and I release the breath "It must be their choice."

He stands and places his hand on my shoulder. "You are a good leader. All will see that."

"It is with the Goddesses."

"You are worried. About what?" Father asks.

"If Luther would risk his army, what else is he capable of? He has already tried to have me removed once. What if he accuses me of being in league with the dark souls, paints me also as being an evil sorceress? Holden knew of my magic, knows that is how I got out of Lower Earth when the dark angels tried to trap me and that I used it to kill the locusts. Not all may be so inclined to believe that I have been granted these powers by the Goddesses. Many will fear them."

"You risked much exposing yourself, but you have many friends who know your heart. They will witness to your virtue."

"I pray it is so. I may be exiled to Willhelm along with Luther, but for now, I should sleep." Kissing Father's cheek and hugging Mother, I exit their chambers.

Grant and Foster's father, Matthew, flanked by two guards, stand in the hallway. I look from one fae to the other. "What is wrong?"

"Nothing, we hope." Grant's eyes cut to Matthew. "Foster's father has something to share with you."

Matthew shifts his weight from one foot to the other. His wings twitch on his back. "I do not pretend to know the gravity of your situation. I would guess there is much uncertainty."

"Yes, that is true." My side stiches as I look into eyes that so resemble Foster's.

"Before you … left, I guess, he told me that if anything ever happened to him, I was to give them to you, and that if I could not, to give them to Grant. He also said you would need a witness, someone from the High Council, and a judge."

Sweat forms in my palms. "Give me what?"

"Foster's journals. Every piece of information he learned, he wrote down in ledgers. They are in a locked box in our cellar." Sliding a hand in his pocket, he produces a key.

My eyes fill with water. Even in death, Foster watches over me. I blink my eyes and squeeze Matthew's arm. "Thank you for bringing this to us. Keep the key safe. Grant will provide you with guards for the night. We will have a High Council member and judge sent to your farm in the morning."

Grant gives orders to the guards to escort Matthew home. My heart weighs heavy watching Foster's father walk away. If it weren't for me, Foster would still be alive. My side twitches, and I cross my arms over my middle.

Grant lays a hand on my shoulder. "All will be well. Foster watched King Luther and his family closely. The journals will likely prove his vendetta against you."

I release a breath. "Even if they believe Luther acted treacherously, what they do with me, now that all know I possess powers other fae do not, is a separate issue."

"I guess it is so. You should try to get some rest." He pats my arm.

"Yes. You as well. Goodnight."

"Goodnight."

I beat my wings in slow, rhythmic waves, floating through the empty halls. It feels as if I am in a dream to be back in my home again. My heartbeats come fast, and I slow my breaths, willing the pain away. *How can I hold such joy yet such fear and heartache at the same time? Will all this be ripped away once more? What grief awaits me when the High Council delivers its ruling?*

You are strong. You are in control. I alight in front of my cousins' door. Turning the knob, I find Isla and Makani snuggled together, their breaths matched in slumber. I slide off my riding pants and into a nightgown, and then get into bed beside Isla. I stare at the stone ceiling and think of the timber planks of my cabin and how I used to watch Foster drift to sleep. Tears come, and I do not fight them. They are the only way I will heal.

—◆◆◆—

I TIPTOE FROM ISLA'S ROOM before first light. Two guards wait in the hall.

Motioning them down the passageway, I learn that a High Council representative and Regin, the keeper of the southern Nariel Ring, and as such, one who also serves as a judge, will travel to Foster's home this morning to retrieve the journals. With this development, the High Council postponed the tribunal meant to assess King Luther's actions and my return.

"And all our judges received instructions as to polling the members of their regions, correct?"

"Yes. They all have the ballots."

"Good." I clasp my hands at my center, wondering how I will fill my time this day. Drawing in a long breath, I stride through the halls to the king's study. I find pastries and fruits already set out for breakfast and Quinn at the end of the table, hovering over an accounting sheet.

"Cousin, you are up early," I say.

"I am up early every day, but this day, I hope to relinquish all of this to you. Come, see the state of your kingdom."

"You are getting ahead of yourself. Our countrymen will vote, and tomorrow, the High Council holds their tribunal. Even if our kingdom counts me worthy, the judges and other monarchs may not accept me. We have no responses from the correspondence I sent to each royal family." Taking a plate, I choose a pastry and some strawberries.

"I am sure everyone is in shock. Most of all Mikel and your other suitors. Many are thought to announce engagements soon. It is rumored Mikel will choose a princess from Borean."

My side pangs again, and I fit my fingers over my ribs. *What does Mikel think? Will I be made to honor my marriage contract?* I think back to winter solstice, the last holiday I spent with my family, and Mabon when I attended Holden's wedding. Who could have foreseen that I would have been so close to everything I had always wanted, an engagement to the man I truly loved, and a treaty between long-estranged clans sealed, a crusade fulfilled. My mind jumps to thoughts of Upper Earth.

Did the witches give Sonia Lilith? Did Sonia laugh in their faces as well? Do they feel as used as I do? Used by whom, I am not sure. They could blame DJ and me for time wasted, but who am I to blame? We knew our mission may not yield the results we wanted. Perhaps I feel anger. Anger at who or what, I am not sure. I am as much to blame as anyone. I dig my fingernails into my palms. I pray Alena,

Camille, and Hunter will have better luck in their quest to find Thanatos.

Quinn leans forward. "Are you still with me? I hear Prince Mikel did not fly for months following your death, or supposed death."

"I have much to make amends for." I release a breath as my side ticks. "I owe him, especially, an apology. Perhaps my time is best spent making amends today."

"A personal visit and explanation may go a long way in showing the other monarchs that you recognize what a grievous act you committed."

His words cut into my very soul. *Grievous act.* Tears flood my eyes. "I cannot apologize to you enough. I truly hated what I had to do. Yes, I could have stayed dead. Perhaps it was selfish to ask the witches to preserve me, but every part of my being told me that my purpose had not been fulfilled."

Pushing the ledger away, he takes my hand. "If you had not been there when King Luther came with his threats to our kingdom, there would have been much bloodshed. How would we have defended ourselves against an evil archangel? What is to say Luther would have stopped with Aubren? With her backing, he could take any kingdom he wished. Bedham has but fifty soldiers. They could not defend themselves."

I hold his gaze. "Yet still you call my pretend death a grievous act."

"Yes. It was. The pain I felt for your loss was like none I have felt before. You are like a sister to me. Yet, I am grateful you were courageous enough to save us from Luther and the dark angel. It was a huge risk. I acknowledge that. We yet do not know the ramifications of your actions, but if it were up to me, I would choose you above anyone, any day. That is why I propose we visit the monarchs together. If they see I hold no grievances, it will further convince them to accept you."

I grip his other hand. "You will do this for me, cousin? If so, I will forever be in your debt. Without this post, I have nothing."

"Of course I will do this for you, but please, do not speak of having nothing. I am here, as are your parents, your cousins, and Alfreda. They need you as well."

Looking to the tabletop, I whisper to him that Foster and I were to be married. "So, you see, he was to be my everything. When I say I have nothing, I do not mean to discount the love of my family, but you, of all people, know that when you find that one special person, losing them would be the worst thing that could ever happen."

He squeezes my fingers. "I understand, cousin, and I am here for you."

Wriggling my hands from his, I stand. "We should prepare to travel. We have seven kingdoms to visit this day."

"Seven kingdoms? Can we come?" Isla flits to my side followed by Makani.

Biting my lip, I look between the girls. "I am not sure. What do you think, Quinn?"

"I would think the bigger your party the better. Perhaps our first stop should be Bedham. If King Herman and your father could make the journey, it would be most helpful."

I stand and cross to the fire. "But if sentiments be against me, then they also will be viewed in a negative light. If Father can come, that would be helpful. I do not want to make problems for others."

Makani crosses to me. "I think Isla and I would make excellent traveling companions. The whole realm already knows of our ties to you."

Thinking of my cousins' gifts of magic, I am almost swayed. "We should ask King Herman and your parents. They must agree."

"Who must agree?" Mother on his arm, Father hobbles into the room.

"Quinn and I are thinking about visiting each kingdom today. Isla and Makani wish to come."

"I think it is a good plan for you to visit the ruling families, especially those of Lindleton. King Hector sent the troops promised, and I hear Mikel especially grieved your loss."

Mikel, the prince I accepted a marriage contract to even though I held no more love for him than any of my other suitors, that I pledged to wed although I knew it would never happen. Guilt eats at my stomach, and fear lingers in the back of my mind. *Will he force me to uphold our marriage contract?*

We send advance messages to each kingdom, and I send one to Alemayehu and Yonas, thinking they may help us create alliances with their monarch. I thought Alemayehu would send news as to his conversation with the witches and whether Sonia visited them. I pray Sonia's heart changed when she realized she may truly be reconnected with her mother. Or that maybe Lilith is one part of Sonia's desire for reconciliation, even if not all. Of course, if she holds the ire she reports for her mother, burning the bones may give her some satisfaction. For the vampires' sake, I hope Sonia refused their offering and left Lilith's remains intact. They deserve that much for their willingness to sacrifice one who represented so much for them.

Quinn, Father, and I debate including Gatuika and Lowell on the visits. We wonder if bringing two of my cousins without the third will raise questions. In addition, their presence could detract from my goal of making amends with the ruling families. In the end, we decide the three should travel with us to Bedham to see their family but not farther.

Father agrees to accompany us to Bedham, and we meet in the courtyard. The flight to Bedham is brief, and minutes later, we land to bugles blaring in front of King Herman's castle.

His whole family stands in a line to greet us.

Isla and Makani run to their mother, and Gatuika and Lowell follow behind.

"Titania." Queen Natasha approaches with tears in her eyes and wraps her arms around me. "We are so happy you are safe. I know this brings your family much joy."

"It is good to be home. Thank you."

King Herman eyes me sideways. "My most flamboyant niece. Only you could stage your own death and then return with such flair. Well done with the archangel. That is a first for this realm."

I dip my chin then hold his gaze. "Thank you. I could not stand by and let hundreds die. I do pray you will forgive my deceit. My only intent was the safety of our fae and this realm."

Looking between Herman and Natasha, I hold my breath. My uncle should be the most likely to welcome me back to the circle of monarchs.

He extends his arm. "Welcome back, Titania."

I wrap my palm around his forearm. "Thank you, Uncle."

"Come, enjoy breakfast with us." Herman motions to his castle.

"We could have some tea." I explain my goal of visiting each kingdom this day.

Aunt Cassia approaches, and I relish her embrace. My mother's sister shares so many traits with my mother, I feel as if in hugging Cassia, I hug a piece of mother's spirit, too.

Enjoying a quick cup of tea, Quinn and I bid farewell to Father and my cousins. I focus on the wind, gusts, pockets of cool and warm air, anything to divert my thoughts from what our welcome will be in other kingdoms. As we near Chastam's capital, my angst grows. We spiral down to the palace where but four fae stand. Landing, I realize King Shen and Prince Minyu, flanked by two guards, have chosen to meet us.

"King Shen." I curtsey. "Thank you for welcoming us."

"Yes, thank you for seeing us on such short notice." Quinn dips his chin to each.

"Your family have always been friends to us. We treasure the support your kingdom provides when needed," King Shen says.

"As have we." I look between the men. "I wanted to ask your forgiveness for my disappearance. It was not how I would have wished it."

King Shen crosses his arms over his chest. "I would guess that your re-entry into fae life was not as you wished either."

"No, it was not. I would have not returned and caused such upheaval if not to save the soldiers of our kingdoms."

"We do not fault either decision. We will continue to call you friend."

"Thank you." I offer my arm.

King Shen then Minyu lock their palms around my forearm one after the other, and the tightness in my chest lightens a smidge.

With a wish for the Goddesses' blessings, we take flight. Heading west, we dip below the dense canopy to Rotuga's capital. Alemayehu and Yonas stand beside their king. Like Shen and Minyu, the monarch welcomes us with forgiveness and friendship. Studying Alemayehu, I hope to see some flicker of communication as to news of Sonia, but I find none. I tuck away my thought to find a way to speak with him in private soon.

My hope for acceptance by the monarchs of the realm grows further with a warm greeting from King Philipe of Elita, but as Quinn and I head north, my side ticks again as I remember the little respect offered from King Joseph of Borean.

"You should let me speak first to King Joseph," Quinn says as we swoop toward the castle.

"He never liked me."

"Tradition is a double-edged sword. The princes speak well of you."

"I will follow your lead."

"Whatever you do, do not argue. Give your apology, ask for forgiveness, and leave it at that."

King Joseph is flanked by Prince James and Prince Maxwell, and we alight before them.

Quinn dips his chin, and I curtsey.

"Thank you for alerting us to your visit. It seems your kingdom is again entrenched in mayhem," King Joseph says.

Quinn nods. "Yesterday was indeed a day of great sadness as well as joy. As you have heard, King Luther marched on our castle with his full army, ready to take our kingdom by force. Through his greed, he drew an evil angel to this realm, but Titania drove her away."

My mind spins with frustration as Quinn so diplomatically describes the events of the past day. I look to James then Maxwell, but their gazes are fixed on Joseph.

"How do we know she is not a witch herself?" King Joseph crosses his arms over his chest.

"I have known Titania all my life. I remember her birth, her first flight."

"Her mother is a witch as well. Rumors are she is a seer and prophesied the beasts that beset your kingdom."

His words surprise me and cause alarm. *I guess all kingdoms use their spies well, but a witch? Really? Give your apology,* I repeat to myself.

"My only wish for today was to express my sorrow for having deceived this realm. This dark angel targeted me and our kingdom. The only way to stop her attacks was to leave."

"If you draw such danger, you should leave this realm for good. Your kingdom needed stable leadership. King Luther could have provided that."

I raise my chin. "My cousin has provided excellent leadership in my absence. I am fae, and I intend to remain fae. King Luther proved that he does not honor our fae values."

"You think your sins lesser than Luther's? The High Council will decide your fate on the morrow. I, for one, will not support you rejoining our ranks if that is your aim."

His words sting. *Are there lesser and greater sins in the eyes of the Goddesses? Of the Creator?* I will make no progress with this man.

"I again apologize for my deception." Dipping my chin, I step back.

Quinn offers his arm. King Joseph wraps his hand around Quinn's forearm as do James and Maxwell. I study them, trying to decipher their feelings, but the princes' opinions will not matter tomorrow. All I can wish for is that more monarchs and judges support me than do not.

We cross the ocean to Lindleton and head south to the capitol. I think of Foster and his opinions of the royals of this kingdom. I can imagine him wondering why I would stoop to ask for pardon from the arrogant ruler. When we hear the bugle, my stomach tightens and palms warm. No matter my opinion, as the monarch of the most populous kingdom in the realm, it would be good to have King Hector's favor.

Two fae stand at the base of the castle stairs when we land, Hector and a guard.

I bow low and raise my chin to meet his gaze. "Thank you for seeing us."

"You are wasting your breath pedaling your apologies here," Hector says.

"I wished to extend my regret to Mikel in person if he is available."

"Mikel counts himself lucky not to be saddled with a marriage to a lying, lecherous witch. He does not need or want your apologies."

Hector snaps his heels together, spins, and marches up the castle steps.

I am greeted with much the same disdain by Ivan of Willhelm. This surprises me as I felt his family held me, and my family, in high esteem prior to my faked death. I did turn down his son's engagement offer, so I cannot guess if that colored his view.

We set our course for home, me feeling downtrodden and dejected. *How could such good intentions be so poorly rewarded? But could I expect more after my treachery?*

My wings and back ache by the time we alight in the courtyard lit with torches as the midnight hour draws near.

"I feel I will need to sleep a whole day." Quinn opens the door for me.

"I too, cousin."

"The last three visits were not as we hoped, but of seven, four kingdoms offer support. With Hilbron's royal family unable to lend their opinion, that is over half."

"Titania, Quinn!" Isla, Makani, and Gatuika speed toward us. "Look at all these scrolls. They are all notice of the election."

Holding out a roll, Gatuika clutches my arm. "And this is from Alemayehu."

"Thank you." I hug each of them. "Give me a minute, and we will convene in the study to count the votes."

Taking the letter, I stride away from the group. I lean against the wall and loose the ribbon.

Seeing one smooth, white sheet with DJ's chicken-scratch handwriting, I fold the page under the other. Alemayehu will have told them what happened with Sonia but also of Foster. I am not ready to read words of comfort from my friend. I read Alemayehu's message.

T,

I wish to relay news from Hunter. They have not had contact with Sonia. They are protecting Lilith's body until the solstice when many will gather on the island of Sardinia. That night, they will call to Sonia and beseech her to reconcile with her mother. Their numbers will protect them.

Blessings,

A

Biting my lip, I flip to the first page.

T-
I am so sorry about Foster. I know
he meant a lot to you. My heart
breaks for you, and I pray to the
Goddesses to mend yours.
I hope to see you soon.
DJ

Perhaps I will go to Sardinia on the solstice after Gatuika's wedding. Goddesses know that I do not wish to be reminded of the one whose absence I mourn most at a wedding feast. I fold the pages and slide them into my pocket. That is a decision for another day. Tonight, I shall know the hearts of my people, whether they hold me with contempt or love.

Chapter 18

I wind to Isla's room, tucking the correspondence in my chest and dousing my face with water. Glancing at the quilted bed, half of me wishes to sink into the down mattress and sleep forever, but I strip my clothes and wipe my skin with a wet cloth. My wings protest as I slide into a clean shirt and vest, and then pull on a riding skirt.

In the study, I find a larger crowd than expected. The advisors line one side of the table, and Quinn sits at the end. The smell of mint invigorates my senses, and I draw in a deep breath.

Alfreda pours tea into cups and loads them onto a tray.

I take one as I pass her, refusing bread and cheese and then cross to the table, finding my cousins sliding ties from the scrolls and laying them out flat.

Quinn marks each on a page in his ledger entitled "First Election of the Kingdom of Aubren."

"I do not see why it needs to be done like this. Just read each one as you open them," Isla says.

"Each region must be accounted for." Gatuika grabs Isla's hand as she attempts to steal a page.

After addressing each of the advisors, I take a seat beside Quinn. I sip the tea, and it settles my churning stomach. Once Gatuika has all the regions' tallies accounted for, she begins reading the counts from the first region of Nariel out loud.

"Yay, one hundred twenty-four, nay, two." She passes the sheet to the First Advisor.

He hands the sheet to his right, and each of the advisors inspect the document. They approve the count, and Quinn records it. This proceeds for each of the twenty regions. With each tally, my heart swells. Less than a handful from each region vote against me.

"Nariel region," Gatuika announces.

I lock my hands in my lap. Regin oversees his ring's region, and in the beginning, he objected to my rule. I hold my breath, for we decided that if but one region have a majority vote for nay, I will not rule. The door opens, and I cut my eyes to it.

Father shuffles into the room. "Who decided not to summon me? I saw the lights from my window when I woke."

Quinn rises. "Sorry, Oberon. It was after midnight when we convened. We felt this should be attended to before the High Council tribunal tomorrow. The High Council may want to know the wishes of our subjects."

"The High Council should know how our fae side on this issue, given it is them who are most affected." Squeezing my shoulder, Father takes the seat next to me and peers at the ledger. "How are you fairing?"

"We have recorded all but the last three regions." Gatuika lifts the page. "The Nariel region, fifty-six, yay, forty-eight, nay."

I press my palms together as Gatuika passes the sheet to the first advisor. Nariel region fae tend to side with Regin more often than not, and if even a majority of these fae want me to rule, then most assuredly the other regions will vote the same.

As Gatuika reads the last two ballot results and they are recorded, we find indeed that the fae of this kingdom wish me reinstated as monarch.

Quinn stands and offers his arm. "Congratulations."

Rising, I wrap my palm around his forearm. "Thank you, cousin. We will see how the High Council rules tomorrow."

Father congratulates me with the greeting of a warrior, and the girls hug me. The advisors file up, one by one, to give praises and well wishes for the tribunal. As the room empties, Alfreda scurries around picking up cups and plates. I help, transferring dishes from the table to her cart.

"I am very happy for you." She kisses my cheek. "Do not bother with these chores. You need rest for tomorrow."

"I fear I shall not sleep a wink."

"Should I draw you a lavender bath?"

"That would be nice. Is there a free chamber? I do not wish to disturb my cousins."

"You may bathe in mine."

"Thank you." I wrap my arms around her. "For so much."

"It is so good to have you home. Promise you will never leave again."

"Not while I still draw breath." I cinch my eyes shut, praying to the Goddesses that I do not have to break this promise.

<hr>

ALFREDA WAKES ME EARLY from the small cot in her room. "Goddesses be. What are you doing here? I looked all over and come back to find you right where I started from."

I push up on one elbow. "Sorry, Alfreda. I was too tired after my bath to go any farther."

"Everyone is gathering for breakfast before the tribunal." She lays a formal, green gown with a high neck and long sleeves on her bed. "You should wear your best today. I will have someone come to weave your hair up pretty."

Within minutes, I sit with a maiden brushing out my strands, winding them into curls, and fixing them on top of my head. She forms ringlets down the side and holds up a hand mirror for me to inspect her work.

"It is beautiful. Thank you."

Rising, I adjust my collar. It feels stiff on my neck after the summer in my loose tops and trousers. I stroll through the dimly lit passages of the early morning to the study. My family and advisors are gathered with bread, cheeses, and fruits adorning their plates. I think of my garden and animals, of Messie, who returned to an empty cabin. I swallow as memories of my meals with Foster surface. I must ask Nicholas or Timothy to retrieve my animals for me.

Alfreda hands me a loaded plate, and I force half down, one bite after the other, knowing it will be a long day. I pack the rest in my pouch for later, and we convene in the courtyard. Our party grows large as the Ring Keepers join us. I thump my fist to my chest, reminding myself we are all fae, all hope to serve our people and fulfill our destiny in the Creator's universe. In the words of Upper Earth: We are all on the same team.

I survey the group, and seeing Lowell lean down and kiss Gatuika, my lungs clench. But to have one more kiss, one more breath, one more day with Foster. I lift my chin. All I can do now is honor him with each breath, each heartbeat, each moment.

Bidding goodbye to Mother, Alfreda, and my cousins, my party takes to the air with Grant, Adam, Timothy, and Nicholas at our sides. We head east over the forest where my cabin stands hidden below the tree canopy. It feels eerie to retrace the route taken just over a year ago when I stood trial for letting the witches pass through our realm. Now, the High Council judges may divulge that they supported my efforts with the witches in previous instances. Alemayehu and his sons may be forced to admit their knowledge of my status and relationship with the trinity and their heralds.

I plan to answer all questions asked of me. Only one causes me grief. *Are there any others like me? Could I, with good conscience, answer no?* My cousins' powers are not like mine, after all. They bend sound, wind, and water, and they cannot blast streams of energy from their palms. It is not, in entirety, the same.

We cross Hilbron's border, and we fly over the desert, descending to the ringed amphitheater. A chill washes over me as I alight on the hard stone, still cold from the night. I eye the high arch, recalling how Luther attempted to prevent Holden from seeing me, and we met in the village by the sea. How Quinn helped distract me while we waited for a verdict. I find it ironic how the council sent Zekiel to watch me as part of their probation sentence and ensure I did not consort with the witches. Now, Zekiel stands as our biggest supporter in our efforts with the witches to neutralize Sonia.

I survey the arena, the white and red uniforms of the council, the flags of each kingdom, the buzz of conversation, the cold stone benches, and the bright rising sun. Each stimulus pricks my nerves, and bumps form on my skin. My breaths come short and shallow. The largest unknown hangs heavy on my mind. *Will they accept one with powers they do not understand?* I dig my nails into my palms hoping to stave off the impending panic.

Warm fingers grip my shoulders. "You are shaking."

Shuddering, I fight the urge to jerk away from Quinn's touch. I straighten my back, summoning my courage. "I will be okay."

"Take my cloak." He slides the garment from his back and wraps it around mine.

"Thank you, cousin."

As Adam hoists the flag of Aubren in the air, I take my place behind Quinn and the judges.

We descend into the arena, sitting in front of the High Council.

Father takes my hand as he sits beside me. "I am glad to be with you today."

"I am grateful you are here." I squeeze his fingers.

Beyond Father and Lowell, Adam winks at me. I cannot let these fae down. I will not. If the council does not bless my reign, I will continue my efforts with the witches. We will figure out how to eradicate Sonia from the Earth realms, or at the very least lock her soul away for all eternity.

"Blessed be."

I raise my eyes to see Zekiel standing, palms out, opening the tribunal with the ritual phrase.

"Blessed be," the crowd repeats.

The low rumble of deep voices echoes through the chambers. Just as before, I am the only female fae in the structure. I think of the human witch and werewolf trials and pray I will not be burned on a stake. I could think of many more pleasant ways to die. Perhaps it would be fine to pass from this life. I would see Foster again.

What thoughts arise in my psyche? I rebuke the path.

Zekiel reads King Luther's charges of treason, sedition, and unprovoked threat of war and occupation. Zekiel turns to me, and I think I note his eyes soften.

"Titania, former Queen of Aubren, you are charged with ignoring a decree of this council and deception unbefitting a fae."

Quinn leans in. "Ignoring that holds promise, and did he just say deception unbefitting a fae?"

I raise my chin and lock my hands together. If they exile me to Willhelm, I will accept my fate. Foster's death already sealed that I might never truly be happy again.

My heart issues an odd thud, and my breath catches.

This will not serve your fae. Mother's voice sounds in my head as if she sits right next to me.

I will join the witches.

This will not serve your fae.

I glance to each side, thinking I will see Mother. *The Goddesses direct their paths.*

Blessed be. Mother's voice whisps away like a down feather swept by a gale.

Father pats my hand. "These are not bad charges, a slap on the wrist at most. The council ignored their own edict in signing the treaty."

They call King Luther to witness, and he descends to the middle, sitting opposite the High Judges. They ask him many questions about his motives for threatening war against my kingdom. His answers do not veer. Yes, he acted alone, commanding the army as is his right as king. No, he does not think he did anything wrong. He proposes Aubren has been poorly run since I ascended to the throne, and the only solution is to combine the king-doms, restore Primus under his leadership. That I pulled such as stunt as to fake my death proves his words.

What happened to the man who dropped to his knees two days ago and begged the Goddesses for forgiveness?

"He is mad. He has eaten some poison berries," Quinn whispers under his breath.

Zekiel lifts his hand. "King Quinn, can you testify as to the state of your kingdom?"

Quinn stands. "Yes. I have seen no faulty leadership. Our kingdom flourishes, even with the challenges we have faced. Before her departure, Titania prepared for the rainy season, assured livestock and harvests were enough, and restored the farms damaged by the ogres that ransacked our land. The people are happy and have just voted to re-instate Titania as monarch."

Rumbles of conversation grow throughout the arena.

Luther jumps to his feet. "Who ordered a vote? She is charged by this tribunal. She is not fit to rule."

"I ordered the vote. I love my people and was happy to serve them, but this post is not my calling. She is the rightful heir, and further, she is who her people want to lead them."

"This council must rule first!" Luther bellows.

"Titania and I recognize and will honor any decisions of this council."

Leaning on a cane, Zekiel stands. "King Luther, thank you for your testimony."

Luther ascends to his seat as Zekiel calls Princes Brandon, Holden, and Lowell in turn. Each testify of no knowledge of Luther's plan. As Lowell retakes his seat beside Father, Grant raises his arm.

"I am Grant, Fae at Arms of Aubren. I have served King Oberon as warrior and guard, as well as Queen Titania and King Quinn in this post. May I present to the council?"

"Do you have information pertinent to the testimony given here?" Zekiel asks.

"I do." Grant reaches in his pack and produces a leather-bound book. "This is but one of the journals written by the late Foster of Westshire. He served as chief security officer to Queen Titania and King Quinn. He gathered information throughout both their reigns as to King Luther's family and his bias against Titania. The writings show that he sent Holden to try to make Titania his wife, and when a better arrangement presented in Lindleton, sent Brandon to sway Titania's heart, thinking that her zeal for protecting her people would lead to her untimely death, giving Luther's family Aubren."

I press my palms together and cut my eyes to the sky as waves of sadness wash over me. *How can I repay Foster's debt? He did not deserve to have been taken from this realm so soon. Not before—*

"These are ludicrous and unsubstantiated accusations!" Luther yells above the murmurs rising from those gathered.

"Those with me, the Ring Keepers of Aubren, and the officers gathered here, can attest that these are the true findings of Foster of Westshire."

Zekiel and the High Judges question each of Aubren's ring keepers, and they question Adam, Nicholas, and Timothy, who interviewed other officers present when the information was obtained. All back the story told by Foster's journal.

"We have all the ledgers here in our possession. We are willing to hand them over for inspection. They are all signed by witnesses from each day's entry." Grant takes to the air, landing before Zekiel and placing his pack on the center altar.

My heart beats fast in my chest as I try to reel in my emotions. There is Foster's life laid out for the whole realm to see. I swallow as a lump forms in my throat and dig my nails into my palms.

Grant bows to the judges. "Dear sirs, I believe there is another piece to this that has not been discussed yet. We who were present when King Luther sought to take Aubren witnessed something else. An evil demon professed that Luther and his followers had bestowed her power in this realm. She killed the comrade who penned these journals with daggers shot from her fingertips. Everyone in the courtyard witnessed such. There is no better evidence against King Luther than the demon's own words."

I look at Luther who sits with his chin up, but his skin has taken on an eerie green pallor and glistens as if dampened with the finest mist of rain.

"Luther, what were your words that day?" Grant asks. "Goddesses, forgive me?"

As my eyes cut to Grant and back to Luther, a cacophony of voices lifts from the crowd. The large, bulging protrusion of his throat rises and falls. I hold my breath. He cannot deny it. All saw. All heard.

Hands pressed to knees, Luther pushes to a stand. "I am not a monster. I am truly sorry for Aubren's loss that day, but the fact remains that Titania is not fit to rule."

The arena falls silent.

Grant raises his hands to his middle, dropping his shoulders back. "Yet you were willing to risk soldiers' lives, even your own, in pursuit of our kingdom."

"It is what should be done." Luther's skin flushes red.

Quinn leans toward me. "He has eaten a whole poison berry tree."

Heads turn to their neighbors, and murmurs rise again.

Zekiel pounds his gavel to the altar. "Order! I believe we have heard all the testimony as to Luther's charge. We will now move to the charge of deception brought against Que"—Zekiel clears his throat—"Titania, former Queen of Aubren."

With a slow, full swoop of my wings, I rise then float down to the arena floor, landing beside Zekiel. I take the seat opposite the High Judges. When Zekiel asks for my testimony, I pan the crowd, taking in each hard stare.

I lift my chin. "I do not deny that I ignored edicts of this council or deny my deception. I am heartily sorry for the hurt I caused. You have all received my correspondence laying out my reasons for abandoning my kingdom, friends, and family. These same reasons apply to my decision to aid the trinity witches in fashioning a treaty with the Guardians and other sects of Upper Earth, a treaty ratified by the fae gathered here."

Zekiel requests comment from those gathered, and many stand. All comments concern Sonia and my powers. Who is she? Where did she come from? Why is she threatening our realm? What can be done to prevent her from entering Middle Earth, from gaining power here? What other powers do I possess? How can a fae have these powers? Where do they stem from? Who else knew of them?

At this question, Zekiel raises a palm.

The crowd grows silent, so quiet I feel I could hear a worm pushing through the dirt beneath the block.

He lowers his head. After taking three long breaths, he raises his chin. "The High Judges knew of Titania's powers and her quest to rid the realms of Sonia before her death. We, in part, aided a group that continued to work with the witches in Titania's supposed absence."

Whispers spread like a wave on the sand. As they grow, I strain my ears to make out the words. A chant forms as the syllables align and, one by one, judges rise to their feet.

The words become clear. *The One. The One. The One.*

Cheeks flushing red, motion catches my eye, and I find Luther, hands high, crossing them over each other. His mouth opens, but I cannot hear him over the other, now almost deafening, cheers. Tugging Brandon's arm, he coaxes his son into the aisle and starts up the stairs.

King Herman of Lindleton throws his wrap over his shoulder and, waving to his sons to join him, heads toward the exit. On the other side of the arena, King Joseph of Borean also gathers his sons, and they process to the top of the arena and outside.

Zekiel rounds the altar and holds out his palm to me. Taking it, I stand, fingers shaking between his. The crowd quiets, and looking into my eyes, he dips his chin.

Taking a great breath, I raise our hands between us and push a small tickle of power to my fingers. My skin glows green, and Zekiel lays his other hand atop them, showing he is not harmed. Releasing my hand, he takes a step back. My heart beats wildly in my chest, and my stomach feels as if a million birds flutter through it. I have hidden for so long, feared ridicule and judgment. *Is this what the Goddesses want? Is this my path? Whether it be or not, I am here, and there is no space for retreat.*

I raise both my palms, stretching my arms out straight and pushing my power to my fingertips. They tingle with the transfer, and bright beams flow into the air, lighting the sky above.

Zekiel steps to my side. "This is the future. A future without fear of dark times, without fear of beings that may take our realm, without fear of the evil lurking below."

He holds a high bar for me, and the million wings of the birds in my stomach bat against my insides. Drawing in my power, I lower my arms. My throat clenches, and I swallow.

"I do not know why the Goddesses have blessed me with these powers, but I attest that each step I have made since rising to the position of monarch has been to secure the safety of the fae and to fulfill our charge to protect the human realm. This will always be my aim."

I lower one hand and, taking Zekiel's, lift our palms.

"Long live the fae!"

"Long live the fae," the crowd answers.

These chants continue until Zekiel releases my hand and motions for quiet. "The judges will now recess to decide on the charges put forth for King Luther and Titania."

As he spins toward the other judges, he winks at me. He pats my shoulder, his rough fingers sliding down to my palm and squeezing it.

"Well, done, child. Well done."

"Thank you." I lean in and kiss his cheek.

The High Judges climb the stairs and exit the arena into their chamber. Not knowing what to do with myself, I look to Quinn and Father.

Father's eyes shine brightly.

I smile at him and lift my skirt to climb the steps.

A judge from the front row jumps to his feet, stepping into the aisle to block my path. He holds out his palm. "Titania, may I?"

"What?"

"Feel your powers." His wide eyes dart from my face to my hands.

Wary, but not feeling I can deny him, I cast my power to my fingers.

"Blessed be." A smile grows on his face.

"Blessed be." I dip my chin.

Clutching my dress fabric, I start to take another stair and glance up to realize a host of judges crowd toward me. *Goddesses be.* I grip my middle. *Am I to show each?* Perhaps it must be this way. *For without seeing for themselves, how can they know?* Uncertainty brings fear and misunderstanding, and the likelihood of me ending up dropped to the bottom of a deep well or being banished to the human realm grows in that environment.

Evening nears before the last of the judges have witnessed my gift.

"You are quite pale." Quinn holds out a chunk of bread and cheese as I rest on the nearest bench.

"Thank you, cousin. I do not believe I could fly in this state. I am most drained."

"The High Judges called the judges of Hilbron to confer with them. It may not be long before there is news of a decision."

"I pray it is not."

Father rubs my back and hands me a flask.

I take a big gulp and almost choke. "Father, what are you bringing to the High Council?"

"Just some spirits Alfreda gets for me. It warms my joints. Also good for calming nerves. I figured you could use a bit of liquid courage right now."

Taking another sip, I hand him the flask. "It has been a most unexpected day."

I study the space. Small groups of judges mingle about, but I see no other royals. I guess they are enjoying meals on the coast as I did while waiting for the last High Council. My head pounds with the weight of the day. *What will become of Luther and his family, his kingdom?* Drawing in a slow breath, I release it. *A few more hours, and you will be back with your cousins. In your kingdom, in your castle, Goddesses willing.*

A bugle sounds, and a page announces that the monarchs of each kingdom are summoned to meet with the High Judges. Quinn climbs the stairs, disappearing into the dark doorway. As the kings arrive and file into the chamber, Kings Luther, Herman, and Joseph, with chins high, I pace the stone in front of the altar. An hour passes, and I sit and stand, unable to settle myself. My life hangs on a precipice yet again, my psyche dangling ever so close to the abyss of my grief. If I am left with nothing, no kingdom, no castle, no home, and no Foster, I fear I shall not survive. *But they welcome you with open arms*, the other side of me battles. *They will be grateful to have you securing their realm.*

Sitting next to Father, I clutch my knees. "I cannot abide waiting here any longer. I must take a flight."

His chin rises and falls. "Take a few guards with you. They will summon everyone when there is a decision."

"I will come." Grant stands.

"No, stay with Father." I ask Adam and Nicholas to accompany me.

We climb the stone steps, my feet feeling like lead weights and legs searing, cross the stone ringing the arena, and I jump into the air. I beat my wings hard, letting my feet dangle below. I hold my arms out straight, feeling the wind on my skin. With summer near, the warm air graces my face, washes through my hair, and skims over my wings and skin.

As I am circling over the desert of Aubren, above the sands where I fought the dragons just months ago, a loud bugle sounds, and my heart thuds in my chest.

It is time.

Chapter 19

I want to ignore the sound of the blaring horn, fly straight to my castle, and sit in front of the fire with my cousins, hearing about their day at school, their studies, and their friends. I wish to exist in a realm with no kings attempting to take my kingdom, no evil archangels determined to ruin my life, no dead… I shake my head. I will not think it. *Now especially, what else am I to do but fulfill my fated lot in this life?*

My pulse beats hard through my veins as I lift one wing, turning my body east toward the arena of the high council. I alight on the stone and cross under the arch, descending the stairs with others garbed in their white robes and red sashes. The High Judges sit at the bottom center and monarchs in the front row.

I find Father and sit next to him. "Could you glean any information from seeing the monarchs as they exited the high chamber?"

"Whatever happened in there, their faces showed nothing. I tried to catch Quinn's eye, but his gaze was fixed on the altar."

Folding my hands in my lap, I wait for the count indicating all are present.

Zekiel rises.

For as quiet as the arena seemed before, now it feels as if all suspended our breaths, nay the beating of our hearts. Save for mine, which beats wildly, filling my ears with thumps.

Zekiel's eyes cut down to a page and then up. "The High Judges, judges of Hilbron, and monarchs have discussed the charges against King Luther of Hilbron. King Luther has been found guilty of all charges of treason, sedition, and unprovoked threat of war and occupation."

The eyes of my old adversary turned mentor find me. "As to Queen Titania, she is found guilty of ignoring an edict of this council and deception unbefitting a fae."

"Exile, exile, exile." Chants from the Borean and Lindleton groups grow.

Blood rushes through my veins, pounding in my ears. *It cannot be.*

"Goddesses be with us," I whisper.

Zekiel raises his palms, waiting for silence. "Even so, her heart and mind stayed true to her people, as we believe they always have been. Queen Titania is absolved of all charges. Given this, King Luther is hereby removed from his post, and he is exiled to Willhelm. His kingdom is hereby granted to Queen Titania, ruler of Aubren."

Standing, the contingents of Borean and Lindleton file up the stairs, exiting the arena.

Holden's dark eyes meet mine.

My ears hum. Father grips my arm. Air freezes in my chest. *Hilbron is granted to me? Queen Titania, ruler of Aubren? Ba-boom, ba-boom, ba-boom.* My beats come quick, my hands moisten, and my face heats.

Arms waving, Zekiel calls over the murmurs urging patience. "It is the council's feelings that Primus should be restored. We have strayed too far from our roots, our purpose as fae. That one of our chosen rulers gave an evil being such power in this realm has been an awakening. No longer will our fae be kept in the dark as to the challenges we face. All should have a say in how they will react. We will create a realm guard to protect Middle Earth. Queen Titania shall oversee this army, teaching us how we may defend ourselves and protect the human lives above us."

His words sound as if they come from behind a stone wall. Then, his eyes land on me, and he raises a hand. "Queen Titania, will you accept these posts?"

Mind firing thoughts like explosives and legs like runny sauce, I rise. "I will do all in my power to secure our fae and fight the evil that lurks around us. As to the army, I am happy to assist in organization and training, but as to assuming Hilbron"—my eyes cut to Lowell beside Father, then to Luther, held between two judges—"I believe it may best be served by asking the fae of that land who should lead them as I have in Aubren."

"And it shall be," Zekiel says, lowering his palm. "I hereby call this tribunal closed. Blessed be."

Beside me, Father rises and wraps both arms around my middle. "Good job, daughter."

"Thank you, Father." My hands shake as I hug his back.

Feeling a hand on my arm, I release Father and step back.

Lowell stands before me, wide-eyed. "This is a hard day for my family. Thank you for honoring our people."

"We will figure this out together." I squeeze his arm.

Still in disbelief, I pan the arena. Unlike earlier, the tone in the arena is quiet. Judges speak amongst themselves in hushed tones.

No one fae holds blame, save perhaps Luther. The system our forefathers created worked for a very long time, but now we need something different. My mind jumps back to the last high council when it was I who received negative judgment. Here I am, being handed a new kingdom and a realm army, a confirmed monarch, granted such by my people.

"Cousin." Quinn jumps the row in front of me and lands by my side. "You have done it."

"How did this happen? I cannot believe all the monarchs agreed to this."

"King Joseph of Borean, as you can imagine, did so with disdain, and I believe his agreement was only because he does not want to be seen as an outsider. The others are scared and realize you have more knowledge than they do combined. They want to be part of a solution for peace."

"I am almost too stunned to believe it is true. This is more than I could have hoped for. We should go. It is late." I lift my skirt and turn to Lowell. "Will you come with us, or do you need to be with your family?"

"Tell Gatuika I will come tomorrow."

As we weave with the crowds up to the top portico, I feel everyone's intent gaze. The weight of my charge begins to settle on my shoulders. *Isn't this what you wanted? You are no longer one. I am no longer one, but one of many.* My lungs expand, filling completely for the first time in two days.

—◆◆◆◆—

I LAY AWAKE, STARING AT THE CEILING, waiting for daybreak to start work, figuring out how to mend Hilbron, how to blend armies, planning how we may work together. *What can even a united fae force do to stop Sonia? How can we help her be reconciled, if we even should? Securing Lilith seems to have been a fool's errand. Securing her son Thanatos may be impossible. Theron still eludes us as well. Are these souls the ones we should be looking for, or could they be a mate, perhaps a sibling?*

My other goal for the day is to convince Alfreda and my family that my coronation should be a private affair, if it even needs to take place. I realize this is not to be as all override me at breakfast. Now, more than ever, our fae need to be reminded they are safe, and we intend to keep them that way. A grand coronation and celebration with a few thousand of our countrymen is the best way to do that, I am assured.

I convince them the event should be held before the solstice so families may have time to prepare and gather with their families. The cousins suggest we prepare the event for this very night, and while part of my insides screams it is too much, the rest of me sees their aim of having a way to seal our celebratory mood.

That evening, after the coronation, we parade through Capitolshire and back to the castle meadow, where tables are laid out with as much food as we could gather. Tables ring the space, but most bring blankets to sit on the grass.

I ignore the tightening of my chest when I remember my dances with Foster. I force smile after smile, accept embrace after embrace, and take every good tiding with appreciation. My stomach writhes as the night holds such bittersweet sentiment. Yes, I am grateful to be in my home, serving my people, but that I will experience all without that one person who completed me holds such sorrow I dare not linger on the thought too long.

The jigs last long past midnight, and I trail my youngest two cousins to our rooms after the last dance.

Isla hooks her arm in mine. "I will miss our slumber parties when you move back to your quarters."

"I am not moving Quinn out. Lowell and I will go to Hilbron, and I may be there a while. I need Quinn here for a bit."

"Good." She rests her head on my shoulder.

The next morning, I watch as light grows outside my window. Again. For my people, I would want it no other way. I should be elated at the council's decision, grateful to be back with my family, to be serving my fae once again. I am in my mind, but these things do not reach my heart. It is as if a stone wall has been constructed around it, and nothing can reach the threshold to enter. I know if I feel glad, even for the tiniest speck of time, the grief of losing Foster will come as a tidal wave over the beach, and I will have no wall to stop it.

This day, I swing my legs over the side of the bed, touching my toes to the cold stone. I again have distraction. The solstice harkens, along with Gatuika's wedding and the night I will visit the witches to witness what may pass between them and Sonia. *Will she stay true to her word? Does she not care a stitch for her mother, or had she jested out of spite for me?*

The side of my mouth turns up as I remember her words. The witches seemed to be making better progress than she thought possible. Because of me. I spread my shoulders and stand, feeling just a bit proud. Crossing to my chest, I survey the choices. I would rather have my black leather pants, but a riding outfit will have to do.

"Are we riding today?" Isla asks. "That will be fun before we must sit before the mirror and have our hair brushed and pinned."

I turn to see her lift her head from the pillow. "Sorry to wake you, but no. I must aid the witches."

"What? No." She throws the blanket from her body and bounds from the bed. "Sonia will kill you."

I take her hands. "She will have many targets, but we will all be safe, I promise."

"You do not know that."

"I bested her in this realm where my only advantage is my powers. Many will be gathered. She cannot be powerful enough to do harm in a group so large."

Isla shakes her head, tears forming in her eyes. "I do not care about the others. I only care about you. Do not go."

"I have to go." I say the words, knowing they are not true. "But I will return before the wedding."

I need to go. I must know that all my work the past months was not in vain, that Foster died for something. Even though I hold little hope Sonia will be appeased by our offering, there is a slim chance it will bring us closer to resolution.

Kissing Isla on the forehead, I promise to return before we are to dress. I round to the barracks, and Adam, Nicholas, Timothy, and I take to the air, weaving through the forest to the cabin. Landing on the porch outside, I swallow, thinking of my last moments with Foster. Clenching my eyes shut tightly, I force out a breath, willing the memory from my mind.

Alemayehu and Yonas descend through the tree canopy and alight beside us. They congratulate me on the recent council ruling.

My skin prickles at the mention of Primus. It holds such a foreboding space in my mind, an ancient, old land of long bygone histories. It seems as foreign to me as Upper Earth. Aubren is my kingdom, my birthplace, my home. I cannot imagine it not existing.

"That discussion is for another time." I steer them from the topic. "Today, we go to the witches."

"We are clear, correct?" Alemayehu eyes me. "You and Yonas are to witness, nothing more. Try to stay hidden, and if there is any danger, you retreat to our realm."

"I understand." I nod.

He waves a finger in front of my face. "Even if your friends are in danger. They can handle themselves. You do not need to be a hero."

I cross my arms over my chest. "Someone has been watching too many Earth movies? I promised Isla I would be home before the wedding. I will not break that vow."

Ensuring all know their roles, Yonas and I take flight, heading straight to the Daintree ring above. We glide through the portal, and the familiar hum of magic tingles over my skin. Bright light greets me as we exit the forest, catching a warm draft to rise high over the ocean. I find my body feels lighter, my wings more powerful without the drain of using a cloaking spell. We pass over India, the Middle East, and lower our altitude as we approach Sardinia.

I land on the soft grass ringing the castle and sense the hum of magic.

Yonas's shoulders quake, and he sniffs the air. "Witches. So many witches. And vampires. Thank goodness the werewolves seem to have stayed away."

"They did their part."

"I do not sense any elves either."

Shrugging, I start toward the entrance. "Why would they come? They only helped to maintain their isolation."

As we near the castle, Alena, Camille, Jude, Hunter, and DJ round the side of the structure. Seeing DJ's wide, round eyes, the sympathy oozing from his creased brow and downturned lips, I tense. I came to avoid Foster's memory, not be seeped in it.

Alena bounds to me, wrapping her arms around me in her usual grip-like fashion. "We're so sorry."

I pry her hands from my shoulders. "Thank you."

Camille's embrace is gentler, but her eyes well with tears as she releases me. My lungs catch, and I swallow, accepting her sympathies with nails digging into my palms.

I am grateful when Hunter extends his arm in our typical warrior greeting. "Alemayehu tells us you've been restored to your monarchy and made a general as well."

Narrowing my eyes, I nod. "I am most relieved to be absolved of my deception. I believe the strides toward unity in our realm will make us all stronger."

Beside Hunter, DJ rolls on his heels, and as soon as Hunter releases me, DJ's arms wind around me. My body relaxes into his warm embrace, and I inhale his coconut scent. Tears spring to my eyes.

His hand cradles my head, and he whispers in my ear, "God, T, I'm so sorry. I've been so worried about you."

Batting my eyelashes to stave the onslaught of tears and emotion threatening to spill over my barriers, I wriggle from his hold. "There are many gathered here. I would like to meet them."

"Tyler is around somewhere." DJ motions to the building.

"Any news of Theron?" I glance between the witches.

"We've been focusing on Lilith's casket. It won't open," Hunter says.

"You need it opened?"

"We'd like to know if anything else is inside before we hand it over."

"We've tried everything: magic, crowbars, hammers, axes, chainsaws… They don't even scratch the surface." Alena slides her hand into Hunter's.

My side twitches with a pang of sadness at their show of affection. "It's spelled?"

"We believe so, but by who or how, we've no clue. Tyler's been hunting through his dad's documents for any clue, but we're out of time. The Guardians definitely have someone crafty on their side."

DJ opens the door, and I walk in ahead of him. Bumps rise on my skin as the hum of magic engulfs me.

"How many witches are here?"

Alena skips to my side. "Over a thousand will be in attendance tonight."

Crossing to the elevator, Hunter presses the down arrow. "We want you to try to open Lilith's casket. We're hoping a fae may be the answer."

"Why would a fae be any different? Who else has tried?"

"Just us and vampires, but you're not from this realm, so we're hoping that might work. The werewolves and elves didn't respond to our invitations."

The ding of the elevator has my pulse racing. I evaluate the space as we enter. For even as I have ridden in one of these carts several times, I do not like them. DJ stands next to me, his skin warming mine.

We exit in the carved rock sanctuary deep below the castle. The air is cool and damp, and I stifle a shiver. I recognize the tomb set on an altar at the far end of the dark space lit by torches hammered into the stone. I wonder how I would feel if this were my mother, if we preserved our dead. *Wouldn't I want her near?* At least there would be a physical connection tethering the memories. I think of where I may go to feel connected to Foster: the cabin, our cabin in the wood, where we were to be married. I wince as my side pings with a contraction.

"You okay, T?" DJ stares at me.

"We do not preserve our departed." Balling my fists, I follow the group.

"If this is too much…" He trails after me.

I ignore him, joining the others circling the tomb. Running my hand over the smooth, carved stone, I eye the skulls shaped there, mirror images of each other. I fit my palms under the lip of the lid and lift. The rock stays locked in place. I push on the top but feel no movement.

"Try an opening spell," Camille says.

She recites the lines, and I copy them, but the lid sits fixed in place. We try two other incantations, a release and an unsealing spell, and heft and heave, to no avail.

"Damn." Hunter pounds his fist on the casket.

A cold burst of air blasts my hair around my face. I spin to face the dark chasm not ten feet away, my locks whipping behind me. DJ grips my hand, pulling me behind him, and the witches form a line in front of Yonas and me. Waving Yonas to the end of the tomb, I stand between him and the witches as icy shards pelt my body. A dark cloud rises from the fissure that leads to Lower Earth.

The amorphous, black fog churns, folding into itself, and the particles within coalesce into an angelic form with wings, each feather a sharp, gleaming blade, spread high. My heart drums in my chest as I inch backwards, coaxing Yonas to stay hidden. *Goddesses protect us.*

Sonia.

"Is my timing intrusive?"

Hunter steps forward. "No, we've secured your mother for you."

"Yes, Titania said you retrieved her for me." Tilting her head in my direction, she raises an eyebrow. "I imagine the vampires did not turn her over easily."

DJ steps to his brother's side. "What matters is that you can be reunited with her now."

Her head swivels to face DJ. "You're all so brave. Hello, grandson. We haven't met. Apologies. Some secrets are too important to be shared."

My foot juts forward, my psyche urging me to protect my friend. Yonas seizes my arm, tethering me to him. I glare at him but yield, remembering my promise to Isla and oath to Alemayehu that I will protect his son with my life.

"You may take her now." Hunter takes another step toward Sonia.

DJ copies, as do the three witches behind him. Even though Alena, Camille, and Jude may be some of the most powerful witches in Upper Earth, my heart still flutters with nervous anticipation. Sonia's last visit left Foster dead. I lock on her form with a hard glare. I will not forget that.

Almost faster than my eyes can register, her hand flings out. I throw my body over Yonas, wrapping my wings around us both.

Sonia cackles. "See, Titania has learned to be scared. Thank you for showing the respect I deserve."

I raise my eyes to see her unfold her palm. A deluge of dark specks rush from her fingers. The witches drop to the stone as the surge gushes over them and slams into the side of the tomb, sending it spinning through the sanctuary, decimating the stone benches in its path. Hurling into the air, the casket slams against the far wall, splitting into chunks of rock and toppling to the ground.

"I believe that may answer your question as to whether my mother is the one I require. Her soul may have been worth something to me. Her bones, however, or really any other part of her, can rot in Hell. She started this, and I intend to end it."

A gale sweeps across my cheeks as air is sucked from the space toward her form. Burying my face under my arms, I cling to Yonas.

Bam. A loud crack sounds and echoes through the hall. *Bam. Bam. Bam.* The diminishing pops trail from the space. I lift my head to near darkness as the torches stand dark. Only a faint glow emits from the elevator light in the adjoining passageway.

I lift my head from Yonas's back. "Are you well?"

His body quakes in my grip. "That was her? The one you expelled from our realm?"

"It was."

"The fae owe you so much more than a kingdom and an army."

"My fae owe me nothing. I only ask them to believe."

Releasing Yonas, I stand. My eyes find DJ embracing his brother, Alena's and Camille's arms tightly around them both.

"Okay, okay, we're all fine." Hunter bats them away and paces to the precipice. "Damn it. Now the vampires are going to be even more pissed off."

He kicks the air.

Alena flicks her wrist, and the torches burn anew.

She approaches Hunter, wrapping an arm around his waist. "We'll figure it out. We always have before."

My eyes pan the space, eyeing the stone benches, half toppled from their supports, fragmented into random shapes. This solstice will not proceed as planned. I cross to the closest pew and lift the leg to its upright position. Yonas follows, arranging the stones into small seats. He, DJ, and I span out, righting rocks where we can. We come to the fragments of Lilith's shattered tomb, lining the pieces against the wall.

I overturn a section of the lid, and a skull rolls to my feet. Lifting the bone, I hold it up. I say a silent prayer to the Goddesses for her soul and set the piece with the others.

"What is this?" Yonas lifts a thick stone wedge, sweeping a hand across the surface. "These look like etchings."

Alena is beside him faster than a speeding roadrunner.

He twitches and holds out the tablet.

Taking it, she sits crossed-legged on the rock floor. We gather around as she studies the markings, running her fingers over what seems to be lines of hash marks set in various patterns.

"These are Akkadian." Jude leans in.

"What is Akkadian?" I kneel beside him.

"It's an ancient language. One of the oldest, perhaps over five thousand years old."

"Like when Lilith was alive?" Camille asks.

"Exactly like when Lilith was alive." Hunter smiles.

"So that means we have records, information Lilith, or whoever entombed her, felt held importance." I smile.

What is that Upper Earth saying? Game on?

~~The End~~
Until We Meet Again

About the Author

Tricia Copeland believes in finding magic. She thinks magic infuses every aspect of our lives, whether it is the magic of falling in love, discovering a new passion, a beautiful sunset, or a book that transports us to another world. An avid runner and Georgia native, Tricia now lives with her family and four-legged friends in Colorado. Find all her titles, from contemporary romance and fantasy to dystopian fiction, at www.triciacopeland.com.

Need more of these characters and their stories?

Find all the books of the *Realm Chronicles* series and the *Kingdom Journals* cross-over series, and which books to read when, with the reading guide:

https://triciacopeland.com/
kingdom-journals-and-realm-chronicles-book-guide/

The next installment in the Realm Chronicles series, *Quest of the Realm Defenders*, follows Alena, Camille, Jude, and Hunter and their quest to find Hunter's father. You can find this short story in the *Four Names of Fortune* anthology, now available for pre-order, releasing April 19, 2025. Get it here:

https://books2read.com/FourNamesofFortune

The fifth book, and finale of the series, To be a Fae, will release in 2025! Learn more and pre-order on my website:

https://triciacopeland.com/to-be-a-fae/